A tingle of alarm cha P9-CMX-412 **spine, Valerie stood and surveyed the yard. "I don't see anyone."**

"Damn. He got away," Nash muttered as he drew back his fingers and stared at the red smears there. He blinked hard, squinted, then shielded his eyes as if the early-evening twilight hurt them. "I, um..."

"Can you stand? Walk?"

He waved her off. "I'm fine. I just..." He wobbled when he tried to rise, and she caught him as he stumbled.

"You are not fine. You hit your head."

"No, the intruder hit it for me."

The idea of an intruder attacking Nash sent a chill to her core. Axel had been attacked in his home. His head bashed. Now Nash...

* * *

Colton 911: Chicago—Love and danger come alive in the Windy City...

* * *

If you're on Twitter, tell us what you think of Harlequin Romantic Suspense! #harlequinromsuspense

Dear Reader,

Working on a Coltons continuity with my fellow Harlequin authors is always exciting. This book was no exception. Colton 911: Chicago brings all the drama, danger and romance you've come to expect from this dynamic family!

Years ago, Valerie Yates and Nash Colton had a steamy youthful romance...with devastating repercussions. Now the former lovers have a second chance at forever—unless murder and revenge get in the way!

By the way, as I always do, I've included a cat in this book. Kitty, the friendly, somewhat presumptive male calico—yes, male—that visits Nash's house constantly throughout this book is a salute to our neighbors' male calico that spent more time at our house than his own...even inviting himself into our kitchen. Sadly, Kitty passed away shortly after the writing of this book, and he is missed.

Happy reading, and happy holidays to all!

Beth Cornelison

COLTON 911: SECRET ALIBI

Beth Cornelison

Special thanks and acknowledgment are given to
Beth Cornelison for her contribution to
the Colton 911: Chicago miniseries.

HARLEQUIN®
ROMANTIC SUSPENSE™

Recycling programs
for this product may
not exist in your area.

ISBN-13: 978-1-335-75949-8

Colton 911: Secret Alibi

Copyright © 2021 by Harlequin Books S.A.

This edition published by arrangement with Harlequin Books S.A.

For questions and comments about the quality of this book,
please contact us at CustomerService@Harlequin.com.

Harlequin Enterprises ULC
22 Adelaide St. West, 40th Floor
Toronto, Ontario M5H 4E3, Canada
www.Harlequin.com

Printed in U.S.A.

Beth Cornelison began working in public relations before pursuing her love of writing romance. She has won numerous honors for her work, including a nomination for the RWA RITA® Award for *The Christmas Stranger*. She enjoys featuring her cats (or friends' pets) in her stories and always has another book in the pipeline! She currently lives in Louisiana with her husband, one son and three spoiled cats. Contact her via her website, bethcornelison.com.

Books by Beth Cornelison

Harlequin Romantic Suspense

Colton 911: Chicago
Colton 911: Secret Alibi

The McCall Adventure Ranch

Rancher's Deadly Reunion
Rancher's High-Stakes Rescue
Rancher's Covert Christmas
Rancher's Hostage Rescue
In the Rancher's Protection

Colton 911

Colton 911: Deadly Texas Reunion

The Mansfield Brothers

The Return of Connor Mansfield
Protecting Her Royal Baby
The Mansfield Rescue

Visit the Author Profile page at
Harlequin.com for more titles.

Acknowledgments

Thank you to Kasey Witherington, MEd, LPC, for her assistance as I researched borderline personality disorder and sought to better understand Valerie's mother. Kasey generously answered questions for me and shared further sources for my research. Any mistakes I have made in portraying the disorder are mine alone.

Prologue

Twelve years ago

Three minutes. Just three minutes.

Good God, who knew three minutes could last so long?

Valerie Yates tried to clear her mind, shift her focus, but waiting had never been her strong suit.

She bent over the paper in front of her and resumed sketching. A face began to take shape in the squarish oval she'd started. Eyes, nose, lips…

Soft, demanding lips. Skilled lips that made her breath catch and her toes curl.

With that unbidden thought, she pressed too hard and the tip of her charcoal pencil snapped off. Huffing her frustration, she leaned back in her desk chair, shook the tension from her hands. Checked the clock.

Seriously? It had only been one minute and fifteen seconds?

She scrubbed a hand down her face and took a deep breath to quell the churning in her gut. The added nervous tension did not help the swirl of nausea that had plagued her lately.

One minute thirty seconds. Halfway.

Groaning, she found her sharpener and fixed the tip of her pencil. Resumed sketching. A smudge with her thumb to soften a line and add shadow, contour. She was drawing Nash again, she realized. Without even considering what she was doing, her fingers, her mind, automatically created the image that filled her thoughts these days. She set down her pencil, closed her eyes and allowed herself to go to those magic nights and stolen moments. To sweaty skin. Adoring hazel eyes. Whispered promises.

Nash Colton. Her first love. Her first lover.

"I wish you didn't have to leave," he'd said morosely that last summer night, two months ago.

"Me, too." Valerie had shifted to her side, pressing her lean, naked body against his. Even at eighteen, he had the taut, muscled body of an athlete. Not gross, bulky muscles like those weight lifters they'd watched on the summer Olympics last year. No, Nash was more… What was that swimmer's name? Michael… Phillips? No, Phelps.

Valerie drew circles on his flat, bare chest and sighed. "I'll come back next summer. And probably at Christmas. My mom was talking about going skiing in Colorado at Christmas, but I'll tell her I want to come back here instead."

"You'd give up skiing in Colorado to see me?" he asked, his tone both surprised and wistful. Grateful. Hopeful. Her heart broke a little for him. She knew how the death of his mother and strained relationship with his father had hurt Nash.

"Of course, I would. I——" She caught herself before she blurted "I love you." Instead she finished with "I think you're special. We have fun together."

He wiggled his eyebrows seductively. "Lots of fun."

She playfully punched his arm. "You know what I mean."

"And how will you explain your preference to come back to Chicago instead of skiing to your parents? Are you ready to tell people about us?"

Val furrowed her brow. "No. We can't tell yet. If my mom ever found out we were…well, whatever this is." She waved her fingers between them. "She'd freak. She probably wouldn't even let me come back to visit Uncle Rick next summer."

"She's really that strict?"

"Yeah."

Nash frowned and folded his arm behind his head. "Has she ever explained why she doesn't want you spending time with my family?"

"Not really. She just says 'Stay away from those Coltons! They're trouble!'"

"Well, I can understand that a little if my father and Uncle Axel are the only Coltons she knows," Nash said, his dark blond eyebrows furrowing, "but has she even met any of the rest of us? We're not so bad."

"It's more than that. I'm pretty sure she got pregnant with me in high school. I mean, all you have to do is the math. So she's worried that I will——" She didn't finish the sentence because it was obvious what her mother was worried she'd do. And because she and Nash had. Recently. More than once.

He flashed an impish grin. "Yeah, well…"

Valerie felt a flush sting her neck and cheeks. "Nash!"

He stroked her face with his fingers. "Don't worry. We've been careful."

Valerie leaned on one elbow and bent her head to kiss him. "I know."

"It's hard, not telling anyone. I really want to tell Damon. He's not just my brother. He's my best friend. And you make me so happy…"

Beaming her own bliss, she framed his face between her hands. "You, too. But…for now, let's not say anything. If my mom found out—" She sighed, knowing how badly that conversation would go and not wanting to risk anything that would push her mother to the edge. To drink. "Maybe next summer—"

A hungry growling sound rumbled from his throat as he captured the back of her head with his free hand and tugged her down for a deep kiss. "I don't think I can wait for next summer, Val. God, I'm going to miss you."

Tears pricked her eyes, and so he wouldn't see her weakness, she kissed him again. Long and hot and full of the love she was scared to put into words.

His hand moved down her spine, cupped her bottom. She scooted on top of him again, her body on fire, and he rocked his hips up, moving—

Ding.

The tiny bell sound of the timer she'd set on her clock yanked Valerie out of her memories. Back to her Ohio bedroom. And the reality that faced her in her en suite bathroom.

"Well," she said, glancing down at the sketch she'd made of Nash, "Time's up. Here goes nothing."

Her knees shook as she crossed her bedroom and approached the bathroom sink. She lifted the washcloth

she'd used to cover the plastic stick, as if to hide it from…
what? She wasn't sure. So she wouldn't peek early?

Her hand trembled as she lifted the corner of the rag
and flipped it aside. Leaned in to read the display.

Positive.

The nausea in her gut surged, and she lost what little breakfast she'd managed this morning. After wiping
and rinsing her mouth, then flushing the commode, she
sank to the floor with the plastic pregnancy test stick in
her hand. What was she going to do? Her mother would
kill her. Worse, would her mother retreat into the bottle
again? She'd just gotten sober this summer at the clinic.
But any little thing could push her to the brink.

A sob rose in Valerie's throat, but she choked it back.
She had to be brave, had to figure out what to do next.

"Oh, Nash. I guess we weren't careful enough."

Chapter 1

Twelve years later
Late October

"It is flat-out unacceptable to me that your father has access to millions of dollars and hasn't offered one penny of it to help get Jackson back!" Nash Colton raged as he paced tight circles in the kitchen of his cousin's suburban Chicago home. "It's infuriating!"

"Yeah, well," Myles Colton replied from the ladderback chair where he was watching Nash pace, "my dad was cut from the same cloth as your dad, so…you know how that is. They might not be identical twins, but Axel and Erik Colton are exactly alike in all too many ways."

Nash slammed a cabinet door too hard, his frustration boiling over.

"Hey, cool it!" Myles said. "Faith is trying to rest. We

haven't gotten any sleep lately, and the stress is wearing on us both."

Nash took a deep breath and scrubbed both hands on his face as he exhaled. "Of course. I'm sorry. I know that anything I'm feeling has got to be a hundred times worse for you."

Myles, whose four-year-old son Jackson had been kidnapped a few days earlier for a ransom of thirty million dollars, balled the hand he'd been resting on the table-top. "I'm trying to keep it together for Faith's sake. But the waiting, not knowing…"

"I'm sorry," Nash said. "My grumbling isn't helping. I just wish I could *do something*!" He scraped out a chair across from his cousin. "If I could help raise the ransom money—"

Myles angled a skeptical look at him. "You have thirty mil lying around you'd like to donate to the cause?"

"Hardly. Architects in my firm don't make that kind of dough."

"Right. So we have no ransom money. Which means for now we do what Brad Howard, our FBI contact, is telling us. They're working on a plan."

At that moment, Myles's phone sounded with an incoming call. "Speak of the devil…" He lifted the phone to his ear. "You got news?"

Nash signaled to his cousin that he was leaving so that Myles and his FBI contact could work on the plan to bring Jackson home safely and catch the cretin behind the kidnapping and extortion.

He hated not being able to help Myles. He hated even more that the people who *could* potentially do something to make a difference seemed indifferent to Jackson's kidnapping. His father, Erik Colton, and his father's fraternal twin, Axel, received a substantial stipend from the estate of their late father, Dean Colton. They lived well. Very well. But none of that wealth seemed to trickle down to their children. Not that Nash or Myles or any of the younger generation of Coltons wanted the rather tainted money. They all had their own lives and careers. They'd managed to rise above their flawed paternal relationships to become independently successful.

But even if all of his siblings and cousins pooled their resources, they wouldn't come anywhere close to the thirty million that had been demanded for Jackson's safe return. But he knew who did, and Nash found it unconscionable that Axel wouldn't donate any of his sizable wealth to save his grandson.

Nash couldn't let that rest. He dialed Axel's home. The housekeeper answered.

"He's at the racket club, having a tennis lesson as I recall," the maid said. "Is there a message?"

"No. Thanks." Nash disconnected. The racket club. He knew the hoity-toity club the housekeeper meant. "Perhaps this calls for an in-person conversation," Nash said to no one in particular as he headed outside into the late October chill to confront his uncle.

From Myles's front steps, he heard a car door close and glanced up to see who was arriving. And his heart slammed against his ribs.

Valerie stopped in her tracks, her breath catching when she spotted Nash coming out of Myles and Faith's home. Twelve years of heartache, confusion and anger roiled inside her. Flashes of memory blinked in her mind's eye like a painful slide show—holding Nash, her mother's scornful shouting, sharp abdominal cramps, laughing at Nash's corny jokes, a bittersweet goodbye kiss under the arbor, an incriminating picture. So much history. So much hurt.

Releasing the air she'd snagged in her lungs, she took a couple of slow steps forward. She'd known that eventually she'd run into Nash. Before she'd left Ohio, she weighed that particular risk against her desire to be near Myles and Faith and help the family during the crisis they faced with little Jackson missing. She'd hoped she could minimize her chances of seeing Nash by avoiding large family gatherings and spending the majority of her time at her Uncle Rick's house. Foolish thinking. Nash was woven too tightly into the fabric of the Colton family for her to not run into him.

She gathered the courage to speak to him, to show a modicum of civility and calm, even if her pulse scampered and her thoughts were in a whirlwind.

But then, tightening his mouth, he turned without speaking and marched across Myles's lawn to an Infiniti coupe parked at the curb. He climbed in and sped away, leaving her standing there. Alone. Again.

She couldn't say how long she stood there, staring down the street where Nash had long ago disappeared. And she made a decision. Enough was enough.

Earlier in the month, as she'd driven into Illinois and gotten closer to Chicago, a nervous energy had twisted tighter and tighter inside Valerie. One part of that tension, she knew, was an excitement to be returning to a place where she'd spent happy summers and found a second home with her uncle's stepfamily. She'd loved the warm and welcoming home that sat behind Yates' Yards Plant Nursery, her Uncle Rick and Aunt Vita's business. She'd loved spending hours helping in the nursery's greenhouses, among the beautiful plants and fragrant blossoms. As an only child with a part-time mother who'd let it be known she resented her daughter, Valerie had loved getting to know Vita's family and forming deep bonds of friendship and camaraderie with her Colton "cousins."

Quite simply, over the last twelve years, she'd missed them. Missed the passion for art she'd shared with Lila, missed the playful teasing of Myles and Aaron, missed the maternal conversations she'd had with Vita and missed her Uncle Rick's dorky dad jokes and made-up excuses to get the extended family together for picnics or outdoor games. Water balloon fights on so-called "wet Wednesdays." Homemade ice cream on National Strawberry Sundae Day. Potluck picnics in his flower garden to honor Red Rose Day. Cheese hors d'oeuvres on the lawn for Moon Viewing Mondays. She smiled to herself remembering all the wonderful, silly times. Good grief, she'd missed those laughter-and-love-filled days when she'd returned to her mother's tumultuous brand of parenting.

But she'd stayed away from Illinois. Because, of all the Coltons she'd met and loved when she'd spent blissful summers in Chicago, one Colton in particular had rooted himself deep in her heart…and shattered her world.

But enough was enough.

She'd sacrificed enough—too much—because of Nash Colton. The time had come to put a few things straight with Nash and reclaim the family that meant so much to her. She didn't want to fear seeing Nash, didn't want to hide from a confrontation with him, didn't want to miss any more family events and celebrations because Nash would be there.

It was time for a reckoning.

With effort, Nash shoved aside the image of Valerie, standing on Myles's front lawn, gaping at him with a world of pain in her eyes. He had a mission and needed to focus on his reckoning with Axel.

Nash jogged up the steps of the racket club and paused at the glass door. Entry was allowed only if you had a membership card to scan. He growled his frustration, but within a few minutes a member in his tennis whites exited and flashed Nash a smile.

Nash nodded a return greeting and caught the door before it closed. He slipped inside and scanned the lobby, orienting himself.

"Can I help you?" a young woman behind the front desk asked.

"Maybe. I'm looking for my uncle, Axel Colton."

The woman sat up straighter, clearly recognizing the name, and she squared her shoulders. If she hadn't been starstruck at the mention of his uncle's name, Nash would have sworn her body language meant she was about to throw him out on his ear. But she flashed a bright smile and said, "Absolutely. Mr. Colton is on the tennis courts, having a lesson." She aimed a finger past the men's locker rooms. "The exit to the courts is just down there."

Nash thanked the desk attendant and made his way through the posh lobby, past a floor-to-ceiling trophy case and a juice bar decked out to look like a tropical beach stand, to the exit. He shielded his eyes from the late October sun and followed the sidewalk to the rows of tennis courts until he found the one where his uncle was flirting with a woman half his age.

Stopping behind the perimeter fence to watch for a moment, Nash observed his uncle's charade as Axel went through the awkward motions of the worst backhand Nash had ever seen. Nash scoffed. He'd played tennis before against his uncle. Axel had won by two points in the last set because of his killer backhand.

The pretty woman with Axel smiled patiently then stepped close and put her arms around his uncle to angle his hand and guide his arm through the correct motion. Axel's expression during the demonstration was pure cat-that-caught-the-canary.

Irritation spiked in Nash. Uncle Axel's grandson had been kidnapped, but he'd taken time to have a fake tennis lesson, the object of which appeared to be tricking his attractive teacher into pressing her ample bosom against Axel as often as possible.

Nash barged through the gate and onto the court without waiting to be invited, then called to the pretty tennis pro, "Did he tell you he was the Bingham Country Club five-oh champion for six years straight in the nineties?"

Both the pro and his uncle turned to face him, clearly startled.

"Nash? What are you doing here?" Axel barked.

He ignored his uncle's question and kept his attention on the blonde pro in the short black tennis skirt and tank top. "His backhand is legendary. In fact, I think he won a tournament here last spring. Or was it the year before? You can check the trophy case in the lobby if you want to see for yourself. Either way, I'm afraid you've been duped, ma'am."

The woman blinked her confusion and divided a look between Axel and Nash. "I'm sorry?"

"Now see here!" Axel huffed. "I—"

"No, he's the one who should be sorry. For wasting your time." Nash stopped a few feet from his uncle and pinned a hard stare on him. "Right, Uncle Axel?"

The older man returned a glower. He waved a dismissive hand and told the young woman, "Take a break, Tiffany. We'll finish after I get rid of my nosy nephew."

The tennis pro gathered a few loose tennis balls and sauntered off the court with a puzzled knit in her brow.

Nash continued to glare disdainfully at Axel, saying nothing as his uncle walked to the players' bench and tossed aside his racket. Axel retrieved a towel and mopped his neck and face before draping it around his neck and facing Nash with his mouth pinched in a grim line. "Well, what do you want? What was so damn important you had to interrupt my lesson?"

"You're unbelievable, old man!"

Axel raised his chin, frowning. "I beg your pardon?"

"Do you even care that Jackson hasn't been found? You're out here farting around with that poor girl, pretending you can't already swing a backhand better than anyone in your age category, while your son and his wife are going through hell!"

Axel stiffened. "I'll thank you to keep your voice down!"

Nash ignored him and shouted, "Everyone in the family is busting their ass to find your grandson or collect the ransom, except you. To you, today's just another day to screw someone over. To lie and cheat and be a selfish prick. You don't care how badly your family is hurting or worried, as long as you get your jollies tricking poor Tiffany into snuggling up next to your sorry hide!"

Axel cast a glance around the other courts, his jaw tight and his hands fisting. "You're making a scene. Do you really want the Colton name sullied again? People will talk!"

"About how you could be so callous regarding your own grandson's safety? I say let them talk! You're a selfish bastard, Uncle Axel. I know you have the money for the ransom. Why haven't you volunteered it yet?"

Axel snorted. "What? You think I have thirty million

dollars to pay an extortionist? Do you think I got where I am in life by buckling under every time someone tried to blackmail me for money?"

Aghast, Nash rocked up on the balls of his feet and down again, flexing his hands at his sides as he tried to rein in his temper. "We're talking about saving your grandson. Jackson is an innocent. He shouldn't suffer because you're too greedy to help get him back."

Axel dismissed his plea with a haughty sniff and tossed the towel aside. "What guarantee do I have that they'll even give the boy back if I did come up with the money? I can't risk losing that much cash!"

"But you *can* risk losing the life of a child? Your grandchild!" Nash gaped at Axel, appalled, outraged—and yet, tragically, not really surprised—at what he was hearing.

Axel huffed loudly, as if terribly put out by being held to account. "Look. I'm sorry that the boy is missing, but I can't be responsible for bailing out every family member that—"

"The boy?" Nash interrupted. "*The boy* has a name. Can you not even bring yourself to say *Jackson*? And he's not just missing, he was *kidnapped*. He's a four-year-old in danger!"

"Enough!" Axel stood and stepped closer to Nash, scowling, jamming his face right in Nash's. Nash was sure the older man had used this gruff and aggressive move to intimidate countless others in his life.

But Nash had a good three-inch height advantage and an equally stubborn glare to rival his uncle's. He was not impressed with the other man's posturing.

"I'm perfectly aware of the situation and the child's relationship to me," Axel growled, his breath smelling of old coffee. "You don't need to thrash me with it over and again. You've said your piece, and I've said mine. Now kindly leave the premises before I call security and have you thrown out." With that, Axel turned, picked up his racket and towel and headed off the court.

"That's it?" Nash called after his retreating uncle. "You're just going to walk away?" Nash muttered a curse under his breath, then shouted louder, to be sure Axel heard him. "You're going to be sorry you walked away, old man! One day soon, you're going to pay for turning your back on your family!"

Nash stood on the tennis court for several long seconds, seething, fighting to get his ragged breathing back under control. How could Axel be so selfish? So disinterested in the well-being of his own family?

No sooner had the rhetorical question filtered through Nash's brain than the not-so-rhetorical answer presented itself boldly and with certainty. *Because he's your father's twin brother.* Erik Colton had been a distant, cold, unsympathetic father to Nash and his younger brother, Damon. In fact, if not for his father's wife, Nicole, Nash would have grown up not knowing what a truly caring and nurturing parent was like. He'd overlooked and tolerated a lot of crappy behavior from his father and uncle in deference to Nicole and his equally kind Aunt Vita. As he often did when he thought of the more senior Colton women, he said a word of thanks to the fates that had brought the loving women and their children into his life.

With a last sigh of frustration, he stalked off the court, encountering Tiffany on his way out. She stared at him with suspicion and a bit of wide-eyed fear. Clearly, she, along with anyone else in the vicinity, had heard a good bit of his argument with Axel.

He shrugged at her. "What? Don't you have family members you want to strangle now and then?"

If possible, Tiffany's eyes grew rounder. "No. I love them all."

Nash grunted and grinned. "Well, consider yourself lucky. We can't all say the same."

He hurried up the sidewalk and through the racket club, nodding to the front desk clerk as he exited. He took a moment in his car to further calm himself before he got on the road. Driving and rage weren't a good mix. Leaning his head back, he closed his eyes and took deep breaths. He should be used to the callous and cold behavior of the Colton patriarchs by now. His father, his uncle and even his grandfather, Dean Colton, had been bastards, to hear his grandmother Carin talk. But then Carin had a chip the size of the Millennium Park Bean on her shoulder concerning Nash's grandfather and much of the rest of his family.

Focus on the positive, he could hear his adoptive mother whisper in his mind. She'd been the bright beacon in his life and his brother's when their real mother died. Nicole knew as well as anyone how screwy Erik and Axel Colton's priorities were, how distant and disappointing they were to their children. But her love and kindness, her encouragement to count their blessings rather than dwell on the broken paternal relationships had made all the difference to Nash, Damon and his cousins.

"Right," Nash said, opening his eyes and cranking his engine. "I have people who care. People I care about." People who needed his love and support. Like Myles and Faith, whose precious son had been taken. That's where he would focus his energy.

A hum of purpose and focused energy filled Valerie, as she drove down Lake Shore Drive along the Lake Michigan waterfront. She'd taken a circuitous route to her destination, just so she could cruise the famous, scenic highway. That, and she was stalling.

She may have made up her mind that she had to face her past once and for all, but she'd gotten cold feet halfway across town. She'd taken the detour specifically to practice what she was going to say. One more time. But even with her delaying tactic, her stomach felt like it was being turned inside out. Her hands shook harder as she got closer to the terminus address on her GPS app, and she felt as if she had frayed electric wires for nerve endings.

But no matter how scary or painful this errand was, the time had come. She'd spent too long hiding from her past, had stayed away from people she loved, respected and, frankly, needed in her life. Her own parents had been part-time and uninterested in her at best, and harshly critical and toxic at their worst. Valerie longed for the support and warmth she'd found those cherished summers as a teenager. In order to reclaim her uncle's family and reconnect with her loved ones, she had to deal with the proverbial elephant in the room. So now, when the disembodied voice of her GPS told her to make a right turn into one of the gentrified neighborhoods nestled in the city, she exhaled. And turned.

Soon she was parking in the narrow driveway of a Craftsman bungalow that stirred a bittersweet memory from the dusty corner of her mind.

"Whatcha doing?" seventeen-year-old Valerie had asked eighteen-year-old Nash when she'd found him sketching something on one of Lila's art pads.

"Oh, nothing," he'd said dismissively, trying to hide his work.

But she grabbed it, smoothed out the paper on a table and marveled at the neat, precise lines of the sketch he'd made. A house. A precise, perfectly even drawing of a house with a small floor plan in the top corner.

"This is good. Really good. Whose house is it?"

"No one's. I was just…playing around with ideas." He cast an awkward side-glance at her, and added, "I want to design houses and stuff when I get out of school. Maybe be an architect?"

She gave him her best smile. "You'd be good at that. This is really great."

He took back the paper, encouraged by her praise, then frowned. "It doesn't feel right yet. Something's missing. Maybe a dormer window? An upstairs? But that would mean reworking the first-level floor plan to include stairs."

"I know what it's missing," she said, taking back the paper and retrieving some art supplies from Lila's things. Leaning over the table, she began drawing shrubs and trees and flowers blooming in a flower bed. She added a wreath to the front door and a cat sitting on the steps. She tweaked and blended and shaded until the stark lines of his blueprint came alive with color and depth. Turning it, she said, "Ta-da! Now it's more than a house. It's a home."

Eighteen-year-old Nash's face had warmed, and he'd canted close to kiss her. "Perfect."

Now, more than twelve years later, Nash was living in a bungalow not all that different from the home they'd drawn together. The home she'd dreamed they'd one day share. Before…

She squeezed the steering wheel and sighed. Before life had taken their drawing and ripped it to shreds.

Shoving aside the memory, she climbed the steps to the front porch. After she knocked, she turned to take in the shady street. A woman walked by pushing a stroller while a toddler pedaled along behind her on a tricycle. Val's heart gave a sharp pang.

When no one answered her knock, she raised her fist to knock again, then jolted when something brushed against her leg. She glanced down to find a calico cat rubbing its cheek against her jeans at her calf. She exhaled and pressed a hand to her scuttling heart. "Cat, you scared me. Maybe give a meow to warn a girl next time?"

She reached down to scratch the calico's head, pleased with the idea that Nash owned a cat. That matched the compassion she remembered him having. She straightened as a sleek Infiniti sports coupe pulled in the driveway behind her car and parked.

She held her breath as she watched Nash unfold his tall, trim body from the low seat and scrutinize her car as he passed it.

"Hello, Nash." Valerie stepped out of the shadows of his porch.

His head came up, and his steps faltered when he spotted her. He said nothing for a beat, a hundred emotions playing over his face, as if shuffling through them, deciding which one to keep. When, at last, he spoke, his voice rasped softly from his throat. "Valerie." He approached the steps slowly, eyeing her warily. "Why—? What are you doing here?"

Chapter 2

"Wow. Earlier you walked away. Now you ask why I'm here." She gave a strained laugh. "Is that how you always greet a friend you haven't seen in years?"

He mounted the steps and narrowed his familiar emerald gaze on her. Colton green. So many of his siblings and cousins had the same mercurial green eyes. "Are we friends?" When she didn't answer right away, he added, "Seems to me friends keep in touch. Friends don't cut friends out of their life without explanation."

A shaft of pain arrowed through her heart. "Well, nothing like getting to the crux of things without polite small talk and hospitality." She lifted a corner of her mouth with a weak, tremulous smile. "What would Nicole say?"

The dark shadow that crossed his face sent a quiver to her belly. This was a bad idea. She should go.

But like the wind blowing a puffy cloud on its way,

allowing the sun to shine once more, Nash's face brightened a bit, and he flashed a stilted smile. "You're right. My apologies." He moved past her and keyed open the front door. When the calico tried to run inside, he blocked it with his foot. "Nope. Go home, Kitty."

Valerie experienced a pang of disappointment. So much for the heartwarming image she'd been drawing in her mind's eye. "She's not yours?"

"No. *He* lives two doors down." Standing back, he swept an arm grandly, motioning for Valerie to precede him.

She decided against countering his use of the male pronoun for the cat with the argument that thanks to genetics, calico cats were female. They had enough to discuss without starting with her contradicting him on something so trivial.

"Please, come in. May I get you something to drink?"

Okay. She recognized that he was being a bit patronizing now, but she understood his anger. Until she'd had her say, had a chance to try to correct the wrongs she'd done, she'd give him grace. "No, thank you."

Valerie moved into the living room and turned to face him. Nash chucked his car keys onto a small table in the foyer and marched straight to a bottle of something amber in a decorative glass decanter. He unstoppered the bottle and splashed a small amount in a glass. "Are you sure? I have beer and wine if you don't want scotch."

"No. Nothing. I don't drink."

He bobbed a nod, took a sip. "I see."

She doubted he did understand all the reasons she'd sworn never to drink alcohol, but that point was moot at the moment. Maybe someday she'd explain…

"Then maybe water? Or I think I have orange juice."

He took another sip of his drink before setting it down on the wet bar.

She shook her head. "No."

"Food then?"

She sighed. "Nash."

He turned up his palms. "Just trying to be hospitable. How am I doing?"

She gave him a long, silent stare. She imagined that she could hear the tension between them like a hum from a live wire. Finally, after he'd said nothing for several seconds she whispered, "Do you want me to go?"

"I didn't ask you to come."

"I know. But I thought we should talk. I want to explain. To give you some understanding." Tears pricked her eyes as she met his hard stare, then she started for the foyer. "You're right. This was a mistake."

He crossed the room in three long strides and caught her arm. The contact sent a jolt through her. His touch affected her more profoundly than their first kiss had. Because of their convoluted history. Because of the months—no, *years*—she longed for him. Because although she'd mentally prepared herself for confronting him, she hadn't anticipated him touching her. A foolish mistake.

His grip was firm but not rough, and as soon as she stopped, raising her gaze to his, his fingers loosened. But he kept his hand on her wrist. Val knew if he cared to notice, he'd feel the quick, unsteady throb of her pulse there.

"I'm sorry. My foul mood isn't your fault. You caught me at a bad time—"

When she opened her mouth to apologize for her timing, he shook his head. "You didn't know. And you're here now." He drew in and exhaled a breath, on which she smelled the sips of scotch he'd taken. "So say what you came to say."

Steeling herself, she raised her chin. "To start with… I'm sorry. I know my silence hurt you, and…for that, I'm deeply sorry, Nash."

A shudder rolled through him, one she both saw and felt as the hand around her wrist shook slightly. His expression softened, and she saw shadows gathering in his arrestingly green eyes. But then he blinked rapidly, firmed his mouth and released her arm as he strode away from her. He sat heavily on a recliner, but his back remained stiff. She could practically see him pulling his anger and resentment around him like a shield.

She understood the tactic. She'd used her anger toward her mother, toward Nash, toward the unfairness of life as a blanket to protect herself, comfort herself in the early days of their separation. Too much had happened too quickly for her to process it all, so she'd chosen anger as her defense mechanism, to keep herself from shattering.

Clearing the tightness from her throat, she returned to the living room and settled on the edge of the couch across from Nash.

"Okay," he said, gesturing with a flick of his hand. "I'm listening."

The doorbell at Axel Colton's house chimed, and he started to yell to his housekeeper to answer it before he remembered the staff had all gone home. He was alone. If the door was to be answered, he'd have to do it himself.

He scowled and considered ignoring the summons. He wasn't expecting anyone, didn't want to talk to anyone, was in a pissy mood thanks to Mr. Holier-than-thou Nash reaming him at the club. He'd have to talk to Erik about keeping his nephew in his own lane. What he did with his money was his business and his alone.

The bell sounded again followed by an urgent knock. Axel groaned, set aside his gin and tonic and struggled out of his chair.

"What?" he said ungraciously as he yanked open the door.

His visitor glared at him. "Took you long enough."

"I wasn't expecting anyone. Is there a reason you're here? 'Cause if you plan to tear me a new one or air a bunch of grievances, I'm not interested. Especially not today."

His visitor pushed past him. "Hmph. I bet. I heard that Nash showed up at your club and caused a scene. Threatened you. So the rumors are true?"

Axel slammed the front door and faced the look of disdain and disapproval. "No comment." He was tired of his life being the subject of news reports, gossip and family discussion. The dark look shooting at him said his reply was not what his visitor wanted to hear. "And if you don't like it you can leave."

"We have business to discuss."

"No, we don't. Not tonight. I'm in no mood."

"So because your nephew pissed you off, you're going to shut yourself up in here and suck your thumb? Ignore your responsibilities and commitments to—"

"Shut up! Just shut the hell up or get out of here!"

He could feel the crackle of ice, the chill that filled the room. And he was beyond caring whom he ticked off.

"You're a selfish bastard, you know that?"

"Well, you'd know, wouldn't you?" He turned to retrieve his drink, saw a shadow shift from the corner of his eye.

And something hard and heavy cracked against his

skull. Axel staggered. Stunned. Pain exploded in his head, and he slumped to the floor.

"No one talks to me like that! Not even you." His visitor turned and marched toward the door.

And the corners of his vision dimmed. Went black.

Nash worked to keep his expression blank, revealing nothing of the jangling inside him. Of all days for Valerie to show up on his doorstep, why today, when he was already twisted in knots over his confrontation with Axel, worried about Jackson, grieving with Myles and Faith over their missing son? His emotions were raw, and he didn't like starting this potentially explosive conversation with Val when he was already—not vulnerable exactly, but…unprepared.

As if he could ever be ready for rehashing his history with Valerie. Some things were better left in the past. For Nash, Valerie's desertion was one of those things. He'd moved on.

Or so he'd thought, until he'd seen her standing on his porch. Until he'd looked deep into her dark brown eyes and seen real regret looking back at him. And pain.

He could deal with his own heartache and anger over her rejection, but not hers. The idea that Val had lingering hurt, that her disappearing act could have a sad or tragic story behind it…well, that wasn't something Nash thought he could deal with. The mere suggestion that Valerie had scars of her own clawed at his core. Suffocated him.

"The autumn months, after I left here that summer twelve years ago, the last time we—"

Valerie stopped, glanced away, drew a shaky breath. "That fall was the worst time in my life. And thanks to my father's remoteness and my mother's alcoholism and, at the time, undiagnosed mental illness, I'd had some pretty bad times before that."

Nash nodded slowly. "I remember talking about your mother's drinking during those summers when you'd stay with Rick and Vita. Your mother would be in rehab."

"Mmm-hmm. She did several rounds of rehab. None ever stuck."

"What is this about mental illness?"

"I'm getting there." Val tucked a wisp of her light brown hair behind her ear, exposing the delicate skin where the curve of her jaw melded with her throat—a spot he'd traced with his tongue and knew intimately. She flexed the fingers of one hand with her other one, a nervous habit that Nash remembered from their teen years. His heart gave a hard thump of recognition, of nostalgia. A part of him longed to reach for her hand and lace her fingers with his, as he had so many times when they were younger. Instead, he clenched his hands in fists and focused on her story.

"First, I need to explain why that autumn was…my worst by far." Her voice cracked, and she paused to catch her breath. "I wanted to call you, I wanted so badly to hear your voice or even just text you, but then when I heard how you'd moved on without me, I had to deal with that loss, that feeling of betrayal on top of everything else."

Nash sat taller in his chair, confused. *Betrayal? What the—?*

"At first, my mother found ways to block me from talking to you, texting or emailing even, but after I learned the whole truth, I was angry. Hurt. Resentful. And I didn't want to tell you anything. It took me months to forgive you. By then, it felt like water under the bridge, and I didn't think—"

"Whoa, whoa, whoa!" He hadn't planned to interrupt her, despite his confusion. But something deep inside him rebelled. "Forgive me? You had to forgive *me*?"

"Yes. And I did. Well, I thought I had. Forgetting is much harder, and it still hurts sometimes."

Nash scratched his cheek, giving himself time to suppress the righteous indignation that swelled in him. *Hear her out*, a voice in his heart said.

Screw that! You deserve answers! his head countered, and he followed that impulse. "And what was it you had to forgive me for?" He couldn't quell the bitterness that leaked into his tone. "Trusting you with the realities of my own screwed-up parents? Sharing with you my most private hopes for the future? *Loving* you?"

Her brow furrowed over darkening eyes, and her hands clenched in her lap. "Love?" She spat the word at him as if it tasted vile. "How can you talk of loving me when not even two months after I left town you had moved on and had a new girlfriend? One you didn't have to keep secret from your family and were all too pleased to be photographed with."

Nash couldn't decide what startled him more—her venom toward him or her preposterous claim of replacing her. "What the hell are you talking about? I didn't—"

"Don't!" She aimed a finger at him. "Don't insult me by denying it. I saw the picture of you with her. Uncle Rick confirmed that you and that girl had been dating."

He was mentally scrambling to figure out whom she was referring to and what she could have misconstrued while trying not to blow his top. She'd disappeared from his life, broken him with her silence, her lack of communication. And now she wanted to blame *him* for it? To hell with that!

"There wasn't—" He huffed. "Who? Who did Rick say I was dating?"

Val snorted. "Some Lori or Lani or Loni or—"

Click. "Lucy? Lucy Greene?"

She arched an imperious eyebrow. "So you do remember?"

He flopped back in his chair, already exhausted by the conversation, but also relieved to have figured out the source of her confusion. "I took Lucy Greene to some froufrou fall cotillion as a favor to Nicole."

"I know. I saw the pictures. You two looked quite happy together."

Nash gave a bitter laugh. "That's generally what you do in pictures. You'd rather I'd snarled and frowned in the family's photos?"

"You had your arm rather intimately around her."

"Did I? I don't recall. But it seems you studied the pictures pretty closely and read a lot into them."

"Yes, I spent a long time looking at the pictures. They were proof that you'd lied to me. Forgotten me. Betrayed me."

"It was one date! Well…plus a group thing before, so we could meet. Lucy and her mother were new in town, and she didn't have anyone to take her to the dance, so—"

"Did you sleep with her?"

Nash almost choked. "What!"

"Did you sleep with her and get her pregnant, too?"

"No! Geez, Val! I did not 'sleep with her' or 'get her pregnant.'" He mocked her assertion with his tone. "It was one dance, for God's sake!" The accusation was so absurd, spoke so poorly of her opinion of him, that he almost missed the most important word. *Too.*

A numbness crept over him, and he stared stupidly at Val with his heartbeat sounding in his ears.

She brought both of her hands to her face, first pressing them to her mouth, then rubbing her eyes as she heaved a deep sigh. "I'm sorry. That was uncalled for. I told myself I wouldn't do this. I guess I'm still more hurt than I thought. Maybe it's— Sorry." She lowered her hands and raised a beseeching gaze to him. "Can we scratch that last bit and start over. I don't want to argue. I want—" She faltered, tilting her head to the side. "Nash? What? Why are you staring at me like that?"

"Too?" The word sounded strangled, and he cleared his throat. "You said, *too.* Did I sleep with Lucy and get her pregnant…too?"

"I did?"

He nodded slowly.

The color drained from Valerie's face, and he had all the answer he needed. Turning her head away, she whispered, "Oh."

Nash leaned forward in his chair again. A surreal sense of suspended animation engulfed him.

"Val?" he breathed more than spoke.

Trembling and pale, Valerie perched on the edge of the couch like a startled bird ready to take flight. She couldn't seem to meet his gaze for long moments. Finally, she closed her eyes and said quietly, "When I went back to Ohio, after that last summer we were together… I was pregnant." Opening her eyes again, she met his stunned look. "I took a test six weeks after I got home, because I'd been feeling sick to my stomach a lot and had missed my—"

Questions assailed him from so many directions, he didn't know how to process them. He could only stare for painful seconds.

"Nash, say something," she begged while the silence stretched out.

"Why—why didn't you tell me?"

She inhaled and wiped a tear from her cheek. "I wanted to. I was going to, but my mother…"

When she hesitated, he shoved abruptly to his feet, and Val startled.

Nash stalked to the wet bar, where he'd left his scotch, and lifted the drink. He stared into the amber liquid, then slammed down the glass without drinking.

"Why didn't you tell me?"

"I was going to! But my mother found out, and she—" Valerie swiped angrily at the flood of tears that streaked down her face. "She wouldn't let me."

"Excuse me? How could she stop you? It's a simple matter to pick up the phone and call or text or—"

"She took my phone and ripped the cord of the house phone from the wall in a fit of drunken rage."

He scoffed and waved a hand. "So use a friend's phone. Write a letter. Send a damn smoke signal! I had a right to know I was a father!" A chill rolled through him as he spoke the words. A father. He was *a father*?

While that thought buzzed in his brain, Val moved toward him, pleading, explaining. "It wasn't as simple as that. My mother…" She stopped, closed her eyes and started again. "She got pregnant with me when she was eighteen. My father, Rick's brother, isn't my real father. Both my real father and her parents abandoned her when she learned she was pregnant. She was alone when I was born, and she's always hated my real father for ignoring his responsibility. When I told her I was pregnant, she flipped out. She was furious with me for getting myself in the same situation she'd been in. She said she wouldn't let me ruin my chances for a better life the way I had ruined hers." She scoffed bitterly. "That's right. My mother told me I ruined her life. Essentially blamed me for her drinking. For stealing her dreams."

"Yeah, your mom's not a nice lady. We established that years ago," Nash said impatiently. "But let's not brush over the fact that you didn't tell me *I am a father*!"

Valerie stilled, her expression chastened. Releasing a breath slowly, she lowered her eyes to her hands and whispered, "No. You're not."

Chapter 3

Nash thought, in the heat of his anger, he'd heard wrong. He took a moment to replay her words in his head. "I'm not?"

Valerie walked back to the couch and sat down again, not looking at him.

Nash pinched the bridge of his nose, trying to gather his spinning thoughts. What did her last confession mean? Had she cheated on him? Gotten rid of their baby? Had her mother forced her to give away the baby?

"I think you need to explain," he said in a low, growling tone.

Her chin tilted to a haughty angle. "I was trying to when you yelled at me."

He returned to the grouping of his couch and recliners, hovering over her. His whole body was taut, quivering with fury, shock and frustration. "Don't you think I have a right to yell and curse? I can do whatever I feel like when you come into my home and accuse me of betrayal and unfaithfulness and deception! When, now that the truth has come out, you were the one who betrayed and kept secrets, and…hell, maybe you even cheated on me. Huh?"

Her gaze snapped up to his, ablaze with indignation. "What? No! How could you think—?"

"You said you'd gotten pregnant, and now you tell me I wasn't the father. Seems to me—"

"I said you aren't *a* father, not that you weren't *the* father! There's a big difference. Don't twist my words!"

"Gah!" Nash threw up his hands, roaring his frustration as he stomped away. "This is going nowhere. Would you just *tell me* what you're trying to say? Why did you come today? What did you have to tell me after all these years that makes any difference now?"

Val's shoulders drooped. Her whole body seemed to wilt in defeat, and she shook her head. "Maybe none of it does make any difference now. But for years I've avoided coming to Chicago, avoided seeing my family and friends, the place that was once my escape, my happy place, because I was scared of running into you. I was afraid of the pain that would be revived if I saw you. I was afraid of *this* conversation." She pointed at the floor to emphasize her point. "And today I realized I couldn't continue to let my fear rule me, deprive me of things I loved, people I loved. I knew I had to face up to what happened when I was seventeen or I could never really get on with my life." She puffed out a breath and rubbed her arms. "That is why I'm here. I'm trying to put things…if not right, at least out in the open. I don't want to miss out on seeing my uncle and cousins because I'm avoiding you."

Nash shook the tension from his hands. Returned to his recliner. Calmed himself. "Right. Okay. So finish.

Explain to me how it is that I'm somehow not a father, when five minutes ago you said I was."

"You're not, because I never had the baby." Her voice was thin, sad.

He narrowed his eyes on her, his mood growing dark again. "Hang on. Are you saying you—?"

"No! I wanted our baby! As scared and confused as I was about being pregnant, as much hell and grief as my mother gave me, I wanted our child! I would have done anything to save it, but I—" She choked on a sob. "I couldn't. I m-miscarried. And it almost killed me."

Nash curled his fingers into the nubby fabric of his recliner and absorbed the revelation. His chest filled with a hollow ache that swelled painfully when he met the grief and regret in Valerie's gaze.

She swiped at her nose, then ducked her head as she dug in her purse for a facial tissue. She dried her eyes and blew her nose while Nash processed everything he was learning. She'd lived a very different reality to what he'd imagined. He'd written a much harsher script in his mind about her coldly dismissing him, ghosting him, having played him for a fool.

The slow, hammering *lub-dub* in his chest, the vise-like constriction stealing his breath and the sour roil of scotch in his gut all called out his unjust conclusions. Yet another voice scratched in his brain, warning him not to forgive too easily. He had too much experience with rejection to trust that one simple conversation could mend all. Valerie's explanation may have cracked his defenses, but until he had proof of her true heart, her loyalty, her intentions, he still needed to be on guard.

She still clutched the crumpled tissue in her hand when she spoke again, her voice still strangled with tears. "I'm not being melodramatic when I say that, either—that it almost killed me. Because the heartbreak of losing the baby, on top of my mother's campaign against you and the report I'd been told that you'd moved on, was only half of the story."

Nash squeezed the armrests harder, bracing himself. "What do you mean?"

"When I miscarried, there were...complications."

Nash tensed. Opened his mouth to ask questions.

But she quickly added, "Long story short, I hemorrhaged because of problems with my post-miscarriage D and C. I lost a lot of blood and needed transfusions. I was very weak, unresponsive for a while. The nurses told me I almost died."

"I did something...regrettable. And I need you to help me clean up the loose ends."

Simon Wilcox was well into his six-pack when the call came in. "Meaning?"

"Not over the phone. But I'll make it worth your trouble. Never fear."

"Cash. Tonight. I don't take no credit card, you know."

He heard an exasperated sigh. "Fine. Of course. Just... get over to Axel Colton's and take care of things. If you need a fall guy, Nash Colton could use a comeuppance. And he argued with Axel publicly, so it'd be the perfect frame."

"Nash Colton, huh?" Simon rose from his recliner and stretched. "All right. I'm on it."

Nash took a moment to process what Val had said. Complications with the miscarriage? He'd almost lost Valerie for good. To death. Because she'd miscarried his baby. A chill raced through Nash, and he rasped, "My God, Val."

"I don't remember much except waking up in the hospital ICU and learning I'd lost the ba-b-by—" Her voice cracked again, and when she closed her eyes, new tears leaked onto her cheeks. "I'd...l-lost my last tie to you."

Without weighing the ifs, ands or buts, Nash vaulted from the recliner, and as he dropped on the couch, he scooped her onto his lap. Pure instinct and gut-wrenching grief compelled him to wrap her in his arms, as if he could shield her from the tragedy that had already wounded her so deeply.

Without hesitation, she curled against him, draping her arms around his neck and burying her face in his shoulder. Her sobs reverberated in his soul, shook him to his core. "Geez, Val. I wish... Well, a lot of things, but mostly, I wish I'd known what you were going through."

She sniffled and pulled back. "What if you had? What difference would it have made?"

"Well..." Her question had caught him off guard, and after his initial shock, it nudged his ire again. "For one thing, I wouldn't have hated you quite so much for so long."

She made a tiny hiccupping sound and scooted away from him. "You hate me?"

"Hated. Past tense. I had to hate you at first to get over you. Then I just...tried not to think about you. But the underlying hurt was still there."

Val closed her eyes and slumped against the fat sofa cushions. "Oh, man. So much hate and hurt and wasted time. Because I let my mother get in my head."

Nash harbored no illusions about Valerie's mother, but her blame shifting still rankled. It still didn't answer why Val had so easily lost faith in him, denied him the truth about the pregnancy and miscarriage. Her radio silence for years.

"Because she showed you a picture and told you a lie about me?" His tone spoke for his skepticism.

Valerie repositioned herself to fully face him and hugged herself as she spoke, as if trying to hold herself together. "I know I own some responsibility. I can admit that. I let my mother poison me against the Coltons, including you, when I was vulnerable—physically, emotionally and mentally. She was relentless, and I was heartbroken. But I should have known better. I'm sorry."

Poison me against the Coltons. Those words stood out discordantly, like someone striking a gong during a lullaby. He slapped the sofa cushions and grunted. "Again with the Coltons. Why? Why did she hate my family so much? I know my dad and Uncle Axel are no peaches, but Nicole and Vita and my cousins… They don't deserve her disdain. Did Rick say something to your dad?"

She shook her head and flashed an ill-humored smile. "No. It had nothing to do with my dad or his brother. Although Rick marrying Axel's ex was a bitter pill for my mother to swallow."

"Then what? When we were kids you made me keep our relationship a secret because of your mom's ill will toward my family. If her hatred toward the Coltons is the root of what tore the two of us apart, I want to know why." He drilled a finger into the armrest. "Why all the animosity, Valerie?"

Valerie drew a deep breath and held it as she pushed to her feet. She paced over to the floor-to-ceiling window that looked out on his small backyard.

As he waited for her to respond, his phone rang, and he checked the screen reluctantly. He hated to interrupt this discussion when he was finally getting answers, but…

Nicole. Who'd broken her hip recently, and he'd

told her to call night or day if she needed anything. He couldn't *not* answer.

"Sorry, I need to take this." He tapped the answer icon and said, "Hi, Mom. Everything okay?"

Valerie turned and looked out his back window, giving him the illusion of privacy.

"Yes, dear. I'm fine. But I heard through the grapevine that you had a run-in at the racket club with Axel. Care to tell me what that was about?"

He rolled his eyes. "The grapevine? You mean some busybodies from the snobby club wanted juicy gossip."

"Well, your characterization is rather accurate, but my concern for you is genuine."

He didn't doubt that. Nicole had been gracious and warm to him and Damon when their real mother died of an aneurysm when he was eight years old. She'd welcomed the boys into her home and raised them as her own, despite knowing they were the product of one of Erik's affairs. Their parentage wasn't the boys' fault, and they needed maternal love and guidance, she avowed. Damon and Nash loved her with their whole hearts and would move heaven and earth for her.

"I'm fine. Just…frustrated with the a— The old curmudgeon."

"Well, I can only assume you had a good reason for exposing yourself to a dose of Axel's brand of stress and disappointment. I'm here if you need to vent. I'm well versed in his bad behavior and would be a sympathetic ear."

"I know you would. And, thanks, but no. Can I do anything for you? You need groceries picked up?"

"No, thank you, dear. I am enjoying the delights of DoorDash these days. All my favorite restaurant dishes at the tip of my cell-phone finger. I'm having the chicken piccata from my favorite Italian bistro tonight."

"Well, *buon appetito*!" His use of the Italian phrase caught Valerie's attention. After he disconnected the call, he met her querying gaze. "Don't be too impressed. That's one of about five things I can say in Italian."

"Well, then you know three more than I do. *Ciao* and *grazie* are about the extent of my repertoire."

He set his cell phone on the end table beside him, then stretched the muscles in his neck, tipping his head from one side to the other. Nicole's call had given them both a needed break from the tense conversation, and while he still wanted answers, had a hundred questions for her, he was remiss to dive back in. Yet.

Her extended silence echoed his sentiment. She turned back to his window and gazed peacefully out at his fenced backyard, where a pair of cardinals ate from his bird feeder. She rubbed her arms as if cold, though she wore a long, soft-looking sweater over leggings. The pink yarn and cut of the sweater clung to her torso and past her hips, showing off her gentle curves. She'd always been on the thin side, rather flat with a lean boyish shape as a teenager, but the years had been kind enough to soften the bony edges and round out her angular hips. No one could call her voluptuous, but gone was the rangy girl, replaced by a woman with lithe femininity and grace. Like a dancer. Or a lean cat. Or—

She turned and caught him staring, and he blinked, averting his eyes quickly.

"I knew when I came here tonight that this would be a difficult conversation. Contentious." She sighed, walked over and sat back down on the couch, raking her light brown hair from her face with her fingers. "I hadn't realized it would be so exhausting. But deep emotions are exhausting anytime, huh?" Then in a softer voice, "I should know that better than anyone."

He grunted. Nodded. He'd been worn out from his confrontation with Axel, even before he jumped into his tangled history with Valerie. "Yeah. We can put a pin in this and hash the rest out another day."

Her chin jerked up, her eyes widening. "No. That's not what I meant. Now that we're in the weeds... Well, I feel like we need to reach some understanding, finish what we've started."

He rubbed a hand on his belly and cocked an eyebrow. "All right then. But... Nicole's talk of food reminds me I haven't eaten. I'm going to need some fuel if we're going to plow ahead. Mind if I start some dinner while we finish our chat?"

She shook her head. "Not at all. Go ahead."

He stood and started for his kitchen. "Have you eaten?"

She pressed a hand to her stomach. "No. But I'm not really in the mood to eat…if that was an invitation." She chuckled awkwardly. "Way to assume too much, Val."

"That's exactly what I meant. Are you sure? I was thinking I'd mix up something easy like spaghetti and a salad." He opened his refrigerator and started pulling out ingredients. Waving a cucumber toward her, he said, "You were about to explain why your mother hated the Coltons?"

Valerie strolled to his tiny kitchen and propped a hip against the counter. "I only learned the whole truth that autumn, when she discovered I was pregnant. When she dragged out of me that the baby was yours, she went ballistic…which I can see now was a symptom of her illness." She reached for the bag of carrots he'd set on the counter and selected a paring blade from the knife block. "But more on that later."

He aimed his own knife toward the cabinet at her feet. "There should be another cutting board down there." Then, turning over the blade in his own hand, he chuckled wryly, "Are we sure the two of us should be wielding knives while we have this conversation?"

She stilled and cast him a wary look before twitching her lips in a teasing grin. "I'll promise not to stab you, if you'll swear to the same."

He arched an eyebrow, pretending to consider. "Well, okay."

She set to work scraping one of the carrots. "Anyway, all I originally knew, during those summers when I came to visit, was that she'd warned me to stay away from you. She maintained that you Coltons were bad people. That you'd hurt me. That you were liars and cheats and snobby scum, et cetera. She gave me no reasons for her beliefs. She just threatened me and told me to stay far away from you all." She snorted. "Like I could do that all summer while staying with Vita and Rick. You and your Colton cousins and half siblings were always around. And I liked you. All of you. Especially you. Obviously."

"If she hated us, why did she even let you come down for the summer?"

"Let? Heck, she begged me not to leave her to come here. But one of the few good things my dad ever did for me was planning my summers in Chicago. He intervened. Insisted I be allowed to come here. I guess, in his own way, he was protecting me, giving me a chance to experience life with a more normal family. He warned me to be careful not to mention you or other Coltons to her."

Nash angled a glance at her as he dumped diced cucumber in a bowl. "So you just accepted—"

"Let me finish. There's more. Much more."

He motioned with his hand for her to continue.

"Like I said, after Mother found out I was pregnant, she told me the whole sordid story."

Nash stiffened his spine, his gut tensing. A sordid story? Why was he not surprised? Growing up, he'd learned that Coltons attracted drama and scandal like ants to a picnic.

"When my mother was in high school, she and her family lived here in Chicago." She finished cleaning the carrot and laid it on the chopping board to cut. "It's where she met my dad and Rick. And the Coltons. Specifically Axel and Erik." With a short pause, she gave him a side-glance. "They met through the country club they all belonged to. Well, not Rick so much. He had his own friends, but my dad worked there as a bartender. He'd sneak my mom drinks, even though she was underage, because he had a crush on her."

Nash gritted his teeth and fisted his hands, bracing for the bomb, trying to be patient with her story setup.

She must have sensed his impatience, because she bobbed her head once in apology and blurted, "My mom and Erik had a romantic relationship her senior year of high school. It ended badly."

His eyes widened. "Your mother dated my father?"

Chapter 4

Nash wasn't sure what he'd expected to hear, but it certainly wasn't *that*. He swiped a hand over his mouth as he goggled at Valerie, then sputtered, "Are you about to tell me you're my half sister? 'Cause if you are—"

Val gave her head a firm shake, her eyes saying *I know, right*? "No. They dated—if you could call it that—but she wouldn't sleep with him. He was already married by then, but she was crazy about him. Obsessed, really. He knew it, and he pursued her. Tried to seduce her. It fed his ego, I guess, to have a pretty young thing so interested in him. But...she had some warped beliefs about sex, even then. For her it was a tool. A source of power and control. She thought she could string him along by teasing him without ever giving him what he wanted. But he tired of her game. She claims that's why he dumped her. When he started ignoring her, Mother was furious and came up with a twisted scheme to try to win him back." She paused in her carrot chopping and shook her head. "She thought she could make Erik jealous by coming on to one of his friends. Some guy named Jimmy that Erik brought to a country club summer social."

She hesitated and picked up a slice of carrot to nibble distractedly. Then with a sigh, she continued her tale. "Even at that age—she was barely eighteen—she already had a problem with alcohol. The story she tells is that she slept with Jimmy out of spite, a bad decision made when she was way too drunk to think straight. But Erik didn't bat an eye when she told him, which made her even madder. Then, when Mother discovered she was pregnant, neither Jimmy nor Erik wanted anything to do with her or the baby. Her parents were horrified and kicked her out of the house, cut her off. She was alone. Devastated. All of this, of course fed her BPD."

"BPD?"

She set the knife down and faced him. Nodded. "Borderline personality disorder. We only got an official diagnosis a few years ago."

Nash's brow furrowed. "I...don't know what that is."

Val's shoulders drooped, and she pinched her nose. "It's a mental disorder that manifests in several ways. Extreme emotions, fear of abandonment, delusions and paranoia—"

"Hold up," he said. "Let's finish one topic at a time. Huh?"

"Yeah. Right? I told you it was complicated." She nibbled another carrot slice, then mused, "Where was I?"

"Your mom was pregnant and alone. I assume you were that baby?"

"I was. Remember? I 'ruined her life.'" She wiggled her fingers, making air quotes. "Me...and Erik Colton. She blames your dad for dumping her. Betraying her.

Pushing her toward a desperate act with Jimmy." She scooped the sliced carrots into his bowl with the cucumber. "Of course, she also later learned that, in addition to being married, your father had *another* woman on the side, too."

Nausea swamped Nash's gut. Just when he thought his opinion of his father couldn't get any lower… "My mom."

Valerie's eyebrows lifted, her mouth slack for a moment. "Oh, my God. I hadn't put two and two together. I was shocked enough learning why she despised the Coltons—and it is *all* the Coltons she hates. When her family kicked her out, she asked Axel for help, too, thinking he'd be sympathetic. Of course, since the baby wasn't Erik's, wasn't a Colton, he turned down her request for help. Flat. Quite rudely, with plenty of name calling and bad vibes to hear her tell it."

Her comment reminded him of his own attempt to get blood from that particular turnip earlier in the afternoon, and he grumbled, "No surprise. He wouldn't part with a nickel today, even to help his own grandson."

Valerie tipped her head and frowned. "What do you mean?"

He waved a hand. "I saw Axel today. He won't help get Jackson back, but…that's a story for another time. You were saying your mom was alone, and…?"

"Right. Alone. But to hear her tell it, the Coltons, fearing she might try other means to extort money from them, started an underhanded campaign to humiliate her and paint her as unstable and emotionally unwell among their friends at the club." She rinsed her knife at the sink and gave a wry scoff. "Turns out they weren't wrong. Mother is now sober and has doctors and medication helping keep her on a more even keel, but her BPD was

untreated back then. Her emotions, perceptions and re-
actions to people were almost certainly off the charts."

"So she was alcoholic with BPD?" Nash's mind bog-
gled at what that must have been like for Valerie growing up.

She nodded, then added, "Substance abuse is common for people with BPD. They're desperate to numb the
emotional pain and anxiety they live with every day. Her
biggest fear was abandonment, so imagine how she felt
after being kicked out of her parents' house, losing her
financial support. All of her friends sort of went 'poof'
thanks to the Coltons' influence. Your dad and Axel essentially drove her out of town, branded with a scarlet
letter. Only my dad felt sorry for her, offered to marry
her. They moved to Ohio together and were married by
a justice of the peace three weeks before I was born. But
she clung to her bitterness toward the Coltons, would
never let it go."

"Fast-forward seventeen years, and she finds out her
daughter is pregnant with a Colton's baby…" he said,
seeing her situation in a new light.

"Exactly. She could have forgiven me almost anything
but that. But knowing I went against her wishes to stay
away from you, knowing I was in the same situation she'd
been in, because of a Colton… She was merciless. And
my dad had pretty well checked out of our lives at that
point. Living on the road with his business travel more
often than not. He dealt with Mother by avoiding her. So
Mother was the only one home when I started miscarry-
ing. I had to tell her the truth about the pregnancy then.
I needed a doctor."

Nash blew out a slow exhale. "But you knew I wasn't
like my dad. I cared about you. I'd have been there for
you!"

"Maybe I know that now. But hindsight is always twenty-twenty. When I was seventeen, in the hospital after losing our baby and so much blood, her words—her venom—changed me. Hers was the only side I was hearing. She'd taken away my means to call you, and when I wrote to you, I got no letters back, despite your promise at the end of the summer that you'd keep in touch."

"No letters?" Nash frowned. He wiped his hands on a towel and pushed the bowl of salad out of his way so he could lean his hip against the counter. "I wrote a bunch of letters when nothing else I'd done got a response. I'd called, texted, emailed—"

"She took my phone away, remember? And she put these ridiculous parental controls on my computer, where she screened my email and internet use for a year, as punishment, after she learned I was pregnant. She said I'd proven I couldn't be trusted with full freedom. Clearly she was screening my mail, too. Both going in and out. I swear I wrote five or six letters before I gave up."

Nash tried to absorb the truths he was hearing. Tried to decide if he believed Valerie or if she was blaming her mother's condition to alleviate her own guilt. He rubbed a hand on his cheek as he processed it all. "So now, your mother is…?" He waved a hand, inviting her to fill in the blank.

Val pulled a face, twisted her mouth in a way that said she was searching for the right word. "Mostly stable, is the best I can say." She took a tomato from the counter and washed it. "She fought me over seeing a psychiatrist, but it's really made a huge difference. The key is keeping her on track, on her meds and attending her AA and therapy sessions. That's where her AA sponsor, Nancy, and I come in. We monitor her and encourage her." She began dicing the tomato. "It's been a long time coming, but she's been sober, in therapy and on the right meds for several years."

"But she—"

She raised a hand to forestall his arguments. "I'm not excusing her previous behavior, but it helps me to know there was a root cause for it. That she isn't a total monster."

"And your dad? Where does he fit in all this now that she's in treatment?"

"He died last spring."

He didn't detect a great deal of sadness in her tone, but still he said, "I'm sorry, Val. I didn't know."

"Thanks." She finished scraping the diced tomatoes into the bowl and rinsed her hands in the sink. "I'm afraid my relationship with my dad is another victim of my mother's illness. Because he avoided Mother, left me alone to deal with her and her hypercritical, unpredictable brand of parenting, and I resented him for years. That's something I'm dealing with in my own counseling sessions."

He rubbed his chin, relieved to hear she had a professional to talk to, to help her deal with her own stresses and issues of caring for her mother. Stepping toward her, he put a hand at her elbow and nodded. "I can relate to a distant father. Erik being who he is, and my mother having been one of his affairs, I knew him in name only for the earliest days of my life."

She turned to face him, her gaze locking on his as she listened.

"I heard her embittered stories about what a jerk Erik was, how he'd done her wrong until the day Damon and I found her dead in her bed from an aneurism."

Valerie gasped. "You found her? You never told me that. How awful for you and Damon!"

"Yeah, that was no fun. As you know, our dad wanted nothing to do with raising us. Thank God Nicole was of a different mind. I owe her so much. She's been the mother Damon and I needed ever since my mom died." He gave a gentle tug, and she came easily into his arms. Lifting a hand to her cheek, he caressed her face with his thumb. "How did you turn out so kind and good with parents like that?"

"Well, Mother had good moments. They may have been few, but...they gave me hope. And, of course, I saw true love and nurturing when I came to stay with Uncle Rick and Vita. Goodness, but I loved being with your family. Nicole and Vita and Rick gave me roots. All of the kids gave me happy memories and something to cling to when Mother had her bad days."

Nash stared into Valerie's dark eyes, and years of resentment seemed to evaporate like the morning mist after sunrise. "So much hurt and misunderstanding. Do you think we can find our way back to each other?"

She exhaled, her breath a soft tickle on his cheek. "Is that what you want?"

He leaned in and pressed a soft kiss to her lips. "Isn't it worth a try?"

"Oh, Nash, I—I don't know." She pulled gently away and pressed a hand to her mouth. Then, raking that hand through her hair, she whispered, "I've spent so many years getting over you. Moving on. It scares me to think of going back, to opening myself to that kind of pain again."

"Yeah, well, it's scary for me, too. I spent most of my life feeling cast aside by one person or another. You, my dad, even my mom when she died. As a kid, I was angry with her for leaving us." He put a hand on her shoulder and turned her to face him again. "Maybe it's stupid to think we can recapture what we had. But I've felt like we had unfinished business for years. Don't we owe it to ourselves to explore whether we had something real or if we were just two kids with raging hormones and idealistic views of love?"

"Is that what you've told yourself all these years? We just had raging hormones and idealism?" Her tone was hurt, and beneath his grasp of her shoulders, he felt her shudder.

"I had to believe something. The evidence, your disappearance and silence, gave that theory credence."

She frowned, hesitated. "If we did rekindle our relationship, what—what would I tell my mother?"

He jerked back as if slapped. "What?" A bitter laugh escaped his throat. "Seriously? After she tore us apart once, do you really care what she thinks?"

Her shoulders squared, and obvious affront swept over her face. "No, of course not. But she's fought hard to get her life on track. She has a job and her days now bear at least a semblance of normalcy after so many years. I have to worry about what hearing I was in a relationship again with you, a Colton, might do to the fragile balance of her mental state."

"So...what? Because your mother might not be able to handle the idea of you with me, you won't even consider the possibility?"

She threw up her hands and shook her head. "I don't know! I haven't thought it through. I never imagined when I came here today that we'd be talking about a reconciliation. I simply thought it was time that you knew the truth and that I exorcized the ghosts that had kept me from the family I love and need in my life."

Nash scrubbed a hand over his face, paced across his kitchen floor and back to her. If he'd learned one thing in his life, it was not to let opportunity pass you by. Life didn't hand you anything. He'd had to work for every bit of love, success and happiness he had today. This house, his education, his job with the architectural firm downtown. If he wanted Valerie, he couldn't let her walk away without a fight.

"Well, while you debate whether our love is worth a chance, consider this..." With a long step toward her, he drew her close and captured her lips with his own.

Chapter 5

Valerie stiffened, stunned by Nash's bold move. Adrenaline pumped through her, spiking her heart rate. But her surprise passed quickly as pleasure swept through her. Her fight-or-flight instinct yielded to a focused attention on the pressure of his mouth on hers, the way his lips commanded compliance, molded to hers, wooed her to respond.

Her body relaxed, and she sank against him, not analyzing the wisdom of what was happening, only following the lead of her desire. She looped her arms around his neck and feathered her fingers through the short blond hair lying against his neck. His touch and his lips were familiar and welcome to her starving soul. She'd been reluctant to date in the years since her miscarriage. Not because she feared getting pregnant again, but because the whole experience of losing the baby, losing Nash and living through her mother's bitterness and scorn had scarred her.

Was she crazy to even consider reigniting the passion and emotions she'd locked away for Nash? Surely doing something so foolish would only open wounds best left scabbed.

"You taste just the way I remember," Nash muttered as he trailed kisses along her neck. "Like berries and summer sun and a hint of cinnamon."

She canted back and flashed an impish smile. "And you taste like trouble."

He grunted fake indignation.

"Pure temptation and forbidden pleasure. With a hint of scotch."

He wiggled his eyebrows devilishly, and using a deep, mysterious voice, said, ""Come into my parlor," said the spider to the fly...""

She pulled a face and shuddered. "Ooo. You'll get nowhere fast with me talking about spiders."

He chuckled. "Oh, right. I remember having to peel you off the ceiling because of a harmless daddy long-legs once."

She arched an eyebrow. "You're still talking about spiders."

"How about...?" He leaned in and took her mouth with his again. "Better?"

"Much." She reciprocated, angling her lips to deepen the kiss and pressing her body more fully along his.

Heat sluiced through her. Sheer lust pulsed to life in her blood, as he stroked his hand down her spine to cup her bottom. He drew her hips closer to his, and she felt his shiver of pleasure as her body found his groin.

His hands hooked behind her legs, and he lifted her, carried her to sit on the counter as he leaned her back and nipped the tendons of her throat. "I want you, Val. I never stopped wanting you."

The husky growl matched the fervor of his searching hands, his hungry lips and his straining muscles. When doubts nudged her brain, she shut them down, allowing a sweet, muzzy oblivion to fill her head as she surrendered to the lead of her heart, the pleasure of his lips guiding hers in an erotic dance.

"Not here. Not like this," she rasped, and he raised his head to meet her gaze with bright eyes. "Take me to bed, Nash. We've never made love in a real bed."

In a back seat, behind Nicole's bushes, in a storage closet and on a blanket under the stars, yes. But never on a bed. His eyes blazed as if he, too, was remembering their youthful liaisons. The reckless passion, hurried joining and awkward fumbling. Rarely did they have time to savor, to cuddle, to explore.

He swallowed hard and scooped her into his arms. "One bed coming up."

The last rays of the day's sunlight had been peeking through the blinds when they'd tumbled onto his bed some time ago, but now his room was dark. He angled his head, looking for the spot his phone had ended up as they'd stripped and clothes had been tossed aside without care. He didn't see his pants from where he was lying with Valerie tucked close against him, dozing. Naked. Sated. At least he'd slaked his need with the frantic coupling, followed by long, patient lovemaking that had ended with them napping in each other's embrace.

After several minutes of listening to the soft soughing of her breath, he wiggled out from under her carefully, trying not to disturb her.

"Nash?"

"Oops. Sorry to wake you."

"What time is it?"

"That's what I was just gonna check." He snapped on the bedside lamp, and she groaned and threw her arm over her eyes.

"Do you really need that?"

He found his pants but not his phone. Then he remembered putting it on the coffee table after talking to Nicole...

"Hmm. Phone's in the living room so...still no idea what time it is." He reached for the lamp again, but paused when he saw the curve of her breast at the top edge of the sheet. Without dousing the light, he stretched out next to her and tugged the sheet.

She gasped, lowering her arm to grab the sheet. "Nash! What—?"

"I wanted to look at you. In the light. You're beautiful, you know."

"I—" She clutched the sheet, hesitating, clearly dubious.

"Shy now, huh?" He grinned and, swinging a leg over her hips to straddle her, he slipped his fingers under her arms with a teasing nip.

She yelped and squirmed, laughing. "Nash!"

"Shy and still ticklish. My, my, my..." His tone was playful, as was the narrow-eyed warning look she shot him.

"Nash, so help me if you—"

He tickled her again, and she squealed, kicking her legs and slapping at his hands half-heartedly as she giggled. "Stop! That tickles!"

"That's the point, love." He ducked his head to kiss her, then went for another tickle. The bubbly sound of her laughter tripped down his spine. Filled his soul. He much preferred the effervescent joy to the anger and tears they'd shared earlier that evening. But that was the way his relationship had always been with Val. She awoke in him the full spectrum of emotions, made him feel things he'd worked his whole life to lock away. Which was why she could be dangerous to him, to the carefully ordered life he'd built where only a select few were allowed close to him. Val had been one of them. And he'd gotten burned. So why was he even considering letting her back in?

A loud rumbly gurgle interrupted his thoughts, and he blinked at Val. "Was that your stomach?"

She winced and pulled a sheepish grin. "Not too subtle, huh?"

"Well, we never did get around to eating, and we burned quite a few calories earlier." He climbed off the bed, unembarrassed by his nudity. "I'm peckish myself, and I did promise you dinner, so…"

Valerie sat up, raking her hair back from her face as a frown twisted her mouth. "Thanks, but I should probably head back to Uncle Rick's. He and Vita will worry if I'm very late."

Nash found his pants, and after putting on clean briefs from his drawer, he started dressing. "So text them. Tell them you're having a late dinner with a friend." He poked his arms through his sleeves, then arched an eyebrow. "In fact, tell them you're spending the night."

She paused with only one bra strap up, her face incredulous. "Spend the night?"

He dropped on the bed beside her and cupped the base of her skull with his hand. "Why not? Don't you want to stay? We could make love all night, and I'll even call in sick to work tomorrow if you want. I just got you back, Val. I'm not ready to let you go so soon."

"I don't know. Nash—"

He cut her off with a blazing kiss, pulling no punches to remind her of the heat and passion that could be theirs if she stayed.

When he broke the kiss, she was breathless and touched her fingers to her mouth. She slanted him a glance. "Feed me first, and we'll play the rest by ear."

He smacked another kiss on her lips, not bothering to hide his cocky grin. "Good enough."

The next morning, in the soft golden light from his window, Nash studied Valerie while she slept, cataloging all the changes the last twelve years had made to her face. Her cheeks were still high and round, hinting at her familiar youthful appearance, but the rest of her face was slimmer, more womanly. He ran a fingertip down her narrow nose, and her dark eyes blinked open.

"Hi," he whispered huskily, overcome with a tangled sense of tenderness and flare of lust. Valerie had always been a blend of soft and sensual to him. Innocence and seduction. So full of contradictions. Mysteries. Magnetism.

Her smile was slow and sleepy. "Good morn—"

A yawn swallowed her words, and he chuckled. "Same to you."

"What time is it?" she asked, turning her head to squint at the room with her elfin nose adorably wrinkled. "I'm blind as a bat until I get my contacts in."

"Early still. No need to rush." He eased closer and tugged her into his arms. With a smirk she couldn't see from her position, he said flatly, "Chocolate is disgusting. People who like chocolate are idiots."

Predictably, he felt her stiffen. "What! Are you kidding me? Chocolate is the best! Where did that even come from?"

"Well, it's just that for all our arguing last night, I had a rather wonderful time making up. So I thought I'd pick a fight now so maybe we could—" he gave her a squeeze and kissed her forehead "—make up again?"

He felt as much as heard the vibration of her laughter against his chest. "And what if I said I agreed that chocolate was nasty?"

He angled away from her, then, mimicking her, said, "What! Are you kidding me? Chocolate is the best!"

She grinned and shook her head at him. "Goofball. As I recall, our post-dinner, completely amicable entertainment was pretty noteworthy, too."

"How about this morning we skip the fighting and get right to the main event?"

"I'd like that." Curving her hand behind his head, she drew him down to her and kissed him. Deeply. He rolled with her, pulling her on top of him, and stroked both of his hands down her bare back to cup her bottom. Heat coiled in his blood and sparked in his veins.

But Valerie ended the kiss abruptly, and her face creased with concern. "Nash, at the risk of starting a real disagreement…"

"Uh-oh."

She slid off him to lie on her side, her head propped on her hand. "There is one thing we need settled."

He made a low growling sound in his throat. "Okay, what?"

"The thing is… I was serious when I said we can't tell anyone about this. About what happened last night. About us."

His stomach swooped, and tension filled his muscles in an instant. "Oh, my God! It's twelve years ago again!"

He smacked a hand on the mattress and frowned at her. "What gives, Val? We're not kids anymore. Why the hell do we have to sneak around this time?"

"Because my mother is—"

"For crying out loud, Val!" He sat up quickly, taking the sheets with him and leaving her to tug the quilt up around her naked breasts. "You're twenty-nine years old! You do not have to answer to your mother or cower from fear of her reprisal anymore."

Giving the sheets a sharp, firm tug, she narrowed a glare on him. "Will you let me finish?"

Nash flexed his fingers and blew out a breath. "Sorry. Go ahead."

"Mother is fragile. I explained that to you last night. In recent months, she'd finally been making progress, taking her medicines, seeing a counselor regularly, attending AA. Then, since Dad's death this spring, she's been on shaky ground. Losing him shook her more than I'd have imagined."

"Okay, so we don't tell your mother. It's not like I had planned to call her up and say, 'Hey, Mrs. Yates, it's that Colton guy you detest. Guess what? I slept with your daughter!'" He tried to keep the exasperation out of his tone, but her expression said he'd failed.

"If your family finds out or if Uncle Rick finds out… *Arrgh*…" She put her forehead against her knees for a moment before looking up at him again. "Word will reach her. I don't know how or who or any of that, but my gut is telling me, she'll find out."

Nash drew a slow breath and swung his legs off the side of the bed. Reining in his composure, he said calmly, "If we decide that this is the beginning of something we want to pursue long-term, she's going to eventually find out, Val. Or were you planning to keep us a secret forever?"

She covered her face with both hands. "Oh, God! I don't know. I don't have a plan. I, for sure, hadn't planned to fall into bed with you last night. Our sleeping together changes everything! It's such a mess."

A prickly sense of defensiveness crawled over his skin. "Are you saying you think it was a mistake? Are these morning-after regrets?"

She dropped her hands and sat up. "No! I don't regret anything."

He remained still, a flat stare pinned on her, and with a pleading look in her eyes, she crawled over to him.

"Nash, I swear to you—" She straddled his lap, the bedcovers falling away so that her nakedness pressed against his. Looping her arms around his neck, she leaned her forehead against his. Her tone was soft and seductive as she whispered, "I regret nothing about last night. Clearly we still have an incredible chemistry together." She punctuated her assertion with a kiss.

His body reacted with the expected rush of blood to his groin, and a crackling energy in his veins. He ran fingers up her spine and savored her breathy sigh as she wiggled closer. "I loved everything about last night, Nash." She kissed him again, then levered back to meet his gaze. "But I'm just not ready to share it with the world yet. Is that so wrong?"

He traced her cheekbone with his thumb and sighed. "Not wrong, just…frustrating. I remember how it was when we were teenagers. How I felt like a thief or something, skulking around to find ways to be alone with you, lying to my family…"

"I'm sorry, Nash. I know it's not a great solution but

I need time to…process. Figure out what to do. What I want. Where we are."

He clenched his teeth, already hating the arrangement. He wanted to talk to Damon or Nicole about what had transpired last night, simply because they knew better than anyone else what he'd gone through after Val left last time. They knew how hard he'd worked to rebuild his life, and he wanted an outside perspective on this strange twist his life had taken. Valerie. Not just back in his life, but in his bed. The chance of a new future before them. And yet, so much painful history still between them.

Sliding his hand to cradle her chin, he nudged her closer, leaned in for a gentle kiss. "All right. I promise."

Her relieved smile broke his heart, but he quashed the rise of pain and pulled her back down on the bed with him, deepening the kiss. When she shivered, he pulled the covers around them, creating a warm nest where they cuddled together, kissing, touching, connecting…

Until the jangling tones of his cell phone, which he'd retrieved from the coffee table after their dinner, broke the quiet of his bedroom.

"Don't answer it," she whispered, clearly as desperate as he was to shut out the rest of the world for a few more minutes, prolong this moment together as long as possible.

Nash huffed a sigh. "I have to. Jackson is still missing, and I promised—"

He moved away from her embrace regretfully, rolling toward his nightstand to check his caller ID, willing to talk to a select few people at the moment, but knowing certain family matters did need his attention. Eventually.

"Myles," he told Val as he touched the screen to answer the call. And only because his nephew hadn't been found.

"Tell me you have good news," he said by way of greeting.

"I have very good news."

Nash sat upright, his pulse accelerating. He could hear the cheer and relief in his cousin's tone. "Really? What happened? Did you find Jackson?"

Now Val sat up, clutching the sheet to her chest. She watched him with wide, hopeful eyes. *What?* she mouthed.

"Yes, we have Jackson back. Safe. Unharmed." Myles's voice cracked with emotion, and he paused to clear his throat.

"Oh, thank God!" Nash exhaled, feeling as though he'd been holding his breath for weeks, and in place of the air, joy and relief poured in.

"I know it's early, but I knew you'd want to know," Myles said.

"Hell, yeah, I did. I do. I—"

Valerie tugged on his arm, and whispered, "What? What?"

"Jackson's home and safe," he relayed to Val.

"Who are you talking to, man?" Myles asked.

Nash stilled. Scrunched his face in a silent *oops*!

"Uh, no one. Just…saying the good news again out loud 'cause it's just… Whew. I'm so glad. I'm— Did they catch the guy who took him? Did you pay the ransom?"

Was it possible Axel had come around after their acrimonious altercation on the tennis court yesterday and come up with the money? Was that just yesterday?

"No, the guy wasn't caught. Look, Vita wanted us to bring Jackson over there for a while. If you want to join us, I think some of the rest of the family is going to be there, too. We'll update everyone at the same time."

Nash glanced at Val again, knowing they had some

unfinished business of their own to discuss. But that discussion would keep. For now. A bridge had been built and as long as no bombshells were dropped to destroy it, they'd made a first big step toward reconciliation. "We'll be there."

"We?"

Nash grimaced again and rolled his eyes. "That, um… was a royal we. *I'll* be there."

Myles half grunted, half laughed. "Whatever. We'll see Your Highness in a few."

Nash disconnected the call and groaned. "I'm not going to live that down anytime soon."

Valerie laughed and kissed his cheek before tossing back the covers and strolling naked across the room to his en suite bathroom. "Thanks for the discretion. For now, do you want to share a shower before we head out?"

Then her phone jangled, as well.

Chapter 6

Despite taking separate cars and using different routes to get to Vita and Rick's home in Evanston, Nash and Valerie arrived at the Yateses' house at the same time.

"So much for our ruse to keep our secret," he murmured, as they walked up the pansy-lined sidewalk to the front steps of the two-story home.

Even with the cool autumn well entrenched, the landscaping around the Yateses' home boasted color and thriving seasonal plants and decor. The abundance of fresh foliage, bright blooms and fragrant blossoms was one of the things Val loved most about her uncle's home. Being surrounded by the beauty of nature, of things growing and scenting the air, inspired and buoyed her spirits even on the most difficult days. Her Aunt Vita kept fresh flowers in every room of their home and replaced fading blooms frequently. Currently, pots of chrysanthemums in shades of rust, crimson and yellow featured prominently in the house, while snapdragon, calendula and pansies populated the family flower beds, as well as Yates' Yards, their plant nursery.

Valerie inhaled the crisp scent of autumn leaves and damp earth as she climbed the steps, invigorated by the clean scents, the morning sunshine…and the sweet ache in her muscles from a night—and morning—of lovemaking. She smiled and sighed happily. Certainly her good mood was boosted by the safe return of little Jackson, but having made positive progress with Nash, having finally unburdened her weighty secret to him, left her feeling infinitely freer, lighter, more upbeat than she had in years.

"Easy, love," Nash said with a droll grin. "I'm glad you are happy and all that, but if you look too pleased with yourself and well-sated, you might raise suspicion."

"Are you saying my smile is so unusual as to be suspect?" She arched an eyebrow and sent him a mock scowl as she reached for the brass doorknob.

"Just sayin'. You're the one who wants to keep our relationship a secret."

The knob in her hand slipped away as someone inside opened the door.

"Oh, a secret! I love a juicy secret. Tell me! What'd I miss?" Lila said as she pulled the door wide.

"Nothing," Val said, with a wave of her hand. "The real question is—" she paused to inhale deeply "—what is that heavenly aroma?"

Lila gave Nash a chaste cheek kiss in greeting and guided them into the front room, where the family was gathering. "Nicole has been baking. Cinnamon scones, chocolate muffins, pumpkin bread. That on top of her breakfast quiche and sausage balls."

Nash furrowed his brow. "But her hip—"

"Is healing just fine, dear," Nicole said from the wingback chair where she was sitting with a walker beside her. "I'm not an invalid, and I need something to keep me busy until the doctor releases me to regular activities again."

Nash moved to greet the woman who'd lovingly and selflessly stepped in and assumed the role as his mom when his own mother died. "And you're not overdoing it?"

"Using bones helps them heal. That's what my new PT guy says." Nicole reached for Nash's hand and squeezed it. "But thank you for your concern. Besides, I can do most of my cooking sitting down if I gather the ingredients first."

"Lucky for us," Valerie said, bending to give Nicole a gentle hug. "I'm starving, and I haven't forgotten how good your scones are."

"Hey, hey! If it's not *King* Nash, master of the royal we," Myles teased as he entered from the kitchen. Jackson was in his arms, a half-eaten muffin in the four-year-old's hand and on his face.

"King Nash," Jackson repeated, giggling.

Ignoring his cousin's playful jibe, Nash clapped his hands once and opened his arms. "Hey, there's my favorite nephew! You have a hug for me?"

Jackson wiggled free of his father's grasp and trotted across the floor. Nash squatted, wrapped Jackson in a firm embrace, then lifted the boy from the floor as he pretended to steal a bite of the muffin.

The little boy shrieked a laugh and held the muffin high. No one said a word about the large crumbs falling to the floor. What did crumbs matter when they could have lost Jackson for good?

When the doorbell rang, Myles peeled away from the group to answer the door and returned with Nash's fraternal twin, Damon, a dark-haired woman and a little girl with wide brown eyes. When Damon spotted Valerie, he made a beeline toward her. "The prodigal daughter returns! I can't remember the last time I saw you, Val."

"Um, Myles and Faith's wedding."

Damon blinked. "That long ago? Where have you been hiding?"

"Ohio. I, um…" Valerie fumbled but was spared further explanation of her years' absence when the woman with Damon moved closer, and Damon wrapped an arm around her waist.

"Hey, you haven't met Ruby and Maya, the new women in my life."

"Ruby Duarte." Damon's girlfriend offered her hand and a beautiful smile.

Val greeted her and looked to the little girl, who crowded close. "And that must mean you are Maya. Am I right?"

The child smiled shyly and clung to her mother's legs.

"Maya is—" Damon began, just as Nash appeared, crouching in front of Maya.

"Hi, Maya. How are you?" he said and signed at the same time.

The girl's face brightened, and in a flurry of hand motions, she signed something in return.

A bittersweet twang plucked Valerie's heart. Nash was good with kids. He didn't have the awkward falseness that some inexperienced adults had.

He would make a great father someday. And that thought inevitably reminded her of her reasons for having avoided him and this family for so long. The bittersweet ache sharpened, and Val had to shove aside the hurt to keep her expression from revealing too much.

Nash glanced up at Ruby. "Oops. I'm afraid 'Hi. How are you?' is as much as I've learned so far."

"She said she's fine and asked if you wanted to play hide-and-seek," Ruby said, ruffling her daughter's hair. "I appreciate your effort to learn to communicate with her."

Nash pulled a face. "What? Of course, I'm learning to sign! Would I miss the chance to chat with this little angel? I think not."

Ruby smiled her thanks, then, signing and speaking to Maya, she said, "Let's say hello to Jackson and maybe he'll play with you?"

Valerie dropped to a squat before Maya could sidle away, signing as she said, "After I talk to the adults for a moment, I'll play with you."

Maya looked startled, then glanced at her mother and smiled at Valerie as she nodded.

"There are lots of good things to eat in the kitchen. Are you hungry?" Val said and signed.

The girl's face brightened further, and she nodded again.

When Valerie glanced up at the adults, Ruby's face reflected a pleasant surprise, while Damon and Nash exchanged stunned looks.

"Did you know Val could sign?" Damon asked Nash.

Nash arched an eyebrow. "No. But she's been full of surprises lately."

Valerie shot Nash daggers with her eyes, warning him not to risk exposing any of the intimate secrets they'd shared.

"Has she?" Damon asked.

"Case in point," Nash said. "She's here." He spread his hands. "That's surprise enough, but sign language?" He shifted his attention to Val. "When did you learn sign language?"

"In college. A girl on my hall in the dorm was hearing-impaired. She taught me enough to have basic conversations." Valerie pushed to her feet, smirking. "And curse."

The men guffawed.

Ruby scowled playfully. "Please don't teach bad words to my daughter!" She hitched her thumb toward Nash and his brother. "Or these bozos."

Val winked. "Deal."

"Damon, you bring those lovely ladies over here, dear!" Nicole called, and Damon ushered Ruby and Maya over to greet her.

"Don't worry," Nash said, leaning in close to Valerie's ear. "I promised to keep our relationship on the down low, and I will. No dirty looks needed."

"Hmm." Valerie scanned the room and whispered, "Seems to me if we don't want to raise flags, we shouldn't be hovering with each other all morning."

"True enough." He squared his shoulders and shoved his hands in his pockets as he watched Damon kiss Nicole's cheek. "But that's not a strategy for the long term, so we still need to talk."

Long term. Valerie's breath snagged. Myles's call, before they'd even gotten out of bed this morning, had postponed discussions on that important question. Was there a long term for her and Nash? Was that what she wanted? She didn't know. What she *did* know was that now wasn't the time for such a conversation. "Later. Right now, I'm going to find Uncle Rick for a moment. Apparently he didn't get my text last night that I was staying with a friend. He left a message on my voice mail asking if I was all right. I need to be seen and reassure him I'm fine and not stranded in a ditch somewhere."

"What are you going to tell him?"

"As close to the truth as I can without giving us away.

Last night's missing text could still show up, so I'll stick to the vague line that I was visiting an old friend and was invited to spend the night. Hopefully that's enough to serve my purposes. He doesn't pry or need specifics. Just reassurances I'm safe."

"Right. Well, good luck with that."

Was it her imagination or did his tone darken sarcastically just then? She perceived a slight tensing of his shoulders, a tightening in his jaw.

"Anyway," he added. "Rick's over there with Lila. If you'll excuse me, Myles is motioning for me to come over."

Valerie watched Nash walk away, a strange niggling telling her something had shifted in his mood just then. But why? Although she didn't have any illusions that everything that had transpired over the last twelve years had miraculously been resolved in one conversation yesterday, she'd thought their lovemaking had put them on the right path toward at least a truce. Maybe even reconciliation.

She braced a hand against the wall when the reality of a future with Nash hit her, full throttle. After all the heartache, loneliness and loss, she'd believed that dream was dead.

Whispers of that old pain stirred in her heart. She could never survive losing Nash a second time. She'd have to proceed with caution.

"Val, are you all right?"

Startled from her musings, she glanced up to find Rick studying her with a knit in his brow. "Huh? Oh, um…yeah." She straightened and forced a smile to her face. "I was just…realizing I hadn't had any breakfast, so I think I'll get a bite from the kitchen. But I wanted to talk to you, anyway, so…good timing on your part. Can I get you a plate?"

"I'll go with you." Rick swept his hand toward the kitchen then placed his hand on her upper back as they weaved their way toward the kitchen. "Vita wanted me to take some goodies out to our new hire, Sara, in the nursery. She's watching the register while we celebrate Jackson's return, but I don't want to take advantage of her helpful nature. We didn't hire her to mind the store." He broke his stride and looked at her. "Which reminds me. Would you be interested in sharing your artistic talents to design an advertisement about our holiday plants? Our poinsettias, evergreen wreaths, amaryllises and Christmas cacti will arrive early next week, and Sara is planning a big advertising splash."

Valerie blinked her surprise. In truth, having something productive to do would be a welcome distraction from the unresolved issues with Nash. She liked Sara and the notion of working with her appealed to Val. "Oh, uh…sure. And I wouldn't be stepping on Sara's toes to do the graphic art?"

"Goodness, no. In fact, when she heard of your artistic talent, she suggested we ask for your help. We'll pay you, of course." Rick chuckled and held open the swinging door to the kitchen for her. "I wouldn't presume to ask you to work for free."

Before Valerie could respond, a disturbance behind them, in the corner of the living room, snagged their attention. Then Nash's voice rose over the others, full of shock and tension.

"What! How?"

Rick stilled. "Oh, that doesn't sound good."

Nash gaped at Myles in disbelief. "Did you say *dead*?"

Damon and Ruby squeezed in closer, their eyes wide with concern.

"Who's dead? What happened?" Damon asked.

"My father," Myles said grimly.

"Axel's dead? But how? I just saw him—" Nash began, and Myles, his face reflecting shock and strain, raised a hand to quiet him.

A murmur had risen around them, and more family gathered close as someone asked, "Who? What's going on?"

"Everyone, listen up! Can I have the floor, please?" Myles said with the resonance, volume and authority of a lawyer about to make an impassioned closing argument to the court. He cleared his throat and held up his cell phone as if it were exhibit A. "I just had a call from Dad's housekeeper."

"From his housekeeper? Why in the world is she calling you?" Faith asked, making her way closer to her husband.

Again, Myles raised his hand, silently asking for the chance to explain.

"When my father's housekeeper arrived at work today, she found him on the floor of the den. Dead."

Gasps and low mumbles of shock filtered through the room.

"Axel is dead?" Vita asked, her face pale. Rick hurried to his wife's side and wrapped a supporting arm around her.

Myles sent his mother a pained look. "Yes. I don't know much more at this point, but…" He looked at Faith. "I think we should go home. There will be arrangements to be made." He swiped a hand over his face as he grimaced. "God, I'll have to deal with Carin and Erik."

Myles's conflicting emotions played across his face.

Mention of his own father resonated inside Nash, and he considered how tangled his feelings toward Erik were, how complicated and contaminated his relationship with his father was. Myles had to be feeling a bit of the same confusion and mixed emotions. Axel had been an equally poor and distant father to Myles and Lila. Nash was reminded again how Vita and Nicole had been the source of strength, affection and cohesion that kept him, his half siblings and cousins anchored, bound them with love.

Damon moved up beside Nash. "Draw straws to see who calls Dad?"

Nash shook his head. "Nah. I'll do it."

He cut a glance across the room to Valerie. As if she felt his stare, she tore her attention away from Vita and met his gaze. Like the moment he'd seen her on his front porch yesterday, tension closed around his throat. Maybe it was the high emotion of the morning, but a wave of something troubling and foreboding washed through him.

Twelve years ago, she'd assumed the worst about him based on circumstantial evidence from her mother. She'd denied him the right to know about her pregnancy. She'd shut him out. And although she'd explained her side of events, the fact remained that, twelve years ago, she'd dismissed his needs, his feelings and his rights in order to protect herself. She'd easily bought into a lie that allowed her to justify her actions. She'd been hurting, yes. But she'd also not given him a chance to defend himself, to speak the truth, to give her the love and support he'd wanted to give her.

And now? Could he trust her all these years later, after all the water under the bridge? She still wanted him to keep their relationship a secret. She needed time to "figure some things out." What was there to decide? Did she care about him and believe in him or didn't she?

Acid climbed Nash's throat as his irritation and resentment grew. He'd spent too many years waiting and hoping for his father's love and attention to repeat those mistakes with Valerie. Was it too much to ask for Valerie's unconditional love and faith? He refused to settle for anything less.

She broke eye contact first, turning back to Vita with worry denting her brow.

Nash sighed and pulled out his phone. Enough stalling. He stepped out of the crowded living room to a quiet bedroom down the hall. His father answered with a brusque "What?"

"It's Nash, Dad."

"I know that. I have caller ID. What do you want?"

So much for small talk or a warm greeting. But then, experience had taught him not to expect much from his dad. "You've heard about Uncle Axel, I guess?"

"Of course, I have. Mother called an hour ago with the news. I'm surprised you've heard, though."

Nash rubbed the back of his neck with his free hand. "Damon and I were with Myles and the family when he got the call from the police just now."

"And?"

Nash blinked. And what? "And…so I…thought I'd see if there was anything I could do for you?"

"No. I'm on the way to the hospital now to give a formal identification, then the body will be turned over to the funeral home." Nash heard no real emotion in his father's tone. He might be feeling some grief over losing his brother but was burying it until the unpleasant business at the hospital was finished. Or he could be in shock, the sadness yet to hit home. Or his dad might be more of a distant, unfeeling bastard than Nash had thought.

He sighed. "Want me to come? I could meet you at the hosp—"

"Hell no. The last thing I need is people clamoring around me and getting in the way."

His father's curt response silenced him for a moment, and a familiar river of hurt and rejection spiraled through him. "All right, then. If you change your mind—"

"I won't. The best thing you can do for me is to keep the interfering hordes away."

Nash bit the inside of his cheek to stem his retort criticizing Erik's characterization of the family—especially Axel's children—being a liability to him. They had as much right as anyone to be part of making arrangements for their father's internment. And his estate.

A jolt shot through Nash. "Now that Axel's gone, if Grandmother wins her lawsuit against Dean Colton's estate, you become sole heir to half of the Colton fortune," he mused aloud.

But the line was dead. Of course, his father had hung up on him as soon as he'd delivered his interfering horde dictate. The almighty Colton had said his piece, no further conversation needed. Click. No goodbye needed.

Nash swiped his phone screen to close the phone app while mulling the ramifications of Axel's death. What did it say for his relationship with his father that he could even harbor the notion Erik might be involved with his brother's death? Axel could have had a heart attack or stroke or—

"Need a drink?" Damon said with a wry grin and a steaming mug extended toward Nash. "It's just coffee, but if you want I can ask Rick for a shot of something stronger to put in it."

Silently, brow furrowed, Nash took the mug and sipped.

"Wow. Did the call with our old man really go that badly?" Damon asked, cocking his head to the side.

Nash waved a dismissive hand. "About as expected. Curt, impatient, he didn't want our *interference*."

"Right. Well, I think Ruby and I are going to take off. Maya's going to need a nap soon, and she's smart enough to pick up on the tension around her without knowing what's happening. That scares her."

"Yeah," Nash replied distractedly. "Damon, do you realize that Axel's death threw a rather sizable wrench in the lawsuit Carin was pushing regarding Dean Colton's will? With Axel gone, Dad becomes the sole heir, to the tune of thirty million dollars."

Damon's body stilled, but Nash could almost see his brother's law enforcement instincts kicking into high gear, the wheels in his brain turning.

After a moment where no words, but plenty of understanding, passed between the brothers, Nash spoke the troubling consensus. "Our dad's got a thirty-million-dollar motive for murder."

Chapter 7

The celebration of Jackson's safe return ended quickly following the disturbing news of Axel's death. Valerie did her best to help Vita and Rick send off the family with hugs, reassurances and to-go boxes filled with left-over food.

Nash stayed to keep an eye on Nicole, who stayed to keep her dearest friend, Vita, company in the wake of the upsetting news. Of the rest of the family, only Lila and her fiancé Carter stayed behind, purportedly to help Vita clean the kitchen, but Valerie could tell from Lila's expression that she was concerned for Vita's well-being, as well. Divorced or not, learning the father of her children was dead had to be a blow for Vita. Rather, *another* blow on top of the succession of trying and traumatic events that had already plagued the family in recent months.

Lila hovered. Vita swore she was fine. And Valerie busied herself with any task or errand that she thought would lighten the load, alleviate the stress or comfort the family in their shock and distress. Bonus points if the busywork also helped distract her from Nash's presence.

He cornered her in the kitchen at one point and whispered, "Obviously, here and now isn't the time and place to finish our business from last night."

Valerie nodded discretely. "Obviously."

"What if you came over this evening for dinner? I'll cook."

"I feel like I should stay here tonight. For Vita. And because disappearing two nights in a row would be suspicious."

"Then maybe tomorrow?" He lifted a hand to touch her cheek when the swinging door from the dining room opened.

Rick breezed in with another platter of leftover scones and mini muffins. Nash jerked back his hand and jammed it in his pocket.

Valerie sidled away. "Let me put those in storage bags, Rick. They'll keep in the freezer for a while."

"Thanks, Val." Rick smiled at her then sent Nash a curious look. "Myles tells me you talked to Axel yesterday afternoon. Is that right?"

Nash opened his mouth. Closed it. Then, with a furrowed brow, he nodded.

"Did he seem all right to you when you saw him? Did he complain of not feeling well or look sick to you?"

"He was having a tennis lesson with some young thing he was clearly hitting on." Nash arched one eyebrow. "So, no. He didn't seem at all ill. He was pure Axel in his usual form."

Rick frowned. "Hmm. It's amazing how these things can strike out of nowhere. Perfectly fine one day and gone the next."

"So… Axel's death was a health issue? Have you heard something?" Valerie asked.

Rick pursed his lips. "No. I just assumed… I mean, it could have been a home accident. The only other explanation is foul play, and that—"

"Foul play?" The three turned their glances toward Vita, who stood in the door from the dining room with a stack of plates and dirty napkins in her hands. "I know my ex-husband was difficult and heartless at times, but—"

"Pure speculation. Pointless speculation on our part, darling. Please ignore our thoughtless comments." Rick took the stack of dishes from his wife and set them on the counter. Valerie took over cleaning up those dishes.

"We didn't mean to upset you, Aunt Vita," Nash said.

"Why don't you go sit with Nicole in the living room and let us finish tidying up? Put your feet up and—"

"Rick Yates, I appreciate your concern for me, but I'm fine. I don't need to be coddled or shielded. If there's news about Axel's death, I want to hear it."

Rick nodded as he ushered Vita out of the kitchen. "And you will, love. But there is none now. Come put your feet up…"

Nash returned his gaze to Valerie when her uncle left the room. "Dinner. Tomorrow. My place. Deal?"

Valerie hesitated before answering. Her mother's voice sounded in her head. *The Coltons are a millstone around your neck. They'll drag you down in the mire with them. They're selfish and conniving. Trouble follows them. One day all their sins will catch up to them, and I don't want you to drown in the wake.*

She thought about all the chaos and tragedy that had already plagued the Coltons in recent months. Now Axel was dead. Was her mother right? Was getting involved with Nash a recipe for disaster and heartache? No matter what she decided, she and Nash needed a chance to hash it out. So she nodded and said, "It's a date."

"Myles promised to call when he learned anything," Lila said to her family when Valerie and Nash rejoined the others in the living room.

Nash took a seat in the chair closest to Nicole and reached for her fragile hand. "I can drive you home if you're tired or hurting."

Nicole shook her head stubbornly. "I want to stay." She shot a look to Vita. "If that's all right?"

"Of course. You can help distract me from my fruitless worrying." Vita turned to Valerie. "Val, dear, Rick says he mentioned the winter ad campaign for Yates' Yards to you. Do you think you'll have time to help Sara before you leave town?"

"I will. Definitely. I'd love to help and am already cooking up some ideas. In fact, I'll stop by the nursery and talk with her in a little while."

"Wonderful!" Rick said. "Our first shipment of poin—"

A loud knocking sounded from the front hall, interrupting Rick, followed by the doorbell, and Vita rose to answer the loud summons. From the living room, Valerie heard Vita gasp. "Rick! Lila!"

Hearing the distress in Vita's voice, everyone but Nicole, because of her injured hip, rose and hurried to the front door. The scents of autumn, perfumed with the abundant blooms in the Yateses' flower beds, greeted them as Rick pulled open the storm door.

A woman with a microphone stood on the porch, a bearded man with a large video camera behind her. Seeing the family arrive at the glass storm door, another reporter and cameraman hurried up from the yard, tramping across Vita's pansies, and the reporter shoved a microphone forward.

"Vita Colton, are you aware that Axel Colton was found murdered in his home this morning?" the first woman with a microphone asked.

Nudging Vita aside, Rick opened the door and waved a hand at the news crews. "You're trespassing on private property. Leave now before I call the police. We have no comment."

"And it's Vita *Yates* now," Vita said firmly, her shoulders squared. "I haven't been a Colton in many years." She wagged a finger at one of the cameramen. "You there! In the blue shirt. You're smashing my flowers! Please, be careful!"

Nash and Carter pushed through the door to join Rick in forming a barricade of bodies between the aggressive media and Vita.

"You heard the lady. Get off the flowers and out of the yard. We have nothing to say about Axel's death," Carter said.

"His murder, you mean?" reporter number two asked. The guy looked like he'd just graduated from high school and wore a double-breasted raincoat, red tie and buttoned-up collar, as if he'd Googled the clichéd image of a reporter from old movies and copied it as his uniform.

Beside Valerie, Lila stiffened. "Murder? Why do you say that?"

"Our sources say the police are now treating Axel Colton's death as a murder investigation," the young reporter explained eagerly.

Valerie's gut turned, and dismay bit hard.

"I, uh…" Rick spluttered, while Vita gasped, "Murder?"

"Our source says the word from the crime scene is the

likely cause of death is blunt-force trauma to the head."
Irritation peaked in Valerie, seeing the young reporter's
overly bright and excited expression as he delivered the
news. To him, this was a career-defining story, the family's tragedy be damned.

"That conclusion is pending confirmation from the
coroner," the female reporter interjected, signaling for
her cameraman to get a closer shot of the family's reaction to the news. "The police haven't yet located the item
used to bash Colton on the head and kill him."

Nash scowled at the woman. "A little sensitivity,
please."

"Come on, Mom," Lila said, taking Vita's arm and
encouraging her to go inside. "Let them handle this."

"Do you know who might want to kill Axel Colton?"
the female reporter shouted as Valerie held the door, allowing Lila and Vita to quickly duck back into the house.

"Can you confirm that Axel Colton was embroiled in
a contentious legal battle over his father's will?" the second reporter asked before Rick, Carter and Nash could
follow Vita and Lila inside.

"Our sources say Nash Colton was one of the last
people to see Axel Colton alive and, in fact, threatened
his uncle."

Valerie swallowed hard, only narrowly holding in her
gasp of shock. She felt Nash tense beside her as he angled a sharp look at the female reporter. "Where did you
hear that?"

"Do you have a comment, sir?"

"Have you spoken to Nash Colton this morning,
ma'am?" the second reported shouted.

Rick puffed his chest, irritation vibrating from him.
"We have no comment. I want you off our property, or
we'll call the police to escort you off."

"No need," the bearded cameraman said. "They're already here." He hitched his head toward the yard, where, sure enough, a uniformed officer and what Valerie assumed was a plainclothes detective marched across the grass.

The cameras swung to record the officers' approach, and the plainclothes cop waved his hand at the media personnel. "Enough. You guys, clear out."

"Freedom of the press!" the young reporter said.

"Is yours from the street," the uniformed officer added. "You should know better than encroaching on private property."

The female reporter stood back to allow the police team to climb the stairs, and though they made a show of backing toward the street, Valerie noted they were moving like glaciers, their cameras still focused on the family and the cops.

She inched back toward the entry to the living room with the men close behind her.

Rick closed the front door firmly and heaved a sigh before lifting a wary gaze to the policemen. "Gentlemen, what can we do for you?"

The detective in khakis, a navy sport coat and a blue oxford button-down shirt, open at the throat, introduced himself as Homicide Detective Harry Cartwright. Though his presence was disconcerting, Valerie got a positive vibe from the man. He carried himself with an air of authority and competence, but without any arrogance she could detect. His light brown hair and beard were short and neatly trimmed, and he conscientiously wiped his feet on the welcome mat before heading into the living room. Behind him, the uniformed officer stood stiffly with his hands clasped in front of him.

"Detective," Vita said, her voice unsteady. "That

young reporter claims there's evidence Axel was murdered. Please tell me he was wrong. That he was just angling for a sensational story."

Cartwright scowled and muttered, "I don't know how he'd have that information."

Vita's face brightened a bit. "Then it's not true?"

"Sorry, but it's true."

Vita sucked in a sharp breath, and Rick moved quickly to put an arm around her.

The supportive gesture touched Valerie, even as her own stomach swooped. The shocking news settled in her brain like an electric jolt. She glanced to Nash, who met her eyes briefly, his expression stark, before he returned his attention to the detective. How nice it would be to have Nash rush to her side and lend his comfort the way Rick had for Vita. But, by her own decree, he couldn't give away their relationship. A pang of regret twisted around Valerie's heart. If only...

"I meant that information should not have leaked from the department so quickly." Detective Cartwright's low tone cut into her distracted thoughts. "Someone's been talking out of turn." He glanced at the uniformed officer, who mirrored the detective's disgruntled look. Schooling his face, he added, "I'm sorry to interrupt your party with such grim business."

Vita frowned, and her forehead creased with a deep *V.* "Oh, dear. *Party* does sound rather bad under the circumstances, doesn't it? Earlier we were celebrating the fact that our grandson was safely recovered after being kidnapped. The family all wanted to—"

"No need to explain," Cartwright said with a kind smile for Vita. "Your gathering actually saves us the time of tracking folks down individually."

Vita seemed only mildly pacified by his reassurance.

"Well, whatever we can do to help. This family has seen quite enough drama and tragedy lately. We'll be glad to put it all behind us as soon as possible and are here to help the police however we can." She turned awkwardly and waved toward the living room. "Shall we sit down?"

Cartwright nodded a genial thank you, but Nash knew the man's intelligent gray-green eyes were taking in every detail, from the family's body language, to the layout of the home, which doors were closed and potentially hiding a suspect or ambush. Cartwright might be polite and friendly, but his instincts and training had him making detailed calculations observations and risk assessments. Finally, he indicated the uniformed officer with a hitch of his head. "This is Officer Moody. He'll be assisting me today."

Nash helped Vita to the couch, where she crumpled in disbelief. His own legs were rather rubbery, and his mind felt numb as he replayed the reporter's announcement. *Axel...murdered?* So he and Damon hadn't been off with their speculation. For once, Nash wished he had been wrong.

Immediately, his thoughts flashed to other recent Colton murders. Axel and Erik's half brothers had been killed earlier in the year. Was there a connection to Ernest and Alfred's deaths? And should he betray his father by mentioning the lawsuit regarding Dean Colton's will to the police? Nash had previously tried to stay on the fringes of his grandmother's lawsuit, but with thirty million dollars at stake, the potential motive for murder couldn't be ignored.

Then another possibility occurred to him. Could his newfound cousins, Dean Colton's legitimate grandchildren, be suspects? They had a great deal to lose if Carin's lawsuit prevailed.

Beside him, Lila tensed, prodding him from his spinning thoughts. Nash raised his head and focused again on what Cartwright was saying.

"One of you might be able to fill in some blanks about where Axel had been and who he'd been with. Routine investigation at this point."

"Before we do," Rick said, "can you tell us first why you suspect Axel was murdered? What's going on?"

When the detective hesitated, Rick touched Lila's shoulder and added, "Lila is Axel's daughter. As next of kin, doesn't she have a right to know what's happening?"

"At this point, no."

"No?" Lila echoed, dumbfounded.

Cartwright twisted his mouth in an apologetic moue. "This is a murder investigation, so the details surrounding your father's death are privileged information."

"So then how—" Carter began then cut himself off. His mouth pressed in a grim line, then, straightening his spine, he said, "Don't worry, Lila. I'll get you answers." He marched out of the living room, and they heard the front door open and close.

Nash leaned forward to glance out the front window and watched as Carter confronted the reporter still loitering on the lawn. Carter's warrior-like size and take-no-prisoners demeanor clearly intimidated the young reporter, and Nash bit the inside of his cheek to stifle a grin.

Cartwright was clearly displeased with Carter's actions, but made no move to stop him.

Nash shifted his gaze to meet Valerie's. Her brown eyes held storm clouds, and she gnawed her bottom lip as she held his stare. But was she worried the truth about their night together would come out, or about the public argument Nash had confessed having with Axel just hours before his uncle was murdered? He wished he could say he knew her well enough to know where her loyalties, her priorities lay.

"Do you think Axel's murder is connected to Jackson being found?" Rick asked the detective as the man pulled out a compact voice recorder. "This morning, Myles mentioned that people connected to his son's kidnapping had connections to known crime rings."

The detective furrowed his brow. "Excuse me? What kidnapping? Catch me up."

"Our grandson was recently kidnapped," Vita explained. *"Axel's grandson,"* she added with emphasis as if to be sure the detective didn't miss that point. "We're all here today because Jackson was found safe last night. But the people behind the kidnapping and an attack on my son Myles are still out there."

Cartwright arched an eyebrow. "Can you tell me about that?"

And she did, summarizing the whole situation with a calm, clear voice. "Brad Howard with the local FBI office took the lead on the case. I can give you his contact information."

Cartwright shook his head. "I know him. Worked a case with him earlier this year. I'll get a recap of the kidnapping case from him later and see if we connect any dots to Axel Colton."

"Goodness," Nicole said with a sigh. "When you consider everything that's happened to this family in recent months, you can build a rather long list of suspects. And God knows Axel must have made a few enemies in his life. He wasn't a pleasant man, and he was known to have had a wandering eye and no problem with bed-hopping." She sent Vita a sympathizing glance.

Cartwright raised a hand. "If you have specific information, names or incidents, known threats, I'll take that information down, but right now I'm more interested in tracing the last few hours of Axel Colton's life. Did any of you speak to him yesterday?"

Nash's gut rolled. He had to be honest, even if it painted him in a bad light.

Before he could speak, Vita said, "I talked with him by phone briefly to update him on the whole kidnapping business. Around three thirty p.m. But only for a minute or so. He seemed in a hurry to get off the phone. Some appointment or something."

"A tennis lesson," Nash clarified. "He was at the racket club."

Officer Moody wrote something down and asked, "You know this how?"

"I went there to talk to him. I interrupted his lesson for our conversation."

"Whatever for, Nash?" When Nicole reached toward him, angling a puzzled look at him, Nash took his adoptive mother's hand and gave it a consoling pat.

"I was trying to convince him to help Myles and Faith fund the ransom for Jackson. By all estimates, he's got more money in the bank than any of us. And as Jackson's grandfather, I saw no reason why he hadn't already pledged the money."

"This was yesterday afternoon?" Moody clarified as he jotted notes.

Nash nodded. "At about four p.m. Maybe four fifteen."

"And he seemed well?"

"Well enough to play tennis and flirt with the tennis pro half his age or younger."

"Did Mr. Colton say if he had any plans for—?" Cartwright began, but a firm knock on the front door interrupted him. Vita hesitated, then stood to answer the door. A moment later Vita returned. A uniformed officer stood with her. "Detective Cartwright?"

Cartwright stood. "What is it, Officer Chatham?"

"A word?"

Chatham and Cartwright excused themselves to the kitchen to confer in private for a moment. As the family waited, Nash felt Valerie's eyes on him and cast a glance her way. Her eyes held the same wary concern they'd had earlier that morning, when she'd begged him to keep her night with him a secret. For the sake of her mother.

While he respected her dogged loyalty to her mother, he wished he could expect even a part of the same allegiance to him. *Please*, her troubled eyes seemed to implore, and the small indentation between her eyes reflected both doubt and worry that cut him. He ducked his head slightly, his gaze locked with hers, trying to silently reassure her. Because, damn it, even if she doubted him, he cared for her, and he was a man of his word. He'd keep faith. But for Valerie's sake. Not for her mother.

The detective returned, bursting through the kitchen door with purposeful strides, Officer Chatham at his heels. "Nash Colton," Detective Cartwright said, drawing both Nash's gaze and Valerie's. "Officer Chatham has brought new information to my attention, as well as a search warrant for your home and car."

"What!" Nash shot up from the couch and gaped at the officer. "On what grounds?"

"At this point the warrant has a narrow scope, based on a tip from an anonymous witness." Officer Chatham produced a document from his clipboard and passed it over to Officer Moody. Valerie crowded in beside Moody, trying to read over his shoulder.

"Anonymous?" Nash scoffed. "This is malarkey."

"If your vehicle's here, we'd like to take a look in it now." Detective Cartwright motioned toward the driveway through the window.

"And what is it you're looking for, Detective?" Nicole asked, her voice reflecting the same deep concern that etched her brow.

"I'm not at liberty to say. Let's just go take a look and see what we find." Detective Cartwright motioned for Nash to come with him. When Valerie and Rick moved to the door to accompany them, the detective held up a hand. "Just Nash. Please wait here."

Valerie sent Nash another worried look, as if wanting to say something, do something, to defend him. As if she wanted to protect him from this ludicrous scrutiny.

He gave her a quick, strained smile, and as he passed her, he whispered, "It'll be okay."

Nash hoped he was right.

Nash strode across the lawn toward his car, wishing he were as sure of a positive outcome as he'd assured Val. An anonymous tip that incriminated him for murder? That didn't sound good. The Colton family seemed to be under attack from outside forces of late. Kidnapping, murder, blackmail. Was he the latest victim of this malevolent crusade? Who could be orchestrating this campaign to destroy his family? His newly discovered cousins? Dean Colton's legitimate children and grands? Maybe. But why?

From his peripheral vision, he noticed the reporters and television cameras scurrying to follow him and the policemen.

"Officer, can you tell us what's happening?"

"Is this man a suspect in Axel Colton's murder?"

Then Carter's voice. "Nash, what's going on?"

Nash glanced toward Lila's fiancé in time to see Office Moody step in Carter's path. "Stay back, sir. This is police business."

"Nash?"

He waved to Carter. "It's all right."

If only he could convince his gut and his brain that everything was fine. Acid churned in his stomach, making it difficult to keep his breakfast down. And an eerie foreboding shrouded his thoughts, a prescience and pessimism born of life experience. He'd had the same strange sense of doom before he'd opened his mother's bedroom door and found her dead of an aneurysm as a kid.

With his key fob, he unlocked his doors.

"We'll start with the trunk, please." After wrangling a pair of latex gloves onto his hands, Detective Cartwright moved to the back end of the Infiniti coupe and waited while Nash hit the right button on the key fob. Nash stalked over to stand beside the detective as Cartwright opened the lid of the trunk...

And found a heavy-looking candlestick inside. The piece was approximately one foot long, sculpted from white marble with waves and flourishes, and decorated with a silver initial. *C.*

Confusion, shock and crushing doom slammed into Nash. He knew instantly that the candlestick had been used to kill Axel. And he was being framed.

"Well, well, well. What have we here?" Cartwright turned to Officer Moody. "Document this, please."

"That is not mine! I have no idea how it got there!" Nash said, knowing he sounded like a cliché, but compelled to at least try to set the record straight. In truth, he knew just how it had gotten there. The anonymous tipster planted it. He said as much as Moody snapped pictures with his cell phone, but, of course, Detective Cartwright was predictably unconvinced.

Moody leaned farther inside the trunk for a better look. "Detective." The uniformed officer pointed to something dark at one end of the foot-long candlestick. "Blood."

"Right." Cartwright faced Nash, his expression flat and stern. "Please turn around and place your hands behind your back."

Adrenaline shot through Nash, and he shook his head. "You've got this wrong. It's a setup! I didn't—"

Officer Moody wasn't having it. He seized one of Nash's arms and tugged it behind his back. "Nash Colton, you're under arrest for the murder of Axel Colton."

As the officer spouted Nash's Miranda rights, Nash angled his head to find Carter, who watched from several feet away with anger and dismay creasing his face.

"Call Myles!" Nash shouted to him. "Tell him to meet me at the police station!"

Carter jerked a nod of understanding and sprinted back toward the house, just as Rick, Lila and Valerie raced from the front door across the yard, shouting, "Stop!" and "Nash!" and "Officer, no!"

Nash's mind spun, and his vision blurred as he was led to the police cruiser. The cacophony of voices—his family protesting, the media buzzing and the police calling for everyone to step back and not interfere—were a surreal backdrop to the thundering of his pulse in his ears.

This was wrong. A mistake. He was being framed.

As the back door of the cruiser was closed, he stared numbly through the window at the crowd of gathered spectators and found the one face he needed most to see—Valerie's.

His lover. His best hope. His alibi.

But given her pleading request that morning to keep their liaison a secret, would she back him up, support his defense?

He honestly didn't know.

Chapter 8

A shock wave rolled through Valerie when the uniformed officer snapped the handcuffs on Nash and led him to the waiting police car. She sent Uncle Rick a desperate look, her heart thundering with fear and confusion. "What's happening? Why are they arresting Nash?"

She fought the swell of panic that bloomed in her chest and tried to steal her breath.

"I don't know, but I intend to find out," Rick replied, then squared his shoulders and marched across the lawn. Val followed. They ignored the microphones waved in their faces and the questions hurled at them from the media.

Carter already had his phone at his ear. "He needs you to meet him at the police station. They found something in his car trunk and immediately took him into custody." Seeing Val and Rick rush up to him, Carter held up a finger, signaling them to wait while he finished his call. "I didn't see. The cops kept me back, but I heard one of the officers say something about blood."

Valerie gasped, and Rick grabbed her arm when she wobbled.

Blood? Was it possible that more had happened between Nash and Axel in their confrontation than Nash had admitted? Nash had a temper. He held grudges. She knew that from her own arguments with him, but he wasn't violent. Was he? Certainly not with her. And she'd not seen evidence of it ever before.

Her mother's voice from years ago rang in her ears. *Stay away from the Coltons, Valerie! Trouble follows them. One day all their sins will catch up to them, and I don't want you to drown in the wake.*

She gave her head a determined shake, as if she could dislodge the doubts and niggling questions.

"It's all right, Valerie dear." Rick gave her a trembling smile. "We'll straighten this out."

Carter finished his call and turned to them. "That was Myles. He's going to head over to the police station and sort things out."

The rest of the family caught up and gathered around to hear what Carter had to say. As did the media. Carter sent a scowling side-eye to the female reporter who tried to push her way close enough to record what he was telling the family. Placing a hand on Lila's back, he hitched his head toward the house. "Let's go inside."

Before returning to the house, Valerie glanced toward Nash's Infiniti, where Detective Cartwright and Officer Chatham stood guard at the trunk. From the front entrance of Yates' Yards, Sara Sandoval emerged and edged closer to Valerie. The new hire's face was dark with concern, and she clearly assumed the worst. "What in the world is happening?"

Valerie wrapped her arms around herself, fighting the cold that prickled her skin. She knew the chill was as much the shock and dread she felt as the crisp October morning.

"Val?" Rick called, slowing to wait for her to accompany the rest of the family inside.

"Just a minute. I—I'll be right there." She took Sara's hand and pressed it between her own, needing the human connection as much as she wanted to offer the distressed young woman comfort. "The family had bad news this morning."

"Bad news? But I thought Vita told me they'd found Jackson, and he was safe."

Valerie bobbed her head once. "Right. But then we learned that Axel Colton, Myles and Lila's father, was murdered."

Sara's face paled, and she drew a sharp breath. "Axel… is dead?"

Valerie nodded and squeezed Sara's hand harder. "Yeah. A shock for everyone." She inhaled deeply and cast a lingering gaze toward Detective Cartwright. "And they've apparently found something incriminating in Nash's trunk. They just took him to the police station as if he were a common criminal."

She heard a little whimper and turned back to Sara, just as the other woman crumpled to the lawn. "Sara!"

She knelt beside Sara, patting her cheek and calling her name, until Detective Cartwright appeared at her side and nudged her out of the way.

"What happened?" He removed his jacket, balled it up and gently placed it behind Sara's head. He shot the members of the media that hustled closer a scowl and shouted, "Get back!" Then under his breath, he added, "Vultures." He angled a look at Val. "Is she diabetic? Epileptic?"

"I—I don't know. She looked pale after I told her Axel was killed and then next thing I know—" Valerie heard another soft mewl from Sara and shifted her attention to her new friend. "Sara? Are you hurt? Sara?"

Cartwright patted Sara's cheek lightly and asked, "Are you all right, ma'am?"

Sara opened her eyes slowly, then blinked hard and frowned when she saw Detective Cartwright leaning over her. "What happened?"

"You fainted, ma'am. Do you have a medical condition that might have caused—?"

"No. Nothing like th—" Sara tried to sit up, and her eyelids fluttered.

"Hey, easy there." Cartwright placed a hand on her arm and eased her back to the ground. "Rest a minute. Did you hit your head? Is your vision blurred?"

Valerie eased back down, eyeing the detective, whose handsome countenance was furrowed with what was obviously genuine concern.

Sara closed her eyes and touched the back of her head, then sighed. "No. I'm not hurt. I just…skipped breakfast. Then when she said…" Her face crumpled again, as if hearing the tragic news of Axel's murder again. "Oh, wow. I just…"

Cartwright lifted his gaze to Valerie. "Can you get her some water?"

"Sure." She shoved to her feet and hurried inside Yates' Yards. She made a beeline to the break room, retrieved a bottle of water from the refrigerator and rushed back out. As she approached the spot where Sara was now sitting up on the grass, she slowed her steps to study the scene. Sara was staring at Cartwright, smiling shyly, and Cartwright was gazing at Sara with a rapt attention and a dazed expression that seemed to shut out the rest of the world. She got an odd sense that she was intruding on a private moment.

The dry leaves crunched under her feet, though, and Cartwright cut his gaze to Val. He stuck his hand out for the bottle of water. "Thanks."

"Really," Sara said, getting her feet under her, "I'm fine now."

Cartwright placed a hand under her elbow and steadied Sara as she stood with a stumble.

Another car with police lights arrived, and Cartwright's ensuing sigh seemed full of regret. "That's the forensic team. I need to go."

Sara stooped to collect the jacket that had pillowed her head and handed it back to the detective. "I'm good. Thank you for your concern."

He gave Sara a half smile, his gray-green eyes lingering on Sara's before he returned to his duties. Sara drew a deep breath and exhaled slowly.

Val stepped closer, ready to catch the woman if she wobbled again. "Okay?"

"Did you see his eyes?" Sara asked, sounding winded.

Val's lips twitched. "They were striking."

"I'll say." Then Sara seemed to remember what had precipitated her faint, and her expression darkened again. "Oh, I'm sorry. You were saying…about Axel. And they arrested Nash for it?"

"So it would seem." Valerie returned her gaze to where the forensics team had removed a heavy-looking candleholder from Nash's trunk and were carefully bagging it as evidence. Even from this distance, she could see that the white marble was stained with blood. With a chilling certainty, she knew she was looking at the murder weapon.

How did it end up in Nash's car? Was it in his car all night while she'd been making love to Nash? Had he lied to her? Was it possible that before he'd come home yesterday, Nash had killed Axel…by accident?

No. A person didn't hit someone else with a marble candlestick hard enough to kill them by accident. Whoever had hefted that piece had intended to inflict grave harm.

"You know the family better than I do," Sara said. "Do you think Nash could have done it?"

Val fought for a breath. She wanted to defend Nash, wanted to believe that the man who'd so passionately and tenderly made love to her last night couldn't possibly have taken the life of his uncle, even in a fit of rage. But her mother's warning echoed in her head, and the police had found condemning evidence in his trunk. She gripped Sara's hand tighter and wheezed, "I don't know."

Valerie returned to the house, where Carter was relaying what he'd learned from the reporter. Vita, Lila and Nicole wore similar masks of horror, and Rick paced the floor, scrubbing a hand over his cheek and through his hair in agitation.

Carter glanced up at Valerie as she entered the room and took a seat beside Vita. "He bled from the head. The guy said he overheard Cartwright tell the uniform at the scene that the cause of death appeared to be blunt-force trauma."

That fit, if the murder weapon was, in fact, the candlestick they'd just removed from Nash's car. Valerie's gut rolled.

"So he hit his head as he fell?" Vita's tone was thin and trembled with both hope and fear.

Carter shook his head. "No. There was nothing close for him to hit his head on. And…there were signs of a struggle."

Rick muttered a curse under his breath.

Nicole's face was calm but shadowed as she asked quietly, "And they found something in Nash's trunk, didn't they? Something they suspect was used to kill Axel."

"Yeah." Carter grasped Lila's hand and added, "But Myles is already on his way to the police department. He'll get to the bottom of this and bring Nash home, if at all possible."

No one said anything for several tense moments. The grandfather clock in the front hall ticked loudly, marking the seconds and keeping time with the heavy, anxious beats of Val's pulse.

Finally, Carter spoke the terrifying thought that was clearly on everyone's mind, but no one else had dared to give voice. "Someone is out to destroy the Coltons, one horrible act at a time."

Chapter 9

Once at the police station, Officer Moody escorted Nash to an interrogation room. When he saw the stark room and hard, straight-backed chair, a chill raced through Nash. He was uncuffed and left alone in the room until Detective Cartwright arrived.

"I'm not answering any questions until my lawyer arrives," Nash said as the detective took a seat.

"That's your right, of course." Cartwright folded his arms over his chest as he narrowed his glare on Nash. "Any idea when that will be?"

Nash cast a glance around the Spartan room with the two-way glass mirror on one wall. "Soon, I'd think. But seeing as my lawyer is also the victim's son... Well, Myles is a bit busy today."

"And you don't see the conflict of interest with that? Having Myles Colton as your legal representative?"

"Of course, I see it. Myles will undoubtedly find an-

other attorney to handle my case, but on short notice…"
Nash spread his hands. "He'll still see that my rights are
protected, and that this railroading doesn't go too far
off the tracks."

"Railroading? Is that your way of denying any culpa-
bility in Axel Colton's death?"

While he wanted to shout his innocence from the roof
of the police station, Nash knew better than to say more
before Myles arrived. He'd already said too much. He
clamped his mouth shut, pressing his lips in a firm stubborn line.

After a moment of holding Nash's stare, Cartwright
unfolded his arms and walked to the door. "All right,
then. I'll be back once your attorney arrives."

Nash leaned back in the hard chair. While he waited,
impatiently, for Myles, he tried to discern how, *how in
hell*, that damn candlestick had gotten in his trunk. Obviously it had been planted, but when? He'd been at home
with Valerie from the end of his confrontation with Axel
at the tennis courts until he'd headed to Vita's. Perhaps
the killer, knowing the family would convene after Jackson was found, had picked his car at random while the
family had celebrated inside. Or could—

The interrogation room door opened again and Myles,
looking stressed and rumpled, was ushered in by a uniformed officer. Nash shoved to his feet to embrace his
cousin.

"What the hell is going on, Nash?" Myles asked.
"Carter said they arrested you for Dad's murder. Based
on what?"

Nash waved a hand toward another hard, uncomfortable chair and sat back down. "Planted evidence."

"Planted by whom?"

"That is the question of the hour." Nash filled Myles

in on the whole series of events, starting with his confrontation with Axel the day before, the detective's arrival at Vita's and the execution of the search warrant.

"I won't ask you to divide your loyalties defending me. But if you can recommend someone—"

Myles raised a hand. "We'll cross that bridge if we must, but I'd rather get these charges against you dismissed."

"I'm listening."

Myles steepled his fingers and tapped them against his mouth as he thought. "If we can prove you weren't the one who put that candleholder in your trunk, this goes away. It's the only thing connecting you to Dad's death at this point."

"So we need a witness who saw someone put the thing in my car."

Myles nodded, his expression still thoughtful. "Or a camera. You have a security video at your house?"

Nash exhaled heavily. "No."

Myles groaned. "What about your neighbors? Any chance they have cameras that would catch any activity at the end of your driveway?"

Nash shrugged. "I've never asked them. My next-door neighbor on the left has a line of evergreens that form a privacy wall of sorts. On the right is an older lady that lives alone. And across the street is a banker and his family."

Myles lifted his phone and tapped the screen. "I'm going to get Damon started talking to your neighbors. Where else have you been in the last eighteen hours?"

"Just Vita and Rick's this morning with everyone else."

"Yates' Yards has security cameras, don't they? Maybe your car will be in frame of their video. I'll have Rick review the feed from this morning ASAP." He clapped a hand on Nash's shoulder. "Keep the faith, cuz. We'll figure this out."

Detective Cartwright didn't return for almost an hour. When he did, he set a mug of coffee and a voice recorder on the scarred wooden table. Then, he took a file folder from under his arm, placed it next to his mug and sat down. "Well, gentlemen, shall we begin?"

Nash glanced at Myles, who nodded once. Even though he hadn't killed Axel, Nash's stomach clenched and acid burned a hole at his core. Not knowing who was at the root of the frame job against him and how far it reached left him wary and restless. Were the police involved in this farce? Or some powerful person with the means to sway an investigation? He knew enough from Damon's undercover operations to realize organized crime was alive and well in Chi-Town.

And his best defense rested on an alibi he'd sworn not to reveal. How desperate was Valerie to hide their one-night stand? Would she deny having been with him to serve her own agenda and leave him defenseless?

"Can you tell me the last time you spoke to Axel Colton?" Cartwright asked.

"I saw him yesterday at his racket club." Nash decided his best move was not to play coy. He would be up front about the nature of the interaction, demonstrating he had nothing to hide. "We argued about his unwillingness to help pay the ransom for my nephew Jackson."

Nash exchanged a look with Myles, who frowned but kept silent.

"The little boy that was mentioned earlier at the Yateses'?"

Myles arched an eyebrow. "My son. But he's been located now and returned safely."

Nash sighed and grumbled, "No thanks to his grandfather."

Myles cut a silencing glance to Nash.

Cartwright nodded. "That's what I was told. I'm glad he's all right." He folded his arms over his chest and rocked his chair onto the back legs. "Do you hold a grudge against Axel for his lack of involvement with Jackson?"

Nash saw the trap and weighed his answer carefully. "I was disappointed in him, yes. Angry, even. But Axel's disinterest in Jackson is no more than I've come to expect from him or his brother Erik, my father. They are both arrogant, spoiled and distant. Neither will ever win father of the year. But Axel's character is something my siblings and I have learned to accept and expect. Yesterday, I shouldn't have been surprised Axel refused to help pay the ransom. He's selfish that way. But I was willing to try to talk sense into him for Jackson's sake. I lost my temper, because I was already on edge and stressed out over the situation. My bad. I admit that. But I didn't kill him."

Myles leaned over and whispered to him, "Keep your answers short and to the point. Don't volunteer information he doesn't ask for."

When Myles settled back in his chair, Cartwright continued. "Would you say you *wanted* to kill him?"

Nash scoffed. "I'm not a murderer, Detective."

"Did you want to kill him?"

Nash gritted his teeth. "No. Not literally."

Cartwright opened the folder he'd brought in with him and shuffled through some papers. "You were overheard by a witness at the racket club shouting, quote, 'You're going to be sorry you walked away, old man,' and that he was going to pay for turning his back on his family."

Nash pinched the bridge of his nose. "Like I said, I was angry. I meant that someday Axel would regret not having made his family a bigger priority in his life."

The detective angled his head. "Regret it how?"

Nash sent Myles a glance, but his cousin said nothing, so he answered, "That he'd realize his family, and not money or status, was what really mattered in life. I was talking about an awareness and sadness he'd have, not a physical retribution from someone."

"Did you tell Tiffany Zimmerman that you wanted to strangle your uncle?"

Nash blinked. "Who?"

Cartwright double-checked his papers. "Tiffany Zimmerman. A tennis pro at the racket club where you confronted Axel Colton."

Raking his hand through his short-cropped hair, Nash recalled the pretty young woman with wide green eyes and his flippant remarks to her. What had he said exactly? "She overheard the argument I had with Axel and looked a little nervous as I left. So—just joking—I asked her something like didn't she ever want to strangle anyone in her family? I didn't mean it literally. I was letting off steam."

Cartwright tapped his thumb on the table and sighed. "Did you threaten to kill Axel Colton, Nash?"

"No! Never!"

"Besides Miss Zimmerman's statement, we have several other accounts from club members that describe you threatening Mr. Colton's life."

Nash's pulse accelerated as he sensed the walls closing in on him. He shook his head vehemently. "No. I never threatened to kill him. I joked about wanting to strangle him because I was frustrated, but I didn't—"

"Where were you between the hours of ten p.m. last night and two a.m. this morning?"

The question struck Nash like a fist in his gut. So here it was. Time to ante up.

How did he prove his innocence without betraying Valerie's request of secrecy? Would she deny being with him to appease her mother? His gut roiled. Surely not. The Valerie he remembered wasn't that cold and selfish. And yet...she'd left him in the dark about her pregnancy. Cut off communication with him for years. Bought her mother's lies without giving him a chance to explain himself. Her previous behavior hadn't exactly earned his trust.

But he'd made a promise to her, and he would keep his word. Surely, evidence that cleared him would come to light soon. It had to.

He flattened his hands on the table and met the detective's stare levelly. "I was at home. I went to bed around eleven. Woke up at nine when Myles called to say Jackson had been found."

"Can anyone corroborate your story?"

"It's not a story. I was at home." Then he added evasively, "I live alone."

"So the answer is no? You have no one to back up your alibi of being at home last night and when you went to bed?"

Nash ground his back teeth together and bounced his heel in agitation. "You could talk to my neighbors. They may have seen my car in the driveway." *And Valerie's,* he thought belatedly.

"We'll talk to your neighbors if we can't verify your alibi any other way. A car in a driveway really isn't proof of anything. You could have called a cab or had a friend pick you up."

Detective Cartwright made some notes and narrowed his gaze on Nash. "Look, Mr. Colton, we're not out to pin this on someone just to make an arrest. We want the person responsible. If you didn't do it, you need to help us prove that."

"I didn't kill my uncle. I was home last night. All night."

"Do you have footage from security camera that would place you arriving home and when you left again?"

"No. I wish I did, because I'd love to know who put that candlestick in my trunk."

Myles cleared his throat, and when Nash glanced at him, he received a warning glare from his cousin. His heart gave a hard thump.

Don't volunteer anything you aren't asked.

"Right. Let's talk about that candlestick," Cartwright said, flipping in his file to a printed copy of one of the photos taken earlier that morning of Nash's trunk.

An earthy curse word filtered through Nash's brain.

"Do you recognize this candlestick?"

"No. I never saw it before this morning."

"How do you explain it being in the back of your car?"

"I can't. But I didn't—" Nash caught the denial on his tongue. Don't volunteer anything… God, he wished he knew what Valerie was telling the police right now. Would she speak up about their night together or let him remain under suspicion?

Cartwright sighed. "Mr. Colton, you understand that, right now, you are the lead suspect in your uncle's death, don't you? First-degree murder? If you have anything else to tell me to clear up this matter, I suggest you share it."

A knock interrupted them, and when the door was

cracked open, a female officer with her hair slicked back in a tight bun poked her head in the room. "Sorry to intrude, Detective, but there's a gentleman out here says he has video footage that is relevant to the Axel Colton case."

The detective's brow furrowed. "Tell them I'll speak to them in a—"

"I think we should see the video together, Detective," Myles said. "If the gentleman she mentioned is Damon Colton, he's here with security camera footage that I requested. Footage that can prove Nash didn't put the candlestick in his trunk."

Cartwright held Myles's gaze for long seconds, then let the legs of his chair thump back to the ground. He pushed to his feet and said, "Wait here."

Nash snorted dryly as the detective left the room. "Like they'd let me leave." He rose to his feet and paced the floor, his hands jittery at his sides. "This is a nightmare. Do you think my dad—?" He stopped himself, realizing that Cartwright's voice recorder was still on the table capturing everything he said. And no doubt someone was behind that mirrored glass watching.

"Keep the faith, man. If Damon's here with security footage then—"

The door burst open again, and Cartwright bustled in. With him was Damon, wearing one of his official DEA jackets and clearly using his own connections in law enforcement to gain entry to the interview room. Nash's brother gave him a stern look. "You and I are going to have a talk about the importance of a home security system when you get out of here. You're lucky Cynthia Myer was home." He set a laptop on the wooden table and switched it on. "She was about to leave town to meet her family in Colorado for a wedding." Damon pulled a flash drive from his pocket. "Her husband and kids left Tuesday night, and she was just finishing up a work project before joining them." He plugged the USB drive into a port on the side of the laptop and clicked through a few screens to open a video-viewing program. He selected a file with yesterday's date. Directing his attention to Detective Cartwright, he said, "Security camera footage from Nash's across-the-street neighbor. She's willing to testify to the veracity and authenticity of the tape, that it hasn't been altered. Notice the date and time stamp. Yesterday at four twelve p.m."

Cartwright didn't look happy that Damon had taken matters into his own hands, but turned his attention to the screen. The shot was of the Myers' front yard, but Nash's house and empty driveway were plainly visible, as well.

Nash rubbed his hands on the legs of his jeans—he knew full well what would play out in the next couple of minutes. The other three men leaned closer to the screen when Valerie's car pulled in the driveway.

"Who's that?" Cartwright asked.

Nash clenched his teeth, his gut in knots.

"That looks like…" Myles squinted at the screen. "Is that Valerie?"

"Valerie?" Cartwright repeated. "She have a last name?"

"Valerie Yates. She's in town visiting her uncle, Rick Yates," Nash explained. "She was at the Yateses' home earlier this morning when you arrived."

Cartwright stared intently at the screen as Valerie walked to his door, knocked, then waved to a woman on the sidewalk with a baby stroller. "Oh, yeah. I remember her."

Then Nash's car appeared, pulling into his driveway behind Valerie's. Nash tensed as he watched himself and Valerie on screen, knowing the questions that would come.

"Why was Ms. Yates there? Had you been expecting her?" Cartwright asked.

"I hadn't. She came to talk." He wanted to leave it at that, but heard himself adding, "We were close as kids, and I hadn't seen her in a long time. We were catching up."

Nash felt more than saw Damon turn a querying gaze on him, but he kept his own eyes on the laptop screen. After a minute or two of nothing else happening in the camera angle, Damon hit fast-forward. Anytime a car or person appeared on the video, he stopped and replayed the footage. Several cars drove down the street as his neighbors returned home from work. Children and dogs ran down the sidewalk, the mother with the stroller returned from her walk the way she'd come. Night fell.

And Valerie's car remained in his driveway.

Patiently, without comment, as Damon continued fast-forwarding, stopping and rewinding, the four men watched and rewatched the security footage. Then when the time stamp read two twenty-six a.m., a vehicle stopped just past Nash's driveway.

"Hold the phone," Damon mumbled. "What's this?"

A large figure dressed in a dark jacket with the hood up stepped out of the driver's side and took something from the back seat. Opened Nash's trunk. Placed the object inside. Wiped Nash's car with a cloth. And hurried back to their car. The taillights of the pale sedan blinked as the car pulled quickly away.

Even knowing he had to have been set up, Nash's lungs squeezed as he saw the scene play out in the security video. While he'd been inside, making love to Valerie, some jerk had been in his driveway, framing him for his uncle's murder.

Damon hit a key on the laptop to pause the video playback. "There you go, Detective Cartwright. Someone planted that candleholder in my brother's car."

Cartwright leaned back in his chair, folding his hands behind his head as he exhaled a slow deep breath. "So it would seem." He chewed the inside of his cheek, his eyes unfocused and his forehead dented in consternation. Then, tapping his fist on the table, he said, "Play it back. What model car is that? Can you see the tag number? The person's face, even for a second?"

All four men leaned in to study the replay, and Nash's pulse bumped so hard, he could feel every throb in his throat, could hear the whoosh echoing in his ears.

They replayed that twenty-two seconds of video five times, but the angle was wrong for capturing the license plate. Between the poor light and the hood shielding the perpetrator's face, making a positive ID was impossible. But knowing the item used to kill his uncle had been placed in his trunk was compelling evidence in his favor.

That, and the fact that he had an alibi.

Once Cartwright was convinced they wouldn't get the license plate from that camera shot, he had Damon fast-forward through the footage until Nash and Valerie could be seen leaving his house in the morning and climbing in their respective vehicles. Without him saying a word, Myles and Damon were now fully aware of the fact that Valerie had spent the night with him.

As the men watched Valerie back out of Nash's driveway and her car disappear from view, Myles reached over and slapped the back of Nash's head.

"Hey! What the—"

"Why the hell didn't you say you had someone who

could verify your whereabouts during the time the murder took place?" Myles asked, glaring at Nash.

"Same question." Cartwright nodded his head toward Myles, then narrowed his eyes on Nash.

"Because…" Clenching his fists, Nash sighed. Explaining the truth—that Val asked him to keep their liaison secret, because her mother's mental health was fragile, because Val was unsure of what she wanted—was as big a violation of trust and her confidence in him as their one-night stand. Half of the truth was out, but he still had a chance to protect some of the intimate details of what Val and he had shared, the full scope of their past.

Cartwright flattened both hands on the table and leaned toward Nash. "Do you need me to repeat the question, Mr. Colton?"

"No. I didn't say anything out of deference to Val's privacy, her reputation. I don't kiss and tell."

"Even when under suspicion of murder?" Cartwright arched an eyebrow.

"I knew I hadn't done anything wrong. I didn't kill Axel, and I had faith that *you*—" he paused briefly to give the word more weight "—would do your job correctly, and the evidence would clear me." He flipped a hand toward Damon's laptop. "Case in point. Video proof I was home all night and someone planted the murder weapon to frame me."

The detective grunted and scratched his chin. "Which begs the question, why you? Why were you, specifically, singled out to frame?"

Nash gritted his back teeth and shook his head. "I wish I knew."

Chapter 10

After the forensic team finished with Nash's car, a young police officer, whose name tag read *R. Tandy*, came to the Yateses' home to talk to the family. Everyone was clearly shell-shocked after having seen Nash put in handcuffs and shoved in the back of a cruiser. No one more so than Val herself. She knew with a simple few words—*he was with me*—she could clear Nash's name. But...

If he was innocent, wouldn't the evidence clear him?

Her stomach swam. *If* he was innocent?

Was she seriously doubting him? The man she'd made love to so gently and passionately couldn't possibly be guilty of murder. Nash had been genuinely stunned to find that marble piece in his trunk.

The truth was, if pressed on the matter, she had no idea what he'd done, how far the argument with Axel had reached before he'd gotten home and found her on his porch. And what was she supposed to do with these awful nagging doubts?

While she could keep quiet about her uncertainties, she knew she couldn't keep quiet about where she'd been last night—or rather, with whom—as much as she'd like to.

Nash's arrest suddenly made her one-night indulgence relevant in a bigger theater. Uncle Rick and Vita already knew she'd been gone all night. They hadn't yet pressed her on her whereabouts, but suspicions were sure to rise soon. She exhaled slowly as she took a seat in the living room and followed the conversation in progress.

"He arrived around ten forty-five or so," Rick said. "Or that's when I first saw him here." Her uncle turned to her. "Val, did you see when Nash got here this morning?"

Valerie's breath snagged. "Uh, ten forty-five sounds about right." *Same as me.*

Did her guilt show?

"It's hard to say for sure. The whole family was here, Officer," Vita said. "It was very busy and confusing… in a good way. We were celebrating. Until the call came about Axel, at least."

"Are any of you aware of a beef of any sort between Nash and his uncle?" Officer Tandy asked.

Lila huffed loudly. "Look. I know you're just doing your job. But Nash did not kill my father. He wouldn't. It's ludicrous to even consider! This whole line of reasoning is a waste of time. The better question is who put that candleholder in his trunk? That's the path that will find the killer. Not these crazy rabbit trails!"

"Ma'am," the young officer said, addressing Lila, "we have to follow where the evidence takes us. The best way to clear your brother is to—"

"Cousin," Lila corrected, her tone reflecting her edgy mood. "We want to keep the facts straight, don't we?"

"Cousin, then. And yes, we do." Tandy used his pen to scratch his head, then asked, "Does anyone have anything to add? Any details or clarifications to what's been said? You never know what might be the tip that helps solve this case."

Valerie held her breath, knowing she needed to speak up. Keeping silent was tantamount to withholding key evidence in an investigation.

Admitting the truth, here and now, would mean she'd face many more questions from the family. Questions she wasn't prepared to answer. She hadn't fully processed for herself what her one-night stand with Nash meant. She'd let her emotions and memories lead her instead of keeping her head, keeping her distance. What had she been thinking? She'd worked too hard and too long to get over him, and then she'd fallen into bed with him again the first time they were alone together? So careless. An obvious mistake. A lapse in judgment she needed to keep quiet. To protect her privacy, to shield her mother, to sweep her recklessness under the proverbial rug.

When the young officer got no further comments or questions from the family, he tucked his pen in his shirt pocket and turned off the recording app on his phone. "Well, if that's all, I'll let you folks get back to—"

"Can—can I speak to you privately, officer?" Val asked.

Lila cut a curious glance toward her. "Val? If you know something about my father, I hope you would feel safe enough to share it with everyone."

Valerie felt her face heat, and her pulse thrummed. "No. It's not that. I just…" She fumbled and spread her hands, searching for the right words.

"If you prefer to speak in private, we can do that." Office Tandy waved a hand toward the foyer.

Well, she'd stuck her foot in it now. With an awkward smile to the room, she excused herself and stepped out on the front porch with the young officer.

The media members, of course, were still camped out in Rick and Vita's yard, waiting for any morsel of information that they could dissect and cook into a story to feed their gossip-hungry audience. At Val's appearance on the porch with the officer, the cameras all swung toward her.

Giving the clustered reporters her back, Valerie scowled at Tandy. "Why do I feel like a tape of this conversation will be analyzed by a lip reader?"

"We could go downtown to the station. An interview room would be completely private."

And completely intimidating. She just wanted to confess her whereabouts, provide relevant details to Nash's defense as simply as possible. Going to the police station to be interviewed felt so...*real*. Significant. Terrifying.

Her expression must have reflected her thoughts, because Officer Tandy gave her a half smile. "It sounds scarier than it is. You're not in trouble. You'd be free to leave at any time. We can even go in separate vehicles if climbing in my squad car with the cameras watching bothers you."

She rubbed her arm as gooseflesh prickled her skin. "I guess..." A glance at the living-room window revealed faces watching her from inside the house, in addition to those out on the lawn. "Yes. The station will be fine. I'll follow you there."

Ten minutes later, she walked with Officer Tandy into the lobby of the police station nearest to Rick and Vita's house. Her nerves jangled, and she felt as if she could jump out of her skin if someone so much as whispered, "Boo."

"Wait here. I'll see which room is available, and be right back," Tandy said.

She nodded and watched him retreat down a long corridor, then stop as someone exited a door halfway down the hall.

Detective Cartwright.

On Cartwright's heels were Damon and Myles Colton. Valerie froze. She didn't want anyone else in the family to know she was here. What if they…?

Damon spotted her and nudged Myles with his elbow.

Damn it. So much for wanting to fade into the background.

Tandy spoke to Cartwright, and Cartwright to Damon and Myles. They all glanced her way before Damon and Myles were clearly dismissed and Cartwright disappeared into a different room with Tandy.

Myles and Damon approached her with knowing grins, and the anxiety inside her morphed into fury. Her disappointment and anger grew as Damon sang a quiet and off-key version of the refrain from Lionel Richie's "All Night Long" under his breath as he approached her. Now Myles poked his cousin with his elbow. "Cut it out."

Nash had promised to keep her secret, but not even six hours later he'd obviously spilled to his brother and cousin the truth about their night together. Sure, he'd had to provide an alibi, answer the detective's questions honestly, but why did he have to spill it all to Myles and Damon?

She wanted to cry. She wanted to scream. Even if she was at the police station to confess the truth, she wanted to rage in Nash's face and tell him how his faithlessness cut her.

In her head, she could hear her mother's voice saying, *I told you the Coltons weren't trustworthy. I told you so…*

Her hands balled in fists, she folded her arms over her chest and tried to ignore the teasing grins as Damon and Myles reached her.

"So…" Damon began, his eyes full of light as he paused to speak to her. "What brings you to the station, Valerie?"

"Judging from your smirk, I'd say you know exactly why I'm here." She didn't even try to hide her annoyance.

Damon frowned. "You sound ticked? Why aren't you happy that Nash—"

"Ms. Yates?" Detective Cartwright approached them, and Damon said no more. "If you'll follow me, I have just a few questions for you."

Her jitters returned. As she fell in step behind Cartwright, she caught Myles's reassuring smile and the confident nod Damon gave her. Sure, they were happy for Nash to have an alibi, but what about the repercussions for her life? They didn't understand how precarious her mother's health was.

The detective directed her into a dingy room with a table and two chairs, then closed the door behind her. She shivered, despite the heat filling the stuffy room. The cubicle—it was really too small to even be called a room— smelled of body odor, mildew and stale food. The tight space was stark. Intimidating. No doubt intentionally so.

Cartwright must have seen the dismay in her expression because he said, "I apologize for the less-than-welcoming accommodations. I only have a couple of questions for you, so I went with expediency and privacy over comfort, but if you'd rather move—"

"No, I'm…" She considered the chair but decided to

stand. The detective remained on his feet, as well. "Can we just get this over with?"

"Certainly. Can you tell me where you were last night between the hours of five p.m. and ten a.m. this morning?"

The specificity of the times left no doubt what Nash had told the detective. Acid puddled in her gut, and anger raised a sheen of sweat on her skin. Or maybe that was just the boiling heat in the small room. Valerie wiped the moisture from her brow and sighed. "I was at Nash Colton's house."

"The entire time?"

Her heart thumped a slow beat of defeat. "Yes."

"And was Nash Colton with you the entire time?"

"Yes."

"Can you tell me specifically where you were at two twenty-six a.m.?"

The oddly specific time surprised her. "At Nash's."

"Can you be more specific?"

She gave the detective a peeved look and huffed irritably. "In his bedroom. Is that what you wanted to hear? That I slept with him? I can't say whether we were making love at exactly two twenty-six a.m., but we were in bed together, and we did make love and took catnaps all night. Is that what you wanted to know?" Her voice cracked, and she was stunned to find that tears had leaked to her cheeks.

Cartwright had the decency to look apologetic. "Detail is helpful. I'm sorry if this is difficult. One last question. Did you hear or see anything in Nash's driveway at two twenty-six a.m.?"

Valerie stilled. There was something here she'd missed, being so wrapped up in her own anger with Nash and worry over how her spoiled secret would impact her mother. Nash's driveway. Where his car had been parked. Has someone planted the murder weapon while they were inside asleep? Her stomach clenched. She struggled for the breath to speak. "I— No. I'm sorry, but I didn't... I don't..."

Cartwright sighed dejectedly. "Well, that's really all I needed from you. Thank you for your cooperation. If you'd stop at the front desk, I'll have your statement written up for you to sign."

She took a few steps toward the corridor before she faced Cartwright again. "What about Nash? He didn't do anything. Can't he be released?"

"Thanks to your statement and some other corroborating evidence, he'll be released within the hour, I'm sure. Just need to finish some paperwork."

The weight on Valerie's chest lifted like a pressure valve being opened to drain away the stress. Yet a lingering ache remained. News of their night together would spread like hot gossip at a beauty parlor...because Nash hadn't kept his promise.

Valerie got back to Rick and Vita's with one goal in mind—holing up in the guest room and being alone with her thoughts, her heartache, her bone-deep fatigue. The roller-coaster emotions of the last twenty-four hours had wrung her out.

The family, however, had different ideas.

Lila met her at the door with Vita and Rick one step behind her. They immediately began lobbing questions in her direction as she took off her coat. Had she seen Nash? What did she tell the police? What evidence had they found in Nash's car? Has she seen Myles and Damon at the station? What was going on?

She raised a hand, trying to get a word in, and finally Carter loosed a shrill whistle that jolted them all into silence.

"Give her a chance!" Lila's fiancé led Valerie into the living room and the family clustered around her. She gave them the highlights. Nash would be released from custody soon. He had a confirmed alibi. She'd seen Myles and Damon, but had not had an opportunity to speak to them at length.

All true. If she felt a flicker of guilt for having left out certain bits of the whole story, she could deal with that compunction later. After a nap. After she ate. After she'd had time to talk to Nash and sort through her tangled emotions. But her desire for time to rest and think was thwarted within minutes as Damon arrived with Nash.

Nash's exhaustion was evident in the lines bracketing his mouth and the shadows under his eyes. Despite being released by the police, his slumped shoulders spoke of defeat and dejection.

The family, of course, swarmed Nash, expressing their relief that he'd been released and peppering him with questions. Like Val, Nash begged off answering more than a few cursory queries.

She tried to ease out of the room unnoticed, but Nash called to her as she reached the living-room door: "Val, hang on. I want to talk to you."

"Yeah, you do," Damon said with a lopsided smile and a knowing wink.

"What's that supposed to mean?" Lila asked.

Nash glared at his brother. "Can it."

Valerie avoided eye contact with the many curious stares she felt boring into her as Nash made his way across the room.

"Let's go somewhere out of earshot, huh?" he said quietly.

Loyal Readers
FREE BOOKS Voucher

We're giving away

THOUSANDS

of

FREE

BOOKS

Sizzling Romance

Passionate Romance

Don't Miss Out! Send for Your Free Books Today!

Get up to 4
FREE FABULOUS BOOKS
You Love!

To thank you for being a loyal reader we'd like to send you up to 4 FREE BOOKS, absolutely free.

Just write "YES" on the Loyal Reader Voucher and we'll send you up to 4 Free Books and Free Mystery Gifts, altogether worth over $20, as a way of saying thank you for being a loyal reader.

Try **Harlequin® Desire** books featuring the worlds of the American elite with juicy plot twists, delicious sensuality and intriguing scandal.

Try **Harlequin Presents®** Larger-print books featuring the glamourous lives of royals and billionaires in a world of exotic locations, where passion knows no bounds.

Or **TRY BOTH!**

We are so glad you love the books as much as we do and can't wait to send you great new books.

So don't miss out, return your Loyal Reader Voucher Today!

Pam Powers

LOYAL READER
FREE BOOKS VOUCHER

YES! I Love Reading, please send me up to 4 FREE BOOKS and Free Mystery Gifts from the series I select.

Just write in "YES" on the dotted line below then return this card today and we'll send your free books & gifts asap!

➡️ YES ⬅️

Which do you prefer?

☐ **Harlequin Desire®**
225/326 HDL GRGA

☐ **Harlequin Presents® Larger Print**
176/376 HDL GRGA

☐ **BOTH**
225/326 & 176/376 HDL GRGM

FIRST NAME

LAST NAME

ADDRESS

APT.#

CITY

STATE/PROV.

ZIP/POSTAL CODE

EMAIL ☐ Please check this box if you would like to receive newsletters and promotional emails from Harlequin Enterprises ULC and its affiliates. You can unsubscribe anytime.

HD/HP-520-LR21

Arms folded over her chest, she glowered at him, but knowing the family was watching, she finally nodded once and headed to the guest room, where she was staying. Once the door was closed behind her she whirled on him, poking his chest with a finger. "This is exactly what I wanted to avoid! It hasn't even been twenty-four hours, and the family already knows we spent the night together! Way to keep your word, Nash."

He gave her a chastened frown. "I'll talk to Damon and Myles, ask them for discretion."

"That's not the point!" she said in a fierce whisper. "I trusted you! You promised me not to say anything and you betrayed that trust!"

"That's not true." He stepped toward her and tried to place a hand on her arm.

She shook off his touch with a scoff. "Oh? So Detective Cartwright is psychic? He asked me specifically about the hours I was at your house last night."

"I can explain—"

"And I guess Myles and your brother just made a really good guess whom you bedded last night?"

"Val…"

"At least have the guts not to lie to me about it!" To her horror, she realized a tear had seeped past her eye and was tickling her cheek. She dashed it away with a brusque slash of her hand.

She fell silent, fighting for composure. She didn't want to fall apart in front of him, didn't want him to know how hurt she was. How much she cared.

Nash moved to the edge of her bed and sat down. "Are you done? Can I speak?"

She gave a petulant shrug.

"I didn't say anything. I did my best to protect your secret like you asked." His tone was calm and reasonable. "In the course of proving the candlestick used to kill Axel had been planted in my car to frame me, the truth came out about you."

"Meaning?"

"Damon acquired the security-camera footage from a neighbor that showed you arriving in my driveway and your car staying until this morning, when we left together."

She held his gaze, digesting what he'd said. Her anger dissipated, leaving her feeling all the more like a deflated balloon—wilted and flat. "Oh."

He nodded. "Oh." After a moment, he narrowed his eyes and tipped his head. "What did you say when Cartwright asked you about being at my house?"

Valerie's pulse spiked. She paced toward the window that looked over the backyard and licked her dry lips. "You were released, weren't you? Doesn't that tell you?"

"I was released because my neighbors' security camera recorded someone planting the candlestick in my car. But it also showed your car parked in front of mine all night. The security video proved my claim the murder weapon was planted and that I had an alibi."

She cut a sharp glance toward him, a surge of relief piercing her dark mood. "There's proof the candleholder was planted?"

He bobbed his head as he pushed off the bed to move toward her. "Yeah. But you haven't answered my question. What did you tell Cartwright?"

Valerie swallowed hard, trying to shove down the knot that swelled in her throat. "The truth. That you couldn't have killed Axel because you were with me all night."

One dark-blond eyebrow quirked. "So *you* told your secret?"

She squared her shoulders. "I couldn't lie to the cops.

Besides…" Her throat tightened again, and she paused to take a slow breath. "I couldn't… I couldn't let you be arrested for a crime you didn't commit."

A slow, sexy smile spread across his face. "Well… thank you."

He reached for her, and when he tugged her into his arms, she went easily. Val melted against him, savoring the comfort his warm body offered. She curled her fingers into the soft fabric of his shirt, and a shuddering sigh rattled from her. "So now what? You've been cleared of murder, but your family knows about us. I'm not mad that you told Cartwright about us to clear your name, but why did you tell your brother and Myles?"

"Myles was there as my lawyer and Damon got the security video from my neighbor. They were in the room when Cartwright and I watched the recording."

Compunction for her castigation, for assuming he'd told their secret washed through her. "Oh. I thought…"

"Is that really such a bad thing, the family knowing?"

"You heard Damon…"

"He's my brother. Brothers tease. I'll talk to him. I promise." With strong fingers under her chin, he tilted her face up to his. He placed a gentle kiss on her lips, and ripples of sweet sensation flowed through her. His second kiss was deeper, and the third stole her breath and made her knees wobble. When he finally lifted his head and brushed his knuckles along her cheek, he whispered, "Honestly, Val, what I want is to shout from the roof that you're my girl. I've waited for you, wanted you since I was twelve years old."

"Twelve? We didn't become a couple until you were sixteen. I was fifteen and—" The tender smile on his face stopped her. "Do you mean…?"

"Like I said. Twelve. You may not have caught on until

later, but that summer we all went to the lake in Minnesota..." He pressed a hand to his heart. "I was a goner. There's a reason I wanted to play so much *Monopoly*. And it wasn't because I liked the tedious game you were obsessed with. No one else would play, so I had you to myself for hours on end."

She bit her lip and shook her head. "You let me win to keep me interested, didn't you?"

"Maybe."

Looping her arms around his neck, she snuggled close to him again. "All I've wanted, since I was old enough to realize my mother cared more about her next drink than she did me, was to have someone I could rely on, someone who'd have my back and love me for me. That's why it hurt so much when I thought you'd broken your promise about our night together. I thought you'd broken my trust."

Nash's brow dipped, and hurt clouded his eyes. "I thought we—"

The jangling notes of her cell phone interrupted Nash and jarred Valerie from the intimate moment. A small shudder of irritation chased through her at the interruption.

"Go ahead." Nash hitched his head toward her purse. "Take it. I'll give you some privacy. I need to call my boss, anyway, let him know what's happening. I had something like twelve messages from him when I got my phone back from the cops."

"Geez. Definitely. Go save your job." Her gaze followed him—she drank in the sight of his lean body and panther-like stride as he left the room. A flicker of heat spread in her belly as she retrieved her phone and remembered those long legs and his taut body wrapped around hers. Making love to her. Cradling her gently afterward. Comforting her when she'd shared her painful past with him.

What was she supposed to do with this complicated, sexy man?

"Hello," she said, answering her call distractedly, without checking her caller ID. Mistake.

"I told you those Coltons were no good!"

Acid pooled in her gut as her mother's sour tone spilled from her phone. She grimaced. "Mother."

"Have you seen the news?"

"No," she said honestly, not bothering to add she'd been living the tragic events with the Colton family.

"Erik's brother, Axel, was murdered! They arrested that boy—the one who got you pregnant—for it!"

Valerie gritted her teeth. Did she really want to hash this out with her mother? "Mother, calm down. It's not like that."

"Oh, it is exactly like that, Valerie Jane! I saw the footage of them putting him in a police cruiser and taking him in. I told you he was bad news, just like his father!"

"He didn't do anything, Mother. The evidence was planted, and he's already been released."

"I— My God, are you defending him? They wouldn't have questioned him without good reason!"

Dropping onto the bed, Valerie scrubbed her free hand over her face. "You're an expert on police investigations now?"

"I know enough to know you need to come home. The sooner, the better."

"No."

Her mother sighed dramatically. "I know you feel a loyalty to your uncle and Vita, and you want to help. But this isn't your problem. If you stay down there around those Colton vipers, you will get bitten! No good can come of—"

"Mother, stop! You're wrong about the Coltons. Well, most of them. And especially about Nash."

"Oh, Valerie," her mother said, her tone heavy with sorrow. "They've brainwashed you. Don't be drawn in by their money and power. And please don't forget how that boy hurt you once."

Valerie's ire surged. It took a moment to catch her breath, but when she did, she snarled, "He's not a *boy*, Mother. He's a man. A good man. A successful architect and respected member of his family and the community."

Her mother snorted loudly. "And a Colton!"

"And for the record, you were far more responsible for hurting me than Nash ever was. You manipulated the situation and—"

"Me?" her mother shrieked. "All I've ever done is protect you!"

Val took a beat to shove down her frustration. Her mother's frantic tone was all too familiar, and a niggling suspicion poked Val. "Mother, are you taking your meds?"

"Don't start with me, Valerie Jane. I know what I'm talking about."

"Did you go to your doctor appointment yesterday? To your AA meeting on Monday?" Maybe she should call her mother's counselor or ask her AA sponsor to check on her.

"I'm not a child, and I'll not have you speak to me that way. And don't change the subject! This is about you and that Colton boy. He's a criminal! A murderer and a liar and—"

"No, Mother. He's not! He didn't kill Axel. Please, take a breath. Calm down…"

"You don't know that. Clearly the police think he's guilty or they w—"

"I do know! Because I was with him! I am Nash's alibi. I was at his house last night. All night!"

Her mother gasped sharply. "What?"

Okay, that wasn't the way she'd intended to break the news to her mother that she and Nash had made a fresh start, but now that she'd lost her cool and blurted the truth, she needed to do damage control. "Mother, Nash is not like his father. He is a good—"

"No!" Her mother made a high-pitched noise, like a growl or whine. "No, no, no! Valerie, you need to come home! Don't do this to me!"

"Mother, I think you should call Dr. Richards. Or Nancy. You aren't alone—"

"No! You are dead to me!"

Valerie heard a clatter, as if the phone had been thrown. "Mother? Mother, are you there?"

Then a shuffling sound and silence. She checked her phone. The screen read, Call ended.

She tried calling her mother back but got no answer. Of course. Next she tried her mother's AA sponsor, Nancy Acree, and left a message. After a quick call to leave a message with Dr. Richards, her mother's psychiatrist, she contemplated returning to Ohio to check on her mother in person.

She'd come to Chicago to support the family she loved during one crisis, only to find herself the center of another. And she had unfinished business with Nash. How could she leave now? Valerie pinched the bridge of her nose and resolved to call her mother later that evening and to keep trying to reach Nancy until she was sure someone knew about her mother's episode.

Valerie bunched the bedspread in her hands and gritted her teeth, feeling a burning resentment bubble up in her. Her mother had been responsible for tearing her and Nash apart once before. She would not let that happen again.

Chapter 11

The next morning, having arranged for Nancy to check on her mother, Valerie walked over to the nursery to meet with Sara concerning the Yates' Yards winter advertising campaign, as she'd promised Rick she would. She found Vita on the sales floor, arranging the new shipment of poinsettias on circular shelves of decreasing width. The display looked like a Christmas tree of red, pink and white blooms with wide green foliage.

"Goodness, Vita! It's still three weeks until Thanksgiving."

"Not in the retail world, my dear." Vita aimed a finger at a pair of scissors. "Will you hand me those, please? I see a bit here that needs a trim."

After handing over the tool, Valerie paused to study the arrangement and wondered what it would be like to celebrate Christmas with Rick and Vita. And Nash.

As a child and teen, holidays with her parents had always been dismal affairs. Her father had been remote, tense, while her mother spoiled what few traditions they'd attempted with drinking and wild mood swings. Knowing the primary source of her mother's behavior had been undiagnosed mental illness did nothing to change the drab gray that colored her memories. A pang swelled in her chest, a longing to stay in Chicago with these people who knew how to love and celebrate and support one another through difficult times. She wanted a real Christmas, with color and warmth and a family that cared about her.

But that would leave her mother alone for the holiday. Vulnerable to her depression, her alcoholism, her isolation. Guilt bit hard. Valerie was the only family her mother had left. How could she abandon her for her own selfish wants?

With a smile to her aunt, she headed back to the small office in the back of the nursery, where Sara was already hunched over a desk, chewing the end of a pen as she studied a notepad. She looked up as Valerie entered, and a bright smile lit her face. "There's my Florence Nightingale."

Valerie snorted. "Hardly. I get queasy at the sight of blood."

Sara shrugged. "Maybe, but I appreciate your help yesterday when I passed out." Her cheeks flushed. "I'm not usually so flaky, but the one-two punch of no breakfast and the horrible news about Mr. Colton..."

Val placed a hand on her new friend's shoulder. "You're not flaky. And I think it's sweet that you care enough about the Colton family to be shocked at Axel's death."

Sara opened her mouth as if to respond, then averted her gaze.

Valerie tipped her head. "Unless the Mr. Colton you mean is Nash and him being taken to the police station. In which case, never fear. He was released without charges. He had both an alibi and evidence the presumed murder weapon was planted."

Sara's chin jerked up, and her eyes rounded. "Planted? Why would someone want to frame Nash?"

Valerie took a seat across from Sara and set the sketch pad she'd brought on the desk. "That is the question of the day. I don't know." She flipped open her pad to the last drawing she'd made. "Enough about all that trouble. Let's talk advertising. What do you think of this? I like the idea you had of focusing on how plants and flowers add a coziness to the holidays. The warm, family gathering theme."

Sara studied Valerie's sketch of a family together in a living room filled with Christmas greenery, poinsettias and amaryllis. "We can do another ad the following week that focuses on winter plants for the yard and the outdoor decorations we sell. Lights and wreaths and the like."

"Do you have a tag line in mind?" Valerie asked.

"I've been toying with a couple."

Excited by the campaign that took form as she and Sara collaborated, Valerie lost track of time. She loved being able to use her talents to help her uncle and Vita. Her artwork was more than a job to her. It was a passion. She'd been drawing, expressing her deepest thoughts and emotions with pencil and paper, for as long as she could remember. Her drawings were an extension of her soul, and sharing her talent to benefit her family filled her with joy.

She and Sara were buried in layouts and in the thick of a free flow of brainstorming when the office door opened with a thump that yanked Valerie from her thought stream.

"Soup's on!" Lila called as she breezed in with bags in her hands.

"Soup?" Valerie asked, peeking in the first bag Lila plunked down on the desk.

"I took the liberty of springing for lunch." She divided a look between Valerie and Sara. "Is now a convenient time for you two to take a break?"

"Sure. Good timing. My stomach's been embarrassing me for the last half an hour. Rumble, grumble." Sara grinned and clicked the mouse to save their work.

"What's the occasion?" Val asked as she pulled a paper-wrapped sandwich out of a bag with the logo *True* on it.

"Do I need a reason?" Lila asked with a coy shrug. "It's been such a long time since we had a chance to just…chat."

Valerie arched an eyebrow, grinning. "We've *chatted* several times since I arrived."

Lila grunted. "Too many of those conversations were tainted by the reigning glum topic of the moment. Kidnapping and murder and funeral plans. Bleh!" Lila unpacked paper bowls with lids from a second bag. "Besides, cumulatively speaking, we need to have many chats to make up for the years you were MIA."

Valerie gave Lila a nod of assent. "Touché."

Sara followed the back-and-forth of the exchange as if she were watching a tennis match, and an amused smile tugged at her lips. "I wish I'd had this growing up. Siblings. Cousins. A big family to share the hard times, the special days, the celebrations of life."

"You were an only child?" Valerie asked, and Sara nodded. "Me, too. I was often lonely. I was lucky to be able to adopt the Colton brood part-time from a young age thanks to my Uncle Rick marrying into the clan. I had many happy summers here." She reached for Lila's hand and gave it a squeeze.

Lila returned a squeeze but pinned a stern, inquiring look on Val. "Then why did you stop visiting? Why did you stay away for so long?"

Valerie paused in the middle of removing a lid from one of the steaming cups. "Oh. That is a long story. Complicated. Not one I want to dive into while we're eating." Seizing an inspiration to change the subject, she opened the container and glanced down at the bright orange puree inside. "Speaking of which, what are we eating?"

"That," Lila said, nodding to the cup Valerie lifted to sniff, "is pumpkin soup. Try it. It's amazing! Everything Tatum does at True is fantastic. And it's all farm-to-table."

"Two questions," Valerie said. "Tatum? True? And what's this?" She unfolded the paper wrapping from the sandwich and inhaled the savory aroma.

"That's three questions," Sara teased as she unwrapped what appeared to be a chicken salad sandwich.

"Tatum is one of the new cousins we learned about this summer," Lila said with a chuckle for Sara. "She's Alfred Colton's daughter and owner of True Restaurant, a local farm-to-table." She waved her hand to the spread. "You have a beef and cheese sandwich, but I'll trade if you'd rather have the veggie. They're both fantastic. The soups are pumpkin, cream of potato and tomato basil. I brought extra bowls and a knife so we can all sample everything."

"Good idea," Sara said. "It all looks wonderful."

"So," Lila said and shot Valerie a side glance as she divided the three sandwiches evenly. "You and Nash, huh? Do tell."

Valerie sighed heavily. "I was wondering when this would come up. Nash swore Damon and Myles could keep it quiet, but families are too much like small towns. News travels fast."

"Why would you want to keep it a secret?" Sara asked. "Nash seems great."

Lila aimed her spoon at Sara. "Yeah. What she asked."

Valerie stirred the pumpkin soup and stalled. "We have a complicated history and... I'm not sure where things stand between us, where we're going. If we are going anywhere. I mean, my life, my job, my mother are all back in Ohio, and Nash is here. His family is here..."

Lila flashed a lopsided smile. "Geography. I get it. Things were a little tricky between Carter and me when we first got together. He travels for his job and I have my gallery here. But we decided we were worth the effort to work out a compromise. We will be together whatever and *wherever* that means."

An ache of longing tugged Valerie's chest. Had she ever had someone so loyal, so trustworthy, so devoted to her that she could lean on them unconditionally? She'd believed Nash was that someone when she was seventeen. And when that dream had shattered, the ache of loss and betrayal almost smothered her. But now her understanding of what had transpired all those years ago had been turned topsy-turvy, and even the jagged, painful beliefs she'd once stood on and clung to for a sense of stability shifted beneath her. The rootlessness was disconcerting.

Valerie smiled politely and took a bite of sandwich. If her issues with Nash were only about geography, things would be so much clearer. But her mother's obsession with the Coltons, her fragile mental health and the whole issue of trust. And commitment. And honesty. And forgiveness—they had a laundry list of baggage to deal with before she could see any future for them. "It's not just that we live in different states. Like I said, our history is messy and—"

"Wait. History?" Lila set down her sandwich and wiped her mouth with a napkin. "Did you and Nash have a thing before this trip? Like…as kids? All those summers you were here…?" Lila's eyes lit with excitement and fascination.

Valerie glanced to Sara as if her new friend could help her out of the awkward spot. But Sara grinned and leaned forward with eager anticipation bright in her gaze, as well.

"Um…"

Lila laughed and playfully swatted Valerie's arm. "Oh, my stars! You did! Your guilty blush is all the answer I need."

Valerie's shoulders drooped. "Okay, yes. But then there were misunderstandings, and broken promises, and disappointments, and—"

Lila took her by the wrist and drilled her with a green gaze so like Nash's it stole Valerie's breath. "The only question that matters is 'do you love him?'"

Once, she'd thought she did. She'd given her heart and soul to Nash, believing he was the one. Now, the honest answer she gave Lila was "I don't know."

Nash didn't see much of Valerie over the next couple of days. He returned to work at Reed and Burdett, the architecture firm where he was rising through the ranks, hoping to make partner in a few years. He put in long hours, knowing he'd taken too much personal time of late. His bosses had, of course, seen the news footage showing him being hauled to the police station, but because they knew Nash, knew his character, they believed his explanation of what had happened. His bosses rallied behind him, even though Nash had to protect certain details of the case, both for the integrity of the ongoing investigation, and for his and Valerie's privacy.

Two days after he'd been hauled down to the police station, Detective Cartwright paid Nash a visit at work. The receptionist who ushered the detective to Nash's office lingered in the hall, pretending to decide whether a plant needed watering and checking her reflection in a decorative mirror.

Nash rounded his desk to shake the detective's hand and closed the door firmly. "What can I do for you, Detective?"

Cartwright pulled a file folder out of a messenger bag and tossed it on top of the blueprints spread on Nash's desk. "Tell me if you recognize this guy."

Picking up the folder, Nash returned to his seat and flipped to the photos inside. Some of the photos were fuzzy black-and-white shots, obviously taken from security-camera footage. Others were mug shots. Others were images likely lifted from social media and cropped to cut other people from the frame. The star of all of the photos was a hefty, middle-age guy with buzz-cut blond hair and a tattoo of barbed wire on his neck. The dude obviously lifted weights. Probably enhanced with one or more supplements that would disqualify him from professional sports. He had a pierced eyebrow and wore a grim expression on his square face.

Nash closed the file and tossed it back toward Detective Cartwright. "I give up. Who is he?"

"Nothing? You're sure?"

"That's not a face someone's likely to forget. No. Never seen him before. Don't have any idea who he is."

He lowered his eyebrows. "But I'm guessing you do and that you have good reason to ask me. So what gives?"

Cartwright grunted and slid the folder closer. He tapped the file against his knee before he returned it to his messenger bag. "His name is Simon Wilcox. We recovered a partial thumbprint from the trunk of your car that matched his."

"He's in the system?"

Cartwright nodded. "Yeah. Mostly minor stuff, but we've long suspected he's a...well, let's call him a thug for hire."

Nash arched an eyebrow. "As in 'dirty deeds done dirt cheap'?"

Cartwright tugged his cheek briefly in a fake grin, acknowledging the AC/DC reference. "As in he advertises his services on the dark web. For the right price, he'll do just about anything. Breaking and entering, terrorizing ex-wives, hiding bodies—"

"Planting evidence of murder?"

Rather than answer Nash's question directly, Cartwright said, "The suspect in the security video that your neighbor supplied has the same body type. We got two numbers off the license plate of the suspect's car. Three nine. Simon's wife has a light blue Cougar coupe. Tag number three-nine-five-G-R-two."

Nash spread his hands. "Sounds like you got the right guy."

"Except his wife swears, hand to heaven, he was with her all night."

Nash groaned. "And you really believe her?"

Cartwright shrugged. "Just saying. We brought him in to question him, as well, but got nothing. Not that we expected much. Not good for his business model if he squeals on the people who hire him."

"So you let him go?" Nash asked, aghast.

"For now. Until we have enough to build a more solid case. That's why I was hoping you had something to help us connect him to this."

Nash puffed out a breath and shook his head. "Man, I wish I did, but I never laid eyes on him until you showed me that picture. And I don't even know how to get on the dark web, much less how to hire a thug from a murky website or whatever."

Cartwright pulled a face and exhaled his obvious frustration. "Okay. Well, I'll get out of your way."

"Wait," Nash said, leaning forward and pinning the detective with narrow-eyed scrutiny. "That's it? You said you had a partial print. Isn't that enough to tag the guy?"

"It's certainly a start. But if that's all we have, his lawyer will claim he could've touched your car in a grocery-store parking lot. We need more that connects him to the candlestick. To Axel's residence. So…" Cartwright stood, ducked his chin in parting. "Thank you for your time."

Nash gritted his back teeth, knowing the cop wouldn't say more about an active investigation. The detective had made it to the door before Nash said, "One more thing."

Cartwright turned. "Yeah?"

"I understand from my Aunt Vita that you know Brad Howard, the FBI man that helped Myles when Jackson was taken."

"I do. We've worked together in the past."

"On the murders of Ernest and Alfred Colton?"

Cartwright pulled back his shoulders and raised his chin. His expression said he was weighing his response. Finally he said, "Yes. Why?"

"Turns out Alfred and Ernest were my half uncles. Dean Colton's legitimate children."

Cartwright nodded. "I'm aware."

"Axel was my uncle. Also Dean's son." Nash waved a hand as if the connection should be obvious. More likely, the detective was just being tight-lipped to see where Nash would go with his theory. "Doesn't that smell to you? Have you looked into a connection?"

"I've considered that angle, and, I assure you, we follow up every possible connection."

"So you don't think there's any link? Is that what you're saying?"

Cartwright hoisted the strap of the messenger bag on his shoulder and shook his head. "Your half uncles were random targets, killed by young sociopaths on a killing spree. One is dead, the other's in custody."

"Right. I know." Nash tried to keep the impatience from his tone. Failed. "We met our half cousins and heard the story. Followed the case on the news. I'm asking if it's possible there was a third guy involved in the killing spree, someone you haven't identified—".

Cartwright raised a hand, cutting him off. "I know you want answers. You're trying to help, but…no. That case is closed. We've not found any link or similarities."

Nash opened his mouth to further his argument, but closed it again with a sigh.

Cartwright reached for the doorknob and gave Nash a confident nod. "We will find the person responsible for killing Axel Colton. I give you my word."

Later that night, Nash sat alone in his bungalow, turning the facts of the murder case and his conversation with Cartwright over in his head, feeling violated and angry over the cretin who'd planted the candlestick. Damon had stopped by earlier in the evening to renew his arguments to install a security system. For the first time, Nash was considering it, which also made him mad, because he hated feeling like he'd caved. But if Valerie was going to be spending more time here, he wanted her to be safe.

But that begged the question—would Valerie be here more often? Or even, at all? They hadn't really settled anything about what was between them. He couldn't say whether they were looking toward the future or simply glad to have some clarity on the past. He'd texted her once or twice, inviting her to come to dinner, to see where they stood now that they'd cleared the air. And gotten quick, if brief, replies putting him off for one reason or another. Already had plans. Migraine. Working late with Sara on ad campaign. Some part of him feared history was repeating itself.

Twelve years ago, she'd assumed the worst about him based on circumstantial evidence from her mother. She'd denied him the right to know about her pregnancy. She'd shut him out. And although she'd explained her side of events a few nights ago, the fact remained that, twelve years ago, she'd dismissed his needs, his feelings and his rights in order to protect herself. Was that what she was doing now, even after all his assurances to her?

Years ago, she'd easily bought into a lie that allowed her to justify her actions. She'd been hurting, yes. But she also hadn't given him a chance to defend himself, to speak the truth, to give her the love and support he'd wanted to give her.

And now? Could he trust her? She'd asked for time, for continued secrecy while she decided how to proceed. But what was there to decide? Did she care about him and believe in him or didn't she?

Acid climbed Nash's throat as his irritation and resentment grew. He'd spent too many years waiting and hoping for his father's love and attention to repeat those mistakes with Valerie. Was it too much to ask for Valerie's unconditional love and faith? He refused to settle for anything less.

Stop it! He squeezed his eyes shut and shook his head as if to jar loose the negative track of his thoughts. He was letting his bad relationship with his father, the resentment over being framed for Axel's murder and a mistaken view of history between him and Valerie color his perception. He was an adult now and needed to view the situation without the warping lens of his emotions. He poured himself a drink at his wet bar and took a sip.

At least she hadn't shut him out, completely ghosted him, like last time. She'd told Cartwright the truth. That was something.

Nash carried his whiskey sour out to the front porch and sat in one of the rocking chairs that Nicole had insisted every front porch required. He sipped his drink and inhaled the cool crisp air and scent of fallen leaves. He blew out a slow, intentional breath and could feel the stress and negativity seep out of him like air from a leaky balloon. Yet a new, overriding sense of isolation and melancholy remained, and he tried to put his finger on the source.

A neighbor he recognized but didn't know by name strolled past on the sidewalk and waved. He returned a kind nod and smile.

His was a calm, quiet neighborhood. Safe. Friendly.

As if to echo that sentiment, the neighbor's calico, who strangely seemed to prefer Nash's house to his own, sauntered up the porch steps and mewed as he rubbed against Nash's calves. Bending to scratch the cat's head, Nash snorted at the irony. "I don't feed you. I don't have a cat to be your buddy. I know your family takes care of you. Why are you always here?"

The cat's bland, even dorky, expression gave Nash a chuckle. "Why do I think you might not be too smart?"

The cat meowed as if to agree.

Nash opened his mouth to comment again and paused. Swore under his breath. He was talking to a cat. Geez, he really was lonely and pathetic if he'd stooped to conversations with his neighbor's feline for company. Taking another sip of whiskey, he realized living alone had never bothered him before. Until... *Valerie.*

One night of arguing, having dinner and making love to Valerie had him reassessing his whole life. Or was it because his siblings and cousins seemed to all be falling in love and finding life partners? He was the last of the family to be unattached, and having seen how happy Damon, Lila, Aaron and the rest were, maybe he was feeling a bit left out. Maybe seeing Valerie awoke old emotions he'd thought he'd safely archived. Memories of losing his mother, being pushed aside and neglected by his father... Valerie's disappearing act.

Dang, but he was maudlin tonight. Why?

A tomato-soup-red VW Beetle rolled past his house and pulled in the driveway two doors down. The cat moved to the edge of the porch, watching his owner get out and walk to the mailbox.

"Your mom's home."

The cat gave him a drowsy backward glance, then moseyed down his porch steps and across his lawn toward home.

Nash tightened his grip on the cold highball glass in his hand. The pang that vibrated like a plucked string in his core was not—*was not*—loneliness over the cat leaving. That was pure nonsense. But...maybe the cat helped highlight to him what was missing from his life. He'd kept people at arm's length most of his life. Letting people get close was a recipe for pain. He'd learned that well enough.

Were surface, distanced relationships all he had to look forward to the rest of his life? Without trusting someone to see his heart, without letting someone into his life and lowering his guard enough for an intimate relationship, all he saw in the years to come was this empty house, this hollow ache and, if he was lucky, visits from someone else's cat.

"Well, that sucks." He needed to make a change. And that change just might start with Valerie.

Chapter 12

Two days later, as Valerie dressed for Axel's funeral, she battled the butterflies that flapped to life whenever she realized that she'd see Nash again. He'd have ample opportunities both at the service and the reception of family here at Vita and Rick's to corner her and demand answers.

She both wanted to see him and didn't. She'd put him off the last several days when he'd asked to see her with excuses as transparent as wet tissue paper. But she'd needed the time to process her feelings. She wanted to be sure she could keep her composure, deflect the gush of emotions that flooded her whenever they were together. She'd been honest when she told Lila and Sara she didn't know what she felt for Nash. The night they'd spent together had cleared up some misconceptions and buried some old anger, but dragged new puzzling feelings and questions into the spotlight, too.

Her mother's calls and texts, begging her to come home, warning her that Nash would hurt her and vilifying the Colton family every way imaginable, only complicated things for Valerie. So many of her mother's theories were clearly rooted in wild speculation and her mother's paranoia. She didn't really give them credence, but she was torn between duty and loyalty to her mother and the love and trust she had for the Coltons. Specifically, the relationship she couldn't stop daydreaming about with Nash. If her mother weren't a factor, would she step over the impediments and shoulder past the roadblocks that kept her from racing to Nash's house and promising him her all? Could she risk that kind of pain again? Did she want to?

After surviving the kind of breath-stealing pain and loss she had at seventeen, had the kind of root-deep suspicion her mother had planted pounded into her for years, a change of heart—going back to the beginning, putting her heart on the line—was so difficult.

She sighed as she looked at her reflection in the full-length mirror. The wide black belt she wore with the navy blue dress she'd borrowed from Lila for the funeral emphasized how much weight she'd lost in just the few weeks she'd been in Chicago. Despite the ample leftovers of Nicole's baking, Vita's generous portions at their family dinners and the discovery of Tatum's restaurant, True, Valerie couldn't be tempted to eat more than a few bites per meal. The stress of murders, kidnappings, arrests and emotional reunions had wrung her out and squelched her appetite.

She applied a little extra blush and chose a lipstick color that wouldn't wash her out, then hurried downstairs to join Vita and Rick for the drive to the church.

"Nash said to tell you he'd save you a seat," Vita said as Rick parked in the crowded lot behind the church.

Valerie snapped her gaze from the horde of journalists camped on the front lawn to her aunt. "Oh?" Then, after a breath… "Oh."

"Good thing," Rick said. "Looks like ol' Axel drew a crowd."

Vita shook her head and frowned. "Nosy Nellies, most of them, I bet."

Rick cut the engine and shrugged. "Don't be so sure. Axel had plenty of business associates and his children certainly had plenty of friends who would be here out of respect."

Vita straightened the stylish hat she wore and checked her lipstick in the visor mirror one last time. "Well, one way to find out. Myles said we'd have seats up front, but not that they'd hold the service so…let's go, huh?"

Valerie opened the back door of Rick's car, deciding Vita was gathering her courage to face the past as much as she was. Vita may have moved on, may have divorced Axel and built a far better life with Rick, but…well, funerals had a way of stirring up the past. Buried memories. Old hurts.

She linked her arm with Vita's as they headed inside. She offered her support to the woman who'd been so kind to her through the years as much as she drew strength from Vita's example.

Chin up. Shoulders square. No regrets. Only dignity and grace.

A few heads turned as they entered, but Vita didn't falter. Her aunt gave her a cheek kiss before slipping her arm free and striding confidently with her husband to the rows down front, where Lila, Carter, Myles and Faith waited.

With a quick scan of the pews, she located Nash, Damon and their half brother, Aaron. Both Aaron and Damon had their girlfriends beside them, and Ruby had Maya tucked close to her side. Nash motioned to the empty seat. For her. Taking a deep breath, she whispered apologies to Damon, Ruby and Maya as she sidled between the next pew and their knees.

Valerie settled on the cushioned seat next to Nash and smiled a silent greeting to Aaron and his girlfriend, Felicia. She glanced around the crowded church then leaned in to whisper to Nash. "Vita, Rick and I were debating. Friends or curious spectators?"

Nash glanced casually over his shoulder as if only noticing the full pews for the first time. "I'm not sure. Most are strangers to me. Some could be here out of respect for the Colton name. Not that Axel did anything to preserve the family's good name. The rest? They're probably busybodies hoping to witness a scandalous scene they can gossip about."

She gave Nash a wry smile. "Careful there. Your bitterness is showing. The man is dead now. Maybe for your own health you should think about letting bygones be bygones and let him rest in peace?"

Nash grunted. "I know." He took her hand in his and squeezed her fingers. "I wish it were that easy."

A loud wailing sound came from the back of the church, and Valerie joined the many other congregants who turned to see what—or more precisely *who*—the disturbance was. She spotted an older woman being led down the aisle by members of the funeral-home staff. The woman was dressed in black from head to toe, and alternately dabbed her eyes and pressed her hand to her breast as she sobbed loudly. Even to Valerie, the wails of distress sounded stiff. Forced. Lugubrious.

Beside Valerie, Damon groaned under his breath, "Good grief."

Val cut another look to Nash—his brow was creased and his mouth was clamped in a taut line. "Who's that?" she whispered.

He leaned close, his aftershave surrounding her and distracting her. "My grandmother. Carin Pedersen."

"That's her fake-mourning cry. Her oh-woe-is-me, everyone-pay-attention-to-me, I've-been-so-wronged tears. What a crock," Damon added, earning an elbow jab and warning glance from Ruby.

"Pedersen? Not Colton?" Val whispered to Nash.

"She never married our grandfather, Dean Colton," Nash explained quietly. "She'd been an affair, and he belatedly gave our dad and Axel the Colton name at the same time he paid Carin some hush money. She's currently trying to claim her sons were Dean's real heirs."

In deference to the public nature of the event, Valerie tried hard to school her face, but a whispered "Wow!" slipped out. "How so?"

The organ music ended, and as the minister appeared at the altar, he motioned for all to rise.

"Later," Nash promised.

Valerie nodded and stood with the rest of the mourners as the prayer of invocation was given. The service was somber, if a bit over-the-top for Valerie's taste. By its conclusion, the ostentatious service felt more like a Broadway show than a funeral, with choirs, speeches and slide shows, concluding with a release of white doves from the front steps of the church as Axel's casket was wheeled out to the hearse.

"Seriously?" Aaron muttered, one eyebrow arched. "Doves?"

"A vulture would have been more appropriate," someone behind Valerie said. She didn't see who, as her attention had snagged on Nash. His eyes were locked on someone across the lawn, and his jaw had grown granite-hard.

Before she could determine who had caught Nash's eye, however, Lila said loudly enough for her siblings and cousins to hear, "Heads up. Incoming." She groaned then added, "I'm not in the mood for this. Come on, babe. Let's make a run for it." Lila grabbed Carter's hand and made a hasty exit toward the parking lot with her fiancé in tow.

Nash gave a muffled groan and fixed a stiff smile on his face as Carin Pedersen marched up to them.

"You!" She aimed a bony finger with a long fuchsia-painted fingernail at Nash. "You have a lot of nerve coming here today!"

Valerie sidled a bit closer to Nash as if for protection—or maybe to protect him from the venomous vibe spewing from the older woman. His family seemed of a similar mindset. Several of them drew closer to Nash, forming a half circle around him, while others, notably Ruby and Faith, led their children away from what they clearly sensed could be an ugly confrontation.

Valerie felt the tension that coiled in Nash when she touched his arm in support. His eyes were cool as he forced a smile. "Carin. A touching service. My sympathies to you."

"Your sympathies?" she snapped at him, her tone shrill and her face screwing up with haughty indignation. "Your sympathies! You should be ashamed of yourself for showing your face here!"

"Oh?" he said in a surprisingly calm tone. "Why is that?"

"You killed him!" She shook the finger aimed at Nash, and Valerie had to battle the urge to slap away the woman's offensive finger. "I saw the news reports! The police had you in custody, had proof you'd killed my son. But thanks to some sort of favoritism or police corruption or other underhanded tactics, you wiggled off the hook."

"Because he didn't do it!" Valerie blurted before she could stop herself. "The evidence against him was planted."

Now the arthritic finger waved toward the other Coltons as Carin's eyes narrowed. "Who said that? Hmm? My son was murdered! And in the last conversation I had with my son—" she paused and squeezed her eyes shut, as if battling a sharp onslaught of emotion "—he told me how Nash accosted him. Threatened him." She squared her shoulders, her sour expression back in place. "I'll find proof you did this and see you pay!"

"What proof?" Valerie asked, unable to stay silent when someone she cared about was being attacked.

Nash wrapped his fingers around her wrist and silently shook his head, as if to say "Don't bother arguing with her."

Carin shifted her narrowed gaze to Val. "Who are you, anyway? What do you know about any of it?"

"This is Valerie Yates, Rick's niece from Ohio," Nash said, as if making introductions at a society soiree. "Valerie, my grandmother."

Shoving down the bitterness at the back of her throat, Valerie held out a hand to shake Carin's, but it went ignored.

"Rick's niece?" Carin grumbled. "Humph. That man has relatives coming out of the walls like roaches."

Valerie coughed to cover her dismay at the characterization of her father and Rick's relations, but recovered quickly. "Yes, we've been blessed with a large family.

Much like the Coltons. Just roaches everywhere!" Behind her she heard a muffled laugh.

Carin angled her chin up and sent an encompassing gaze around to the Colton cousins gathered on the church lawn. Now her focus stopped on Sara Sandoval. "You're new, too. Another of Rick's nieces?"

Sara shifted her feet nervously, clearly awkward with having been singled out. "I, uh…no."

Aaron moved forward and put an arm around Sara's shoulders. "She's a new hire at Yates' Yards. No relation. So back off."

Carin lifted one eyebrow, clearly miffed by Aaron's tone, then gave Sara another narrow look. "Are you sure she's not another one of Dean and Anna's brood? She certainly has the look of a Colton. Those eyes…"

While Aaron replied to Carin's badgering of Sara, Valerie leaned toward Nash again. "So Axel and your father were illegitimate," she said, trying to sort out the details of the family tree that seemed to grow new branches every day.

"Yeah."

As a kid visiting Uncle Rick and Vita's Colton clan, she'd never once considered the legitimacy of various family connections. Why would she? That was hardly the stuff a ten-year-old, or even a teenager, cared about. But now, given the discussions at Vita's dinner table or at other family gatherings, she was beginning to see the tangled web in a new light. "But he gave them the Colton name?"

"A bargain struck between Grandfather Dean and Carin, apparently. We only learned about Anna and her children and grandchildren recently ourselves. Carin hates that side of the family for obvious reasons. It gets rather messy, all the…roaches."

She snickered. "So it seems."

Carin was still wagging a disdainful finger at Aaron when a man with stooped shoulders and graying brown hair appeared at Carin's arm. He tugged her pointed finger down. "Careful, Mother. The cameras are watching."

Carin seemed ready to bark at the man beside her, then his words apparently sank in. She straightened a bit and put her grieving-mother face back in place as she turned slowly to face the gathering news media.

"For God's sake, why didn't you tell me sooner?" she hissed under her breath to the man.

When the man glanced toward Damon and Nash, Valerie saw the resemblance in his square jaw and green eyes, recognized who he must be even before he said, "Hello, boys."

Nash jerked a perfunctory nod. "Dad."

"Hi." Damon shoved his hands in his pockets, his stare flat.

The greetings were so stiff and cool that Valerie felt a prickle at her nape. Or maybe it was just the discomfort of meeting Erik Colton, the man who'd so cruelly rejected her mother that, years later, her mother still nurtured a bone-deep resentment. What would Erik say if she introduced herself as Carol Smith's daughter? Would he make the connection? Would he even remember her mother and the events of that summer thirty years ago?

"Ms. Pedersen! Ms. Pedersen!" the members of the media called as Carin turned toward the assembled cameras and dabbed at her eyes.

"Does Axel's death change anything regarding your lawsuit over Dean Colton's will?" one reporter called.

"Are there any new developments in your son's murder?" another asked.

"Can you confirm that—?"

"Please," Carin said, acting as if the barrage of questions was wearing down her already distressed condition. "One at a time."

"Where does Axel Colton's death leave the lawsuit against Dean Colton's estate?"

Carin lifted her chin. "The lawsuit is unchanged. My sons are—" She paused and clutched at Erik's arm.

Even if the older woman's actions were theater for the reporters, Valerie sympathized with Carin, at least in part. She remembered how difficult losing Nash's baby had been. She'd loved the unborn child immediately, even without ever seeing or holding the baby. Carin had shared decades of life experiences with Axel. She'd seen him take his first steps and learn to ride a bike, and shared dozens of holidays with him. Losing her son had to have left a mark.

"My son Erik is Dean Colton's legal heir," Carin insisted. "We will continue to vigorously pursue our claim to our rightful share of Dean Colton's fortune."

Valerie had heard mentions of the lawsuit that claimed Dean Colton's illegitimate sons were heirs to half of the Colton Connections fortune. Erik and Axel stood to inherit thirty million dollars if Nash's grandmother Carin won her lawsuit claiming her copy of Dean Colton's will was authentic. Valerie's head swam. She couldn't even fathom that much money.

"Are there any new leads in Axel Colton's murder?" another reporter shouted.

Carin's lips pinched, and she sent a baleful glance toward Nash.

Valerie's skin prickled, as if she sensed a predator breathing down her neck. The impulse to step between Carin and Nash and let the woman know, in no uncertain terms, that Nash was innocent and had done nothing to earn her scorn raced through her blood.

"No. The police had in their custody the most likely suspect and saw fit to release him. To say I am dismayed and displeased with the police department's willful disregard for the obvious would be an understatement."

Beside her, Nash sighed and muttered under his breath, "Thanks, Granny."

"Want to leave?" Valerie asked him.

"Not yet." Nash's gaze narrowed on the scene before them, but it seemed to Valerie that Carin wasn't his focal point.

"Mr. Colton, do you have a theory about who killed your brother?"

Valerie didn't see who asked the question, but she felt the tension that jerked Nash's body taut and saw Erik flinch before he firmed his thin shoulders and called back, "No comment."

"Surely you have some idea who might have wanted your brother dead," a different voice asked.

"Some might say you stand to gain the most with your brother's murder, if the lawsuit moves forward," a reporter near the front of the mob added.

Erik's fists balled, and he scowled at the man who'd made the last bold assertion. "I said 'no comment.'" He nudged Carin's arm and took a step away. "Come on, Mother. Don't give these vultures any more fodder."

With a loud *harrumph*, Carin turned to walk toward the waiting funeral home limousine.

"Carin?" Vita called from behind Valerie, then rushed forward when Carin paused.

Nash groaned quietly and whispered, "Oh, don't do it. Don't do it."

"The rest of the family is gathering back at our house.

Would you like to come join us?" Vita asked, and Carin arched a thin eyebrow as if she'd been threatened instead of politely invited to break bread with her grandchildren.

Damon gave an equally dismayed and hushed groan. "Ugh. She did it."

Valerie covered an amused grin as she eyed Carin and Erik.

"Really?" Carin cast a suspicious glance at the huddle of Colton grandchildren and spouses. "You want me at your gathering? In your house?"

"You, too, Erik. You are family, after all." How Vita maintained a pleasant expression, Valerie didn't know. But for as long as Valerie had known Vita, Uncle Rick's wife had always shown grace under pressure and unconditional warmth.

"I, um—" Carin began, and then Erik spoke over her.

"No. Mother needs to rest. Today has been very trying for her."

Carin shot Erik a look as if to say "don't answer for me," but added, "I'll pass. I doubt I'd be welcomed by even your dog, and I have better things to do than make nice with people who don't want me around."

"Make nice?" Myles said under his breath. "When has she ever—?" He let out an *oof* as Faith elbowed him.

Vita managed a smile and gave a nod. "All right then. Take care."

As Erik escorted Carin toward the limo, the assembled Coltons gave a collective sigh of relief.

"Whew. That was close," Lila said.

"Yeah," Myles agreed, then said to Vita, "Mom, you're a saint. But don't ever do that again."

Damon chuckled wryly. "Amen."

Valerie turned to walk to the parking lot with the rest of the family, but paused when she realized Nash wasn't with her. She moved back to his side and followed his line of sight. "Nash?"

"Does my dad look...*old* to you?"

Valerie studied Erik a bit closer as the man circled the back end of the limo to climb in the opposite side. "He *is* getting old, Nash. Maybe not ancient, but...how specifically do you mean?"

"Just...worn down. Frailer somehow. I've always thought of him as this larger-than-life, indomitable figure. A Goliath among men."

"Goliath was beaten by a boy with a slingshot, Nash."

He gave her a brief side glance. "You know what I mean."

"Hmm. Seems to me dealing with your grandmother every day would be enough to wear down even a Navy SEAL."

Nash laughed. "There is that." He exhaled through pursed lips, then placed a hand at the small of her back to guide her out to his car.

"See you at Vita's?" Damon called as he held the door for Ruby.

Nash waved. "You bet."

The family gathering after the funeral was a respectfully somber affair, but the love and support of the Colton children and their respective new love interests was on full display. For Valerie's part, she stayed close to Vita and Rick, helping out wherever she could. She talked with Aaron and Felicia, entertained Maya by signing stories about her visits with the family as a youth and kept Sara company as she watched the Coltons from the sidelines.

But the confrontation with Carin Pedersen at the church had stirred a fresh line of inquiry for Valerie, namely how much Uncle Rick knew about her mother's history with Erik Colton. Did he know the whole story about her parents' past, her mother's hatred for the Coltons and Val's true paternity? The idea that Rick had kept secrets from her stung Valerie, and yet she, of all people, knew that keeping secrets was sometimes done to protect people one loved.

She mulled over the notion of how much Rick knew, had kept from her, throughout the afternoon. Finally, that evening, after helping Vita put away leftovers and clean the kitchen, she found herself alone with Rick as he locked the front door and turned off the downstairs lights.

"Well, good night, my dear. Thank you again for your help today," he said as he turned to climb the stairs.

"Uncle Rick, did you know my dad wasn't my real father?"

Rick stiffened and jerked his head around. "Good Lord, Valerie. Where is that coming from?"

"I've known for about twelve years now. My mother told me. Along with the whole story of my real father... and Erik Colton."

Rick's hand tightened on the banister as he turned slowly to face her. "Is that why you've avoided coming here to visit for so many years?"

Valerie hugged herself as a chilly draft swept over her and left goose bumps in its wake. "Not...directly. I had my own baggage to deal with."

Rick inclined his head and said softly, "With Nash?"

Valerie blinked hard, dropped her arms to her sides as her back straightened. "I— Wha—?"

Rick chuckled warmly. "Don't act so surprised. Vita and I weren't blind. You tried to hide your relationship, but we saw how you looked at each other. Knew you slipped away from the group at the same time for longer than needed to get a drink or use the bathroom."

Valerie gave a short laugh. "Wow. We thought we were so careful."

Rick lifted a corner of his mouth. "I'm guessing that's where you were the other night when you stayed out until morning. Hmm?"

Valerie rolled her eyes, and a you-caught-me sound rolled from her throat. "So that secret is out. Which brings me back to my mother and what you know. What you knew all along."

He raised a palm and twisted his mouth. "I knew enough. I saw most of it firsthand. My brother's infatuation with your mother. Her fascination with Erik Colton. The ruckus when she announced she was pregnant." His expression crumpled. "Are you angry with me for not telling you? I didn't see that it was my place to expose things your mother and father had decided to keep quiet. And you were always considered real family by Vita and me, regardless of who fathered you."

She gave him a smile. "Ditto."

"My brother—" he began and his voice cracked. "He loved you, Val. Even if he did a poor job of showing it. He was flawed, as we all are. Brokenhearted over your mother's drinking, and his own inability to cope with her behavior. He took the easy way out. Avoidance. He wasn't proud of his choices. But…he did love you."

Valerie kept a tight rein on her emotions as she listened to Rick. Until he added, "I tried my best to be the father he wasn't."

Val's breath caught, and tears filled her eyes. She rushed to him and wrapped him in a firm embrace. "You were. You absolutely were. I love you, Uncle Rick."

"What was your word? Ditto? Ditto, Val." He squeezed her back and kissed the top of her head. As he released her, he cast a glance toward the rear of the house. "Oh.

I missed the light on the back porch. Will you get it before you come up?"

She nodded and caught him dabbing his eyes as he made his way upstairs.

When Valerie finally climbed in bed, she was physically exhausted and emotionally spent. She replayed the conversations of the day as she searched for sleep, her mind active even though her body was worn out.

Even though the younger Coltons had distant, often complicated relationships with Axel, it was clear his death had shaken the family deeply. His murder was an attack on the family—one more in a growing list of aggressions against them in recent months. The trend was alarming, to say the least, and Nash's family had circled their proverbial wagons and looked to one another for comfort, protection and support in a way Valerie's family never had. Other than Uncle Rick, Valerie had no one she could depend on for that kind of familial support. Was it any wonder she'd adopted the Chicago Coltons as the family of her heart?

She'd just gotten comfortable, the covers tucked under her chin and her pillow just so, when her phone jangled. She groaned and considered ignoring it. But she didn't dare, not with all the crazy twists and turns in recent days.

Clicking on the bedside lamp, she checked the caller ID and groaned again. Now she *really* wanted to ignore the call. And *really* dared not.

Chapter 13

"Hello, Mother. It's rather late to be calling. Is something wrong?"

"Yes, something is wrong! Something is very wrong."

Valerie raked the hair back from her face, bracing. "What—?"

"I was sitting here, after a terrible day of being harangued by people time and again—your doing no doubt, but we'll get to that later—when what should come on the late news but a story about Axel Colton's funeral."

"Mother—"

"That was hard enough to watch, but then the camera panned the crowd and I saw *you* huddled up with...*them*."

"I went to the funeral with Vita and Rick, yes."

"And—and Erik." She heard her mother take a few shallow breaths. "I saw Erik. They interviewed him and his mother, and he—"

"Yes, he was there. Axel was his brother, but I didn't—"

"How could you do this to me?" Her mother's voice broke. "I've told you what those miserable people did to me. I've asked you to come home. But you… You're still down there. With Erik. With—"

"I'm not with Erik, Mother. I don't think I even spoke to him today. I saw him, but he's not—"

"You're with his son. I saw how close you were standing to him. I couldn't believe it when I saw it, but I rewound the report, and there you were. That boy's hand was on you. You had Coltons all around."

Valerie took a deep breath. "Mother, it's late. I'm tired. Is there a point to this call besides chewing me out for attending a funeral?"

"Honestly, Valerie! It's that kind of flippant attitude that tells me they are turning you against me."

Her heart sank. That kind of paranoia was more evidence her mother wasn't taking her medication. She'd call the doctor's office *again* in the morning. She didn't want to go back to Ohio yet, but if her mother was in a downward spiral…

"You have nothing to worry about, Mother. I'm not turning against you."

"You told Nancy to check up on me, didn't you? She called today. Twice. And so did the nurse from Dr. Richards's office."

"I was worried—"

"Come home, Valerie. I warned you that those people are poisonous. Why won't you listen to me? You need to get away from that boy. He'll hurt you. I can't let him hurt you again. They'll destroy us. They want to destroy us!"

"Mother! Take a breath. Everything is okay." She pinched the bridge of her nose. She'd have to ask Nancy to go by her mother's house tonight. Stay with her. Nancy had volunteered to be her mother's sponsor, because she'd had a family member with similar mental-health issues. She knew the routine. Knew the importance of keeping her mother on her medication.

Quiet sobs filtered over the phone connection, and Valerie sighed. "Mother, I'm going to call Nancy for you. You shouldn't be alone tonight."

"I don't want Nancy. I don't need— I'm not—"

Valerie's heart twisted, knowing what she had to do and knowing it meant letting Nash down, just when they were starting to rebuild their relationship. "Talk to Nancy tonight, Mother. Take your medicines and get some rest, and... I'll drive home tomorrow."

"You're going home?" Nash's grip tightened on his phone, and he grimaced as Valerie's announcement settled in his gut like a rock. Through his open door, the quiet hum of colleagues' conversations and laughter, ringing phones and the ding of elevator bells wafted into his work space. He rose from his desk to close the door, then asked, "For good? We had plans tonight. I thought..."

Never mind what he thought. He'd clearly been wrong. Disappointment made it hard to breathe.

"I know, Nash. I'm sorry. But when my mother called last night it was clear she was off her meds, and I knew I needed to go check on her. Handle things there. In person."

Nash's desk chair creaked as he sat down and rocked back. "Well, you gotta do what you gotta do. Huh?" He knew he hadn't done enough to modulate his tone, to cover his frustration. But knowing he needed to be understanding of Valerie's situation with her mother and not letting it open old wounds were two different things.

"Depending on what I find, how cooperative Mother is, what her doctor says, I could be back by tonight. Toledo is only a four-hour drive. I'm about an hour outside of town now, and my mother's appointment to see the doctor is at eleven."

Nash checked the time on his computer screen. Nine forty-five. Val had been up and on the road early if she was already an hour outside of Toledo. He respected Val for her commitment to her mother, despite the pain and strife she had caused through the years. But he also saw how taking care of her mother wore Val down. "We can reschedule. Don't drive if you're worn out."

"Nash, I'm okay. I have every Starbucks between Toledo and Chicago highlighted on my driving app."

He wished he could do something to help ease her burden. Wished he didn't feel the tug of resentment toward her mother for her part in ripping Val away from him years ago. Wish he didn't feel as if he was on the losing end of a tug-of-war with Val's mother for her loyalty, her time. Her heart. "Be careful, Val. And keep me posted."

"I will."

When Nash disconnected the call, he tried to concentrate on the blueprints for the business complex that were needed for the meeting with their client tomorrow, but Valerie pervaded his thoughts all day. He was about to pack it in for the day and head home, hoping she might be joining him for a late dinner, when she texted him.

Sorry to cancel on you. Spending the night in Ohio. Rain check on dinner? Back in Chicago by lunchtime tomorrow.

He texted back, Sure thing. Tomorrow night then?

Sounds good. Thx.

How's your mom?

Resting. Back on her meds. Still hates the Coltons.

Nash resisted the urge to send a glib reply. Instead he typed, CU Tm. Be careful. Love you.

Then, before he could hit Send, he frowned. His heart rolled. Did he love her? He had once. And they clearly still had sexual chemistry. But love—deep, true, lasting love—required trust and honesty. He wasn't sure they were there yet.

Before sending his reply, he backspaced. And deleted the last two words.

The next day being a Saturday, Nash spent the day at home, culling dead plants from his back garden, straightening his living room, putting clean sheets on his bed… and trying to convince himself he wasn't "house preening" for Val. He tried to distract himself with the Ohio State football game on TV, but every time the announcers mentioned Ohio, his thoughts returned to Val, her emergency trip to Toledo, her torn loyalties. And his agitation and ill ease would return.

He knew that Carol Yates's behavior was rooted in mental illness, knew that resenting Val's mother wasn't a good way to start a relationship with Valerie, knew Valerie needed his patience, understanding and support. And that was what he'd give her, damn it. He would not be the reason this second chance they'd been given failed. He cared about her enough to work at rebuilding their faith in, and their love for, each other.

Groaning his restlessness, Nash clicked off the football game and tossed the remote on the coffee table. An hour later, he put the salmon steaks on the counter to finish thawing and headed to the back of the house to start getting ready.

When he finished showering, Nash returned to the kitchen to start the salmon fillets sautéing. He checked the clock. Maybe it was too soon. Valerie should be arriving in about fifteen minutes, so he should wait a few more—

He stopped short when he discovered his neighbor's cat on his kitchen counter, nibbling the fish he'd left on the counter thawing. "Hey! You son of a— Get down!" He waved his arms at the cat. "Leave that— How the hell did you even get in here?" He snatched a towel from the oven handle and flapped it at the calico. "Go home!"

The cat meowed at him and sat down, licking his lips. Nash picked up the cat and headed to the front door. But it was firmly shut. Angling his head, he glimpsed the multi-paned French door to the backyard standing ajar. One pane in the glass was broken. The one by the doorknob.

He put down the cat and crept forward, staying close to the wall. Across his living room, he saw a shadow move.

A wiry man with his face covered by a ski mask surged from behind the couch.

"Hey! What are you—?"

The man's arm swung up. He had a gun. And he squeezed the trigger.

The gun jammed. With a snarl of disgust, the man turned and ran toward the door.

Adrenaline spiked in Nash's blood. He leaped over the couch, knocking over a lamp. As the cat sprinted back outside, tail puffed, Nash chased the intruder to his backyard. "Stop!"

The trespasser grabbed one of the rocks that lined Nash's landscaping and spun to face Nash.

Balling his fist, Nash swung at the man. Caught him across the jaw. The man staggered back a step then charged again. This time Nash grabbed for the mask, wanting a look at the face of his attacker. The man ducked, as he spun out of Nash's reach, but the mask was unseated enough for Nash to catch sight of wiry, graying brown hair.

He surged forward again, leading with an uppercut that his intruder avoided. Then the man made his move, lifting the rock in his hand. Though Nash raised an arm to block the blow, the large stone cracked against his head with a force that rattled his teeth. The edges of his vision blurred, and his knees buckled. Then…nothing.

Chapter 14

Valerie had just reached Nash's porch and raised her hand to knock, when she heard an angry shout from inside. A loud crash. More yelling. Was it the television?

She leaned close and pressed her ear to the door. No telltale music that would indicate he was watching a movie. A strange sense of alarm skittered through her, a sixth sense that told her the noises inside were signals of danger. She knocked harder. "Nash?"

No answer. Again. Still no response.

She tested the door. The knob turned, and, with her breath stalled in her throat, she opened the door a crack. "Hello? Nash? It's me."

No answer. Her nerves jangling, she entered the house and slowly checked each room as she moved deeper inside. The dining-room table had been set, but the room was otherwise empty. From the kitchen, she could smell raw fish, and with a glance found one salmon fillet on the floor. Odd.

"Nash?"

As she stepped into the living room, a chill autumn breeze reached her through the open back door. Was he in his backyard then? That'd explain why he hadn't heard her knock or call out. She crossed to the open French door, and her foot crunched on something hard.

Broken glass. A fresh spurt of concern swirled through her. "Nash?"

Stepping onto his back patio, she moved quickly, past the low hedge of boxwood, to the point where the yard opened…and found Nash sprawled, facedown, on the grass.

"Nash!" She raced to his side and dropped to her knees. "Nash, can you hear me? Are you all right?"

When he didn't respond, she conducted a cautious search for any injuries. Had he fallen from somewhere? Had a stroke? She didn't dare move him, in case he had a broken neck or—

She gasped as her fingers encountered a bloody gash on the back of his head. She parted his hair gently to examine the wound closer, and he groaned. "Nash?"

He lifted a hand to his injured head as he rolled to his back. "What happened?"

"I was hoping you could tell me. I just got here, but I heard shouting, a loud thump and found broken glass on your living room floor by the door. Now you're here, laid out on the yard with a busted head…"

He jerked his chin up with a sharply inhaled breath. "Where'd he go?"

"Who?"

Turning his head, he searched his yard. "There was a

man—" He cut his explanation short, grabbing his head. "Ow!"

A tingle of alarm chasing down her spine, Valerie stood and surveyed the yard. Saw nothing. No one. "I don't see anyone."

"Damn. He got away," Nash muttered as he drew his fingers back and stared at the red smears on his fingers. He blinked hard, squinted, then shielded his eyes as if the early evening twilight hurt his eyes. "I, um…"

"Can you stand? Walk?"

He waved her off. "I'm fine. I just…" He wobbled when he tried to rise, and she caught him as he stumbled.

"You are not fine. You hit your head."

"No, the intruder hit it for me."

The idea of an intruder attacking Nash sent a chill to her core. Axel had been attacked in his home. His head bashed. Now Nash…

Quashing the anxiety that thumped in her chest, she helped steady Nash. "Either way, we're going to the ER." She placed a firm hand at the small of his back and guided him inside. She let him sit on the couch for a minute while she got a rag to clean his wound and an ice pack to hold against his head in the car. As he hobbled to her car, she took out her phone, scrolled through her contacts and called Damon. "We're headed to the hospital now, but I think you should come take a look at his door and yard. Meet the police. Someone broke in and attacked him."

After assuring Damon that Nash was likely only suffering from a concussion, but that she'd keep him apprised if anything else became evident during the exam, she helped Nash climb into the car and headed to the closest hospital.

On the drive, Nash held the kitchen towel full of ice

to his head and recounted the moments leading up to his injury. "I found the cat in the kitchen. He was eating our salmon."

"What cat?"

"Remember my neighbor's calico?" He explained how he'd searched for the open door or window that the cat had used to get inside, seen the back door ajar…

His breathing grew ragged, stressed. "The guy had a gun. It misfired, or else I'd be—"

"What!" She cut a sharp look to him as she navigated the busy street.

Nash seemed to struggle to recall what happened next. "I guess I chased him, then—"

"My God, Nash! Did you recognize him? Could he be connected to all the stuff happening to the rest of your family? To Axel's—" Her throat clogged with terror, clamping down on the hideous word—*murder.* Could Axel's murderer have come for Nash? Had Nash drawn unwanted attention to himself at the funeral? Or when he challenged Axel at the racket club? When news of his questioning by the police leaked to the media? Geez! What was happening in the Colton family? Who could be behind all the bad luck and tragedy?

Once at the hospital, the ER doctor confirmed Nash had a concussion and stitched up the gash on his scalp. Though Nash couldn't remember past chasing the stranger out of his house, the logical conclusion was the stranger had hit him over the head with something before escaping. No further injuries were found, and the doctor released Nash to go home to rest. They were just getting his discharge papers and about to return to his house when Damon called.

Nash, who was going over the discharge papers and

signing multiple releases, handed her his phone. "Tell my brother I'm fine."

She did, with caveats. Then, putting Damon on speaker so Nash could hear, she said, "We think the intruder hit him with something. Did you or the cops find anything when you searched his house?"

"Besides my brother's continued stubborn refusal to put in a security system?" Damon growled. "Yeah, I, uh…found a rock in the middle of his yard with blood on it. No doubt what was used to bash him in the head."

The contents of Valerie's stomach—a pack of crackers she'd gotten from the hospital vending machine an hour ago—soured. "So it's true. Someone tried to kill him," she muttered numbly, horrified.

"Maybe. Where are you headed? He's welcome to convalesce at my place, you know. Or I'm sure Nicole or Vita—"

"No. I can look after him. I'm sure he'd rather be in his own bed."

Nash nodded his agreement, then raised a hand to his temple, wincing.

"All right. I'm still here at Nash's place," Damon said. "My brother is getting a new security system whether he wants it or not. I'm taking measurements and checking his wiring now. I intend to have his system up and operational by this time tomorrow."

"Good. Thanks, Damon."

Nash handed the clipboard back to the discharge nurse and shot her a disgruntled look. From the phone, Damon said, "I've been telling him since he bought his house he needed one. This isn't Mayberry."

"Right," she said, holding Nash's gaze. "In Mayberry, no one tried to murder Opie. Speaking of which…won't he need to give a statement to the police?"

Damon chuckled without humor. "Way ahead of you. They'll be waiting to talk to Nash when you get here."

Nash groaned and put his arm over his eyes. The jackhammer in his skull was not being helped by the drilling outside his window. Damon had shown up at Nash's house bright and early the next morning and had been creating a ruckus ever since.

"Poor Nash," Valerie said. "Want me to tell him to knock it off?"

He moved his arm and found her standing at the door of his bedroom with a glass of grape juice in one hand and an orange pill bottle in the other. She'd stayed with him, waking him every hour to check on him throughout the night.

"Naw. The sooner he finishes, the sooner I can get some sleep."

She sat on the edge of his bed and offered him the juice. "I know juice is more for colds, but I figured it couldn't hurt for a concussion, so…"

"Thanks." He sat up in the bed, feeling his head swim and throb, and took a minute to let things stop spinning before he took the glass from her.

Val rattled the bottle in her other hand. "Painkiller? The doctor said you could have one of these every four to six hours."

"Mmm. I'll stick with Tylenol for now." He sipped the grape juice while she fetched the bottle of acetaminophen from his bathroom cabinet. "Have the police called with any updates?"

"Sorry. No."

Despite his injured head, he'd given the local police a full account of the intruder's attack as the bits and pieces of the incident slowly returned to him. He'd sat across from the uniformed officer that had come to his house last night and remembered being the subject of suspicion days earlier as questions were asked. Axel's murderer hadn't been caught yet, either. Was this attack on him linked to Axel's killer? Simon Wilcox, the man suspected of planting the candleholder in Nash's trunk, had been described as having short blond hair, but Nash had recovered a distinct memory of his attacker's shaggy, graying brown hair.

Was the break-in connected to Jackson's kidnapping? Were other members of his family at risk while this rogue assailant remained free? Nash gritted his teeth. There were far too many questions, too many assaults on his family and far too few answers.

While he popped a couple capsules in his mouth and washed them down with the juice, Valerie settled on the edge of his bed and placed a warm hand on his leg. "Can I get you anything else?"

He set the juice on his bedside table. "A kiss?"

A dimple puckered her cheek as she grinned at him. "Of course."

She leaned in to brush her lips against his. A teasing, light kiss. And not nearly enough. He caught the back of her head, deepened the connection, angling his head to more fully capture her mouth with his. The kiss woke every cell in his body, made his blood hum with desire. He pulled her closer, tracing the seam of her lips with his tongue and—

"Aha! I knew it!" Damon called from the bedroom window with a laugh. "I've always suspected there was more between you two than you claimed."

Val pulled away, turning to the window with color filling her cheeks. "I— It's not what it looks like. We just—"

Nash's chest tightened. Why was she denying the obvious? Didn't she know that if part of the Colton family already knew about them, then the whole family knew? The Coltons were a bit like a small town in that way. News traveled fast.

"It's exactly like that," Nash said, his focus drilling Val before he turned his attention to his brother. "Stop leering, Damon. You were perfectly aware that Val and I were…" What? A couple? Hooking up? In a committed relationship? What exactly did he and Val have? If she was still trying to dismiss and hide their link, did she even truly have feelings for him?

Val gave a nervous chuckle before pushing off the bed and hesitating awkwardly, as if deciding how much to claim or deny. Finally, without saying anything, she left the room with the rest of the Tylenol and didn't return.

"Was it something I said?" Damon asked.

Nash sighed, the constriction in his chest balling like a rock. He knew these sensations of rejection, disappointment and confusion all too well. From his earliest days of being ignored by his father to the painful months after Valerie shut him out of her life at eighteen, he'd experienced many moments where he felt deserted. Unwanted. Unloved.

"Save the comedy, bro. Just…finish the drilling out there and let me rest, huh?"

Damon's expression shifted from smug to concerned. "Hey, sorry if I stuck my foot in something just now. I thought, well…"

"Yeah. I thought so, too." Nash sank back into his pillow and pinched the bridge of his nose. The attack last night had preempted his dinner, his heart-to-heart with Val. But he wouldn't be put off again. The time had come for he and Val to have a reckoning. If she wasn't committed to a full, honest and open relationship with him, he was out.

What had just happened?

Valerie dropped on Nash's couch, the bottle of Tylenol still in her hand, and stared blankly at the wall. Why had she balked like that when Damon caught her kissing Nash?

She'd already told Uncle Rick and Vita the truth about her budding relationship with Nash. She'd confided her feelings to Sara and Lila. She even confessed the truth to her mother, for Pete's sake! And her mother was the one she'd been trying to keep in the dark all those years, the reason she'd begged Nash for secrecy. So why had she reacted with such reticence, confusion…and fear? Were denial and secrecy just ingrained default settings for her? Or had Damon's teasing called up some aspect of her relationship with Nash she hadn't acknowledged? Some deeper truth about her feelings regarding her rekindled first love?

As she sat there, trying to make sense of her reaction, sort through her thoughts, her unfocused gaze sharpened, and she realized she was staring at the sketch she and Nash had made together, years ago. Of a bungalow with flowers and trees adorning the yard. Of a peaceful home. The utopia she and Nash had imagined together.

A sharp ache pierced her heart. *Together*…

A quiet rattle drew her attention to the pill bottle. Her hands were shaking. In fact, a subtle trembling swamped her limbs, and a disconcerting jangle gripped her core.

She sucked in a breath, trying to fill her lungs, but only managed a shallow gasp. Her instinct was to shy away from the raw emotions. Hadn't she shoved down anything too painful and too difficult for most of her life? Wasn't that the coping technique she'd learned from her father, the reason it had taken so long for her family to get the BPD diagnosis for her mother? But where had hiding from pain, denying truth and ignoring hurt gotten her? It was only in recent years, since Nancy recognized Carol's illness and helped get her to a doctor, that life had begun to approach balance.

Val had glimpsed real joy last week when she and Nash had shared the night together. Even with the heart-rending confessions, the arguing, the painful memories, she'd come through the experience feeling freer, happier. And hopeful.

She stood and walked closer to the colorful bungalow drawing on Nash's wall. He'd kept it. A simple, silly drawing two teenagers had made together. It shouldn't have mattered. He should have tossed it in the trash the first time he'd straightened his room in high school, or when he'd relocated for college, or moved to this house. So many opportunities to discard the drawing. But he hadn't. He'd framed it. Hung it on his wall. Cherished it.

Her tears came fast and hard. That drawing of a landscaped and decorated house was their relationship. Youthful love that she'd hidden, denied, discounted. Because it shouldn't have been as important and meaningful as it was. Nash had seen all along how valuable and true their love was…and he'd treasured it. He'd honored the relationship, kept it close, even though living with his memories had hurt.

She'd run. Denied. Buried. Tried to smother the embers that still smoldered in her core. She lowered her face to her hands as her shoulders shook and tears flowed. She saw now that every bit of hurt and loneliness she'd suffered had been her own fault. Nash had been here, waiting, hoping, the whole time. Loving her despite her rejection, her denial, her silence. She had one last chance to regain his trust and save their love. She meant to make it count.

Later that evening, after a full day of drills and wires and technological trial and error, Damon had Nash's home security system up and running. Nash, his head still throbbing, followed his brother around the premises as Damon explained the main control pad, codes, camera locations and the phone app to view the camera feed.

"The main one is back there and has an angle that encompasses the whole porch." Damon pointed out the small hidden lens. "That's the primary one. The camera over the door is secondary."

"Wait. Two cameras?"

Damon grinned. "Not in reality. Thieves these days are pretty much expecting there to be a security camera somewhere and know how to take them out. When they see this more obvious dummy camera, an intruder might disable it and think they're in the clear. But the more hidden camera, the one that's really monitoring the property, is still recording. I've done the same in the back and side yards."

"Clever. And thorough."

Damon raised his palms. "Do it right or why bother at all?" He flashed a cocky grin, then his expression faltered. "Considering all the sh—" Damon caught himself, glanced at Valerie and twisted his mouth. "Sorry, Val."

"I've heard it all. Don't sweat it."

"Yeah, but I'm trying to clean up my language. For Maya. She's getting good at reading lips." Damon squared his shoulders, looked back at Nash and said, "Considering all the stuff that's been happening to our family, I have to say, my gut is telling me this was a personal attack. And if this wasn't random, whoever jumped you will likely be back to finish the job."

"That's a cheery thought," Nash intoned.

"Are you sure you wouldn't rather come stay with me and Ruby?"

"And bring the danger to your house? To Maya?" Nash shook his head, then gestured to the new equipment. "All this buys me forewarning. Forewarned is forearmed. Let the bastard try again." He clenched his fists and gritted his teeth, relishing the idea of tearing into the man who'd attacked him. "I'll be ready for him."

Simon Wilcox paced his living room, a burner cell to his ear, and waited for his call to be answered. When it was, he said, without preamble, "I want my money. I did your job, now pay me what I'm owed."

"Who is this?"

He snorted. "Don't play games with me. You know damn well who it is. Why don't I have my money?"

He heard a huff, nervous breathing. Then... "I heard you were questioned by the police."

Simon scoffed. "A minor thing. My old lady covered for me. If they really had anything, I'd be sitting in jail instead of waiting over here for my effing money."

"Did you mention me? Can they connect you to me?"

Simon swiped a hand over his face and tried not to lose his cool. If the client freaked out, the whole gig could be blown. "I didn't say nothing. That's part of the service. The service you now owe twenty-five grand for."

"What? No. We agreed on twenty thousand."

"The price keeps going up until I get paid."

"You'll get your money. I swear. But I can't pay you yet!"

Cold fury filled his veins. "You told me you could pay. Do I need to explain to you what happens to people when they don't pay their debts?"

"No. I… Think about it! The cops are watching you. If you get a huge bank draft suddenly, they can trace it back to—"

"That's why I said *cash*, idiot! Put it in a paper sack and take it to the bus station. At exactly nine p.m. tonight, use the restroom and leave the bag in your stall. Someone will be there to collect the bag."

"I can't… What if I can't do that?"

He squeezed the phone and gritted his teeth. "I will come for you. I'll take fingers, ears and teeth as interest, bit by bit until you cough up my cash. The price goes up to thirty grand tomorrow, and I'll take my first interest payment. Understood?"

Through the connection, Simon heard only angry breathing.

"Understood?"

"This is extortion. I will not be ordered around by the likes of y—"

Simon hung up. "Fine. If that's how you want to play this."

He took the burner cell outside, into a cold drizzly rain, and smashed the phone to pieces.

That night at exactly nine p.m., Simon and his wife were at the bus station. The client was not.

"Come on, honey," he told his wife as he rose to head back to his car. He opened his umbrella and held it over them both. "We have another stop to make before we go home."

As Simon pulled out of the bus station parking lot, he

didn't pay any attention to the black SUV that entered the street behind him, one block later. He didn't pay attention to the SUV when it merged on the interstate with him, either. When he did notice the SUV, it was too late.

Chapter 15

Nash was brushing his teeth when the call came in. Lifting his cell, he glanced at the caller ID and frowned. Spit. Wiped his mouth on the hand towel and answered the call.

"Nash, this is Harry Cartwright. I have an update on your case…of a sort."

"Tell me you found something else to tie that Wilcox character to Axel's murder."

"Um, no. It's…"

Nash could hear shuffling papers. Voices in the background.

"I had something come across my desk tonight from the highway patrol. I thought I'd call you before you saw it on the eleven o'clock news."

Nash straightened the hand towel on the rack, trying to be patient, despite the strange buzz building in his ears. "Tell me."

"Simon Wilcox and his wife were both killed in a rather gruesome accident involving an eighteen-wheeler on the interstate. Witnesses say a dark SUV changed lanes without looking, Simon swerved, hit the brakes hard and skidded on the wet road. Ended up under the eighteen-wheeler."

Nash mumbled a curse word. "That's, um…horrible. Was—was anyone else hurt?"

"Truck driver had minor injuries. The SUV had no tag. It left the scene."

A shudder raced through Nash. Just when he thought the strange circumstances of his life couldn't get weirder, darker…

"So, seeing as Wilcox was our best lead regarding Axel's murder, the case just grew rather cold."

"Yeah."

Nash couldn't say what else Cartwright said as they hung up. His mind was already spinning off in a hundred directions. The first call he made was to Valerie. He just needed to hear her voice, know she was safe. The drowsy sweet tone of her "Nash?" when she answered poured a sweet relief through his blood.

After relaying a summary of Cartwright's call, he bid her goodnight and stared numbly at his phone for a moment before dialing another number.

"Hello?" a male voice answered brusquely.

"Hi, Dad. It's Nash."

A grunt. "Do you have any idea what time it is?"

"Late. Sorry if I woke you. I just—"

"What?" Erik asked, his timbre as impatient as ever.

Nash shoved down a spurt of irritation at his father's coldness and focused on the reason he'd called. Axel's death. The intruder in his own house. The murder of his half uncles. Jackson's kidnapping . The fire at Lila's gallery. And the list went on. Coltons under attack.

Nash drew a breath from tight lungs. "Watch your back."

Erik grunted. "Is that a threat?"

Nash's shoulders drooped. Did his father really know so little about him, his character, that he'd truly believe that? The further evidence of his father's lack of faith in him stung.

"No… Dad. It's not a threat. It's…a plea. Be careful. Be smart. Hell, look both ways before you cross the road."

"Why? What's going on? What have you heard?"

"Nothing specific. I just don't like the recent trend of violence against members of our family." He paused then added bitterly, "And my head is healing well after I was attacked, thanks for asking."

"That's right. I did hear something about you and a concussion from Damon."

Nash rolled his eyes. Such deep paternal concern…

"If there's nothing else…"

Why are you such a selfish, distant bastard? Damon and I needed you to be a father, a real father to us. Why was that so hard for you? Why is it still *so hard for you?*

"No. That's all. I just… Well, be careful out there. Okay?"

"Always am." Erik fell silent, and Nash had lowered the phone to tap the disconnect icon when his father added, "You watch yourself, too."

"He told you to watch yourself?" Valerie asked on Sunday that week as she and Nash walked through a neighborhood park, the squeals of playing children and the nip of the coming winter in the air. "How did he say it? Was he voicing concern for you or issuing a warning?"

Nash pulled a face. "That is the question, huh? I'd like to think it was concern but..." He blew a breath that buzzed his lips. "His tone was flat, no warmth to it. But I can't remember my dad every having a soft, fuzzy tone for me. Not his style."

"Well," Valerie said and stooped to pick up a particularly colorful leaf, "keep in mind, he never had an involved father, either. And his mother was Carin. Based on what I saw at the funeral, I don't imagine she was all that loving and fuzzy herself."

"Good point." He laced his fingers with hers, tugging her over to a bench beside the sidewalk. "So...where are we?"

She shot him a confused look and playfully glanced around them as if trying to orient herself. "Um..."

He draped his arm along the back of the bench and scooted closer to her. "You know what I mean. Where do *we* stand? It's been a couple weeks since we first talked, and... I guess I'm needing to know if this is going anywhere? Clearly your mother is still a factor. You dropped everything and left town for her last week. To be honest, I wasn't sure if you'd come back."

His admission shot her with a pang of disappointment. But when she thought about the twenty-four hours she'd spent in Toledo, dealing with her mother's issues and debating what needed to happen, she recognized the truth that caused her ache. And admitted it. "To be honest, I wasn't sure if I would, either. Then. I'm more sure of some things now, though. But to be even more honest..." She bent her head to look at the leaf she twirled as she toyed with the stem.

He placed a hand at her nape and gave the muscles there a gentle massage. "Honest is good. Go on. In fact, let's promise each other going forward that we'll always be truthful and fully forthcoming in everything. Deal?"

She nodded. "Of course. What do we have without honesty?" Then with a sigh, she finished her earlier thought. "The truth is my mother will always be a factor for me. If we're going to have a future, we're going to have to figure out how to do it knowing she's always going to be my family, always going to be one slip away from drinking again or going off her meds. But even with her medications, life with my mother will never be easy, and she may always resent you."

Nash grunted and rubbed the back of his neck. "Hate me, you mean."

She slanted her mouth in rueful agreement.

"Okay," Nash said, spreading his hands. "So tell me what I'm signing up for. What should I expect?"

Val grunted and took a deep breath. "Extreme mood swings. Big emotions. She has medications that help stabilize her volatile mood swings and her anxiety, but she'll always have…a struggle with perspective. People with BPD have trouble processing emotions. Her brain literally works differently. Emotions for her trigger the innate fight-or-flight response, so Mother struggles with the idea that every situation and conversation has a hidden vendetta or danger for her. Paranoia is a problem for her."

"Like her belief that the Coltons are evil and I will destroy you?"

"Among others." Valerie tore a piece of the leaf and let it flutter to the ground as she expounded. "It's likely her drinking started as a means to cope with her mental stress, her extreme emotions."

Nash nodded. "Makes sense. But you said she's sober now."

"She was." Val puffed out an exasperated breath.

"Now? Not sure. She's been really stressed out over me being down here. I've alerted her sponsor. But in addition to AA to keep her on the right track for her alcohol issues and medications for her emotional issues, she attends regular psychotherapy sessions. She has to keep up with all three or…" She lifted a hand. "It's easy for her to falter. She walks a tightrope every day."

Nash scrubbed a hand over his face and shifted to look directly at her. "So she's had this disorder your whole life, but only started getting treatment in the last few years?"

"Yeah. My dad was completely checked out and washed his hands of her when I was in elementary school. He got fed up with her bitter accusations, wild spending sprees and unpredictability—again all symptoms of her BPD we didn't recognize. Dad blamed her alcohol abuse, and I was a kid. What did I know?" She shredded the rest of the leaf and tossed the bits on the sidewalk. "Between them there was lots of denial and not much real understanding. If not for her AA sponsor Nancy and an astute therapist at a rehab clinic six years ago, we might still be in the dark about it."

"Damn, Val. That's— I never realized…"

"Of course not. Why would you? We weren't talking. Rick only knows a little bit. Not the whole story, but he's too discrete to air our family issues."

Nash nodded, processing it all.

Valerie bit her bottom lip, then added, "She…had a fit when I told her I was coming to support Faith and Myles during their crisis. She, naturally, accused me of abandoning her, siding with the enemy—all typical BPD anxieties. Learning I was seeing you again made things worse, made her—" She frowned and waved off the rest of the thought. "The point is whenever I come down here, it stirs up all her ill will toward your family, the trauma and abandonment she went through when she was a teenager. Her hatred for Coltons is deeply ingrained. So…you have to ask yourself if that's what you want to get into. Because I can't abandon my mentally ill mother. I'm all she has. Her illness is not her fault. And while she's responsible for her actions, her drinking, her self-care—" she angled her body to face him "—she's always going to need my support, someone to monitor her, a guardian for her best interests if she ever needs…"

She couldn't bring herself to finish the sentence. Damn, this was hard.

"I suppose if you can live with the fact you'd be taking on the dreaded Coltons if you were with me, I can live with your mother's disdain."

Turning a dubious grin toward him, she caught his hand in hers. "Hardly the same thing. Your family is great. Well, most of them are." She chuckled wryly. "Will you trust me in regard to my mother? It won't be easy. Life with her can be…complicated. But I won't let her change how I feel about you. I won't let her·hurt us again."

"I will trust you. Trust in *us*." He leaned over to kiss her temple. "So…we're officially a couple? We're going to see where this leads?"

A cool wind swept past them, and she shivered.

"Really?" he said, giving her an up-and-down look. "Being with me is that scary?"

She laughed. "What if I said yes?"

He tugged her close for a quick kiss. "Don't be scared. I'm here for you."

His promise and his touch spread warmth through her, chasing away the chill of the late autumn afternoon. After several days of steely skies and icy rain, the sun had peeked out this morning, and Valerie was glad they'd seized the chance to spend some time outdoors before the harsh cold of winter settled over the Great Lakes.

A stiff wind ruffled Nash's hair, and she couldn't resist the urge to comb it back into place with her fingers. Then, looping her arms around his neck, she grew reflective. If she and Nash were going to try again for a relationship, he had to truly understand her dynamic with her mother.

She bit her bottom lip, musing a moment, then said, "I know I've probably given you the impression that life with my mother was always bad. It wasn't. The thing about BPD is that her emotions are all so…big. Just as her criticism and fear can be really out of proportion, her highs—her good moods—can be really good. There were moments where I could pretend everything was normal. Her illness wasn't as bad when I was little…or else I was too young to recognize the reality behind her bad moods. But sometimes, we'd bake cookies together and laugh, or we'd shop for school clothes and go for frozen yogurt afterward." She wrinkled her brow. "Remembering those moments gave me hope as her condition, her drinking, worsened."

She ducked her head, staring at the zipper of his jacket, as a melancholy ache swelled in her chest.

With a gloved hand, Nash nudged up her chin. "But hope is a double-edged sword, huh? It can brighten one moment, lifting you, and crush you the next when it disappears."

"Hmm. Yeah." An odd sensation tripped through her, as if she was being seen for the first time. Truly understood. She tightened her grip on his sleeves. "Sometimes I thought it would be easier to never have those moments of hope, what I came to call her false rainbows. The downs hurt more, the farther you fell."

"I know. When I was small I used to get so excited

when my dad stopped by the apartment, only to be disappointed when he'd brush us boys off or only stay long enough to give Mom money and a hard time."

"So…can you see why it was easier for me to believe the bad about you all those years ago, rather than clinging to a hope that had failed me so many times in the past?"

He took a deep breath, his eyes bright. "And you see why I have a hard time trusting people's commitment?"

She bobbed her head.

"Well—" He kissed her nose and splayed his hand low on her back. "Maybe now we have a starting place. A mutual understanding. I want to be with you, Valerie. I want to make you happy. I want to share more sunny Sunday afternoons with you and find joy in all the simple things life together can offer."

The warmth that his words filled her with was undeniable. Mesmerizing. "That sounds…wonderful."

He cast his gaze around them, then stood, tugging her hand. "Come here." He led her away from the more populated part of the park to a quiet trail, where he found an evergreen shrub that offered some privacy. Drawing her into his arms, he framed her face with his hands and captured her lips.

A half sigh, half moan slipped from her throat as she canted into him, savoring the heat of his body, the caress of his mouth, the security of his embrace. That dangerous hope they talked about moments ago flared deep inside her. Dangerous, but oh, so sweet. She wanted to get lost in the daydream of a future with Nash, where every day held the promise of treasured moments, security and an inner peace.

She angled her head to kiss him more fully, and he whispered seductive words to her. She let herself get lost in his lips, his embrace. His lean body wrapped around her...until a soccer ball crashed through the evergreen branches and landed beside them.

Valerie pulled back from Nash's kiss as a dark-haired girl with cheeks red from the cold and her exertion darted around the bush to collect her ball. The girl gave Val and Nash a shocked look and mumbled, "Um, sorry."

"Hmm," Nash grunted and tucked Val's hair behind her ear. "Enough PDA. What I really want to do with you requires privacy. Shall we head home?"

"Lead on."

"Hungry? I think I still owe you dinner. Between my neighbor's cat eating our fish and the attacker in my house changing our plans, I never made good on the home-cooked meal I promised you last week. What do you say we run by the market and pick up some steaks and a bottle of wi—" He stopped himself, gave her a considering look, then said, "Sparkling cider, and I'll fire up the grill in honor of this refreshing glimpse of fall sun?"

She gave him a smile of appreciation. Maybe his remembering her stance on drinking alcohol seemed a small thing, but to her it represented his cooperation, his attention to detail, to her preferences and choices.

"Sounds perfect."

After a quick stop at the market and a favorite bakery, they arrived back at Nash's house in the late afternoon with enough time for...*privacy*, before they prepared their steaks for dinner.

Nash greeted the calico, which was sunning itself on the front porch—again—with a light scratch behind the ear. The feline answered with a rumbling purr.

"You know, this cat is going to keep showing up here if you keeping rewarding it with attention," Valerie said, chuckling. But then she, too, bent to pat his furry friend.

Nash shrugged. "I don't mind him. He's not bothering anything. And he is pretty charming." He keyed open his front door and stood back to let Val go inside first. As he stepped into his foyer, an odd prickling nipped his neck. Why hadn't his new alarm sounded?

But even without the failed alarm, he sensed something was off. The house was too dark, for one thing. He typically left a lamp on in the entry hall, so that he never came home to a completely dark house. And he smelled something...

"What is that odor?" Val asked as she walked ahead of him into the kitchen. She set the bag of groceries on the counter and reached for the light switch on the wall.

His heart rate jumping, he took a long quick stride and slapped his hand over hers before she could flip the switch. "Don't!"

She clearly sensed the alarm in his tone and raised anxious eyes to his. "What—?"

But then her nose wiggled, and she inhaled deeply. Her brown eyes darkened to nearly black. "It's gas, isn't it?"

He nodded. "Get out."

"But—"

"Get out! And don't turn anything on. Leave the front door open." He cast his attention to his stove, where, sure enough, all four burners had been turned to the on position. The pilot light had been extinguished, and the burners gave a low hiss, like a warning from a deadly viper, as the gas leaked into the room, uncombusted. He bit out a curse and turned the gas jets off.

He pulled his phone from his pocket to call the fire station or gas company or—

His grip tightened on the cell phone as he stopped himself before he woke the home screen. Cell phones could create a spark, same as a light switch could. He exhaled heavily and hurried out to the front yard to join Valerie.

At his front door, the neighbor's calico cat was trying to invite himself inside. Nash scooped up the feline on his way out the door. "No you don't, buddy. Especially not now. It's dangerous in there."

He joined Valerie at the curb, where she leaned against the hood of his car with the phone to her ear. "Yes, we've gone outside. We will. Thank you." Once she'd disconnected the call, she reached out to scratch the calico on the head. "I've reported the gas leak to the gas company. They're sending a guy out. They suggest opening all doors and windows. Airing the place out as much as possible."

Nash nodded and set the cat on the ground. "Right." He scowled and dusted cat fur from his hands. "Val, that was no regular leak. Every burner on my stove was turned on and the pilot light put out."

Her expression darkened. "Excuse me? You're saying it was intentional? Someone was trying to—"

He lifted both eyebrows in answer.

"If Simon Wilcox is dead, then this—"

"Unrelated to Axel's murder, or someone has depth on their roster of criminals for hire."

At her confused look, he clarified the sports phrasing. "More than one skilled person to use if your number one goes down."

"And the money to pay for multiple hits."

"Unless you take out the hitman before you pay them. Dead men don't talk or require payment."

She frowned darkly. "Cold."

"Colder than hiring someone to frame or kill me?"

She wrapped him in a hug. "All of it. Sum total. Cold and scary as hell. Nash…"

He placed a kiss on her forehead. "Wait here. I'm going to open the back door."

Nash made his way through the wrought-iron side gate to his enclosed patio and the flower garden Vita had insisted on building for him when he moved in. A housewarming gift, she'd called it. *Because nothing warms a house like plants and blooms.*

He gave the small backyard and flower beds an encompassing glance, but saw nothing suspicious. He moved carefully to the back door, keyed it open, and left it gaping.

As he retraced his steps to the front of the house, the calico appeared at the gate and wound around his legs asking for attention. He nudged the cat away with his foot, then cut at an angle across his lawn. The cat followed him. "Val, will you report this to the police? I'm going to take Mr. Kitty here back to his house. It's about to get rather busy around here, and he'll just be underfoot."

"Of course." Valerie rubbed her arms, and he guessed it wasn't really the cool day that sent the chill through her. A similar icy sensation crawled through him as the meaning of this incident took root. Someone had intentionally tried to hurt him. Moreover, they could have hurt Val.

When he'd learned Simon Wilcox didn't match the description of the intruder in his house, he'd hoped the attack in his back garden had been random. An interrupted burglary. But a second aggression against him, unrelated to Simon Wilcox, sent a quiver down his spine. What the hell?

Nash leaned in to give Val a kiss, then scooped Kitty back into his arms and chuckled wryly as the feline gave a low purr. "Some watch cat you are. You could have at least tripped the intruder for me."

The calico grew cooperatively limp and looked about as he was carried like they were on a sightseeing adventure. Kitty's owner was in her yard, raking leaves. She set aside her rake and met him at the sidewalk. "I'm sorry. Was he bothering you? He does like to explore."

"No bother, really, but we've had something of an emergency come up, and I thought he'd be safer back home."

"Oh, no! Anything I can help with?" she said, taking Kitty from his arms.

"No. But thanks." He turned to go then paused. "Unless... Did you happen to see anyone, a strange car maybe, at my house in the last few hours?"

His neighbor scrunched her nose in thought, shook her head. "No. I don't recall anything. But... I was inside baking before I came out here. And the Tillsons' trees block my view of your house from inside."

Nash shrugged. "Worth a shot. Thanks, anyway."

As he headed back down the sidewalk toward home, Nash considered knocking on the Tillsons' front door and asking if they'd seen anything suspicious. And then he remembered. He could access the video feed from his security system Damon had installed from the app on his phone. Of course!

He thumbed through his apps until he found the right one and opened it as he hurried back to join Val.

"The police are on the way," she said.

He nodded distractedly. "Thanks."

He propped against the car beside her as the black-and-white image of his front door filled his phone screen.

"You know, you keep calling that calico 'he,' but genetically, all calicos are female," she said, sidling closer to him.

He fast-forwarded through footage from earlier in the

day—him leaving this morning, Kitty crossing the porch to flop in the sun and nap. "Not all. Kitty is a rare exception. Happens like once in three thousand."

"Really?" she said with interest.

He glanced up at her startled expression. She blinked, pulled a what-do-you-know? face. Shifting her gaze to his phone, she asked, "What are you doing?"

"Checking the security camera footage."

He heard her breath catch, and she leaned closer, her floral scent distracting him for a moment. He moved on to the backdoor camera and was soon rewarded with the images he sought. A man with wiry dark hair, liberally threaded with gray or blond—hard to tell which from the black-and-white picture—entered his backyard by climbing his fence.

"There he is," Val said. "Do you recognize him?"

"No. You?"

"Nope. I think I'd remember that messy hair. Geez, man, buy a comb."

A memory teased the edges of Nash's brain. Grabbing his attacker's ski mask...shaggy graying hair...

Maybe...

The man stayed at the edge of the yard, and the camera angle, as he approached the back door. He blasted the dummy camera with spray paint, then donned gloves and turned to survey the back door. He apparently spotted the wires of the alarm system and pulled something indistinguishable from his back pocket.

"What's he doing?" Valerie asked.

"Bypassing the alarm. I couldn't even tell he'd been there just now when I opened the back door." He huffed his frustration. "This isn't his first rodeo." Nash watched as the man fiddled with the door's sensor then slipped inside. "That'd be why the alarm didn't sound when we got back."

She cut a sharp look to him. "That's right. It didn't. Oh, my God. I didn't even realize…"

A few moments later, the man left again the same way he'd come in.

"So not a thief," Valerie said. "He stayed only long enough to turn on the stove burners."

"So it seems."

Valerie snuggled closer to him, a shudder passing through her. "Someone wants you dead. Or at least seriously maimed. Or to send a message. But why?"

"No idea."

"You were cleared in Axel's murder. Surely whoever's behind this knows that!"

"Not necessarily."

Her grip tightened on his arm. "Nash, what if the person who killed Axel is working his way through the Colton family, and you were just the next on the list. Don't forget, the person who took Jackson hasn't been found. Damon and Aaron and Lila have had their share of dangerous encounters lately."

"Or the family is jinxed. I guess I was due."

Valerie gripped the front of his shirt and gave him a slight shake. "Don't say that! That's defeatist talk."

"Oh, I'm not giving up the ship. I'm going to find the person behind this and make him pay, even if only for having put you in harm's way today." He faced her, taking her into his arms and kissing her deeply. "If anything had happened to you…if we hadn't smelled the gas in time and gotten out…" He rested his forehead against hers and sighed. "I've become rather fond of you, Val."

She levered back and shot him a wry grin. "Fond? Oh, you sweet talker! Stop or I'll swoon!"

"What I mean is—"

But before he could explain himself or expand on how much he'd come to care for Valerie, a truck with the emblem of the local gas company painted on the door pulled to the curb in front of them. He pulled free of Valerie's grasp and met the arriving service men with a handshake.

The gas company men ventured into Nash's house with a device to measure and detect the presence of natural gas, and Nash and Valerie settled in to wait. Soon the fire department and a police car were parked in front of the house, as well. Neighbors assembled on their lawns or walked down to watch the spectacle from the sidewalk across the street. A regular circus. Lookie-loos anxious to see what the hubbub was about.

The responding policeman, Officer Jim Hagan, according to his name tag, was an older man with a paunch. He greeted Nash and Valerie congenially, and when Nash introduced himself, the officer arched one bushy white eyebrow. "Colton?"

"Yes, sir. Why?"

"Nothing really. Just that we've been hearing that name a lot recently around the precinct."

"Yeah. My family's had a run of bad luck lately." Nash filled him in on the current situation and pulled up the security-camera footage. He put his arm around Valerie and handed over his phone to show Hagan the images of the intruder.

Hagan moved his glasses to the top of his head and squinted at the phone screen. "Well, we'll file a report, of course, and I'll call a forensic team out to look for fingerprints or hairs, any source of DNA the guy left behind, but it looks like the fella wore gloves. Quick in-and-out. Don't know that they'll find much of anything."

"That was my take, too, but just in case…"

Beside him, Valerie stiffened. Her fingers curled into his forearm, and she gasped quietly. With a low, urgent tone, she whispered, "Nash, he's here!"

"What?"

Hagan and Nash both glanced at her.

She angled her face toward Nash, but used her eyes to direct his attention across the street. "Over there. Be discrete. We don't want to spook him, but isn't that the guy? He's wearing a hat now, but I swear it's—"

"I see him," Nash said, then grumbled. "How bold. Returning to the scene of the crime to watch the fallout."

"Not unusual," Hagan said, handing Nash back his phone. Hagan's glance across the street required him to twist his body, turn his head.

The officer's movement clearly alarmed the intruder, and he took a step back from the gathered crowd and strode down the block at a quick pace.

Nash took one glance at Hagan and knew the older man would never be able to catch up to the intruder on foot. Without overthinking his choice, he shoved his phone into Valerie's hands and sprinted after the fleeing man.

Chapter 16

"Out of the way!" Nash shouted to the milling onlookers as he raced after the intruder. He darted past family clusters and around baby strollers and tricycles, all while trying to keep his sights on his prey. Arms pumping, feet pounding, he pushed himself to eat up ground. His target had a lead on him, but Nash was younger, stronger, faster.

When the intruder cut across lawns, Nash followed.

When the man scrambled over low fences, Nash jumped and swung over with minimal effort.

As the intruder knocked over trash cans, Nash reacted quickly and skillfully negotiated the obstacles with fleet feet.

The man lost his hat, but Nash ignored it, taking mental note where it had fallen.

Within a few blocks, he'd gained ground on the man and waited for the best chance to tackle the cretin. Better to take him down on a grassy yard than the unforgiving sidewalk concrete. Sure enough, his target soon cut sharply to the left to cross a yard, headed for a side alley. Nash pounced. He flung himself forward, grabbing the man's shoulders and using his momentum to knock him off balance.

But, as if he'd expected the move, the intruder rolled as he landed. With a twist, he freed himself of Nash's grasp and lurched to his knees, his breath sawing.

"No, you don't, you jerk!" Nash crawled forward, grabbed one of the man's ankles and tackled him again. He wrestled the intruder to the ground, grappling with the man's arms and dodging knee thrusts aimed at Nash's groin. Nash smashed his fist into the man's face, and blood sprayed from the intruder's nose. When his opponent tried to head-butt him in the nose in return, Nash jerked aside, avoiding the blow. They continued to exchange jabs, until Nash finally caught the man's wrists and worked to pin him to the ground. He almost had the man subdued when his prey bucked hard, shifting Nash's balance just enough that the cretin landed one of his knee jabs in Nash's crotch.

Pain exploded through Nash's belly, fiery hot and breath-stealing. Even so, he made a grab for the intruder as the man shoved free of Nash's grip and scuttled aside. With surprising alacrity, the man sprang to his feet, landed a kick in Nash's ribs and spun to stagger toward the side yard of the homeowner whose grass they'd wrestled in. All Nash could do was writhe in pain and groan as the man disappeared from his view.

"Nash!" Valerie rushed to him, out of breath and her face dented with worry. Officer Hagan was several strides behind her, his face flushed from exertion.

She dropped to her knees beside him, cradling his cheek with her palm. "Are you all right?"

"No," he wheezed. He dragged in a breath. "But I will be. Give me a moment."

Hagan stood over him, gasping slightly.

Aiming a finger toward the corner of the house where the intruder had disappeared, Nash said, "He went that way."

Hagan glanced toward the side of the home, with its rose bushes and tall fence, and shook his head. "He's gone."

"But—" Valerie began, when Officer Hagan keyed the button on his shoulder radio and panted a radio code.

"Please advise units…to be on the lookout for…a Caucasian male in his…mid-fifties, five ten, weight…one-sixty. Black sweatshirt and khaki pants. Graying dark brown hair." He gave their location and more numeric codes, then signed off.

When he turned back toward Nash, his expression was dour. "What the hell did you think you were doing just then?"

Nash blinked. "What?"

"I should arrest you for assault and interfering with an investigation."

Nash had gained more of his breath and managed to sit up. He gaped at Hagan. "What!"

"Are you a policeman?" Hagan asked in the tone of an angry father lecturing an errant teen. "Did I ask you to pursue the suspect?"

"I—"

"I oughta take you down to the station, take your mug shot. Let your pretty gal pal bail you out," Hagan growled, glaring at Nash.

Nash gave Valerie a look that said, "Are you hearing him? Can you believe this crap?"

"Officer Hagan, Nash was only trying to stop the sus-

pect that invaded his home from escaping. He was trying to help—"

"Pbbt," Hagan said, with a dismissive wave of his
hand. "I know what he was doing. But he needs to leave
police work to policemen. He had no right to tackle that
man."

Nash sighed. The officer had a point. At the moment
he'd raced after and jumped the intruder—the *suspected*
intruder, Damon and Myles would be sure to specify—
he hadn't feared for his life or been protecting another's.
He'd seen an opportunity to catch the *suspected* intruder.
His personal sense of violation, indignation and thirst for
revenge had overruled what he had a legal right to do.

Valerie offered Nash a hand and helped him to his feet.
She narrowed her eyes on his swollen lip and soiled shirt.
Concern dented her brow. "You're bleeding!"

Nash glanced down at the stains and flicked his hands
uselessly at the crimson spatter. "No. That's his blood.
I think I busted his nose." A tingle shimmied through
Nash, and he faced the officer. "This is his blood. I'm
sure of it."

Officer Hagan seemed to see where Nash was going.
His jaw clenched.

Nash whipped his shirt over his head and held it out.
"You can take it in and get a sample of his DNA. Match
his blood type. Work whatever forensic magic you need
to and track him down."

Officer Hagan held both hands up, palms toward Nash.
"I can't touch it, put my prints on it. There are chain-of-
evidence rules."

Nash nodded. "Right. Of course."

"Um…" Valerie winced and twisted to pick up something she'd dropped beside her. "I touched his hat. Sorry.
I saw him lose it and thought…"

Hagan sighed. "Look, I won't take you in this time. But consider yourself warned. Both of you. Leave the police work to the police. Got it?"

Nash dusted grass from his clothes and jerked a nod. "Got it."

But as they walked back toward his house, he knew he'd lied to Hagan. Because if anyone came within a breath of Valerie, so much as sent her a threatening glance, cop or not, he'd do whatever it took to protect her.

While the house finished airing out, with windows cracked and his doors locked, Nash took Valerie back to Rick and Vita's house. After explaining what had happened to her uncle and aunt, Nash and Valerie prepared dinner. The steaks, which a fireman had retrieved for them along with the other groceries, were diced, and Valerie added sautéed peppers and onions, turning the meal into fajitas, in order to stretch the dinner to serve four. They enjoyed the meal and conversation with Rick and Vita, even if it wasn't the romantic dinner for two Nash had envisioned.

"We can make up a bed for you to stay here tonight if you want," Vita offered.

"Thanks, but that's not necessary," Nash replied.

Vita blushed slightly and chuckled. "Oh, of course. You and Valerie would share…"

Nash covered an awkward chuckle with a cough. "I only mean that I plan to sleep at my house tonight."

"Are you sure that's safe?" Vita asked.

He nodded. "The air should be clear enough by then."

Vita exchanged a look with Rick. "I mean, what if this guy that's been sabotaging and attacking you comes back?"

Valerie raised a similarly worried gaze to him.

He covered Valerie's hand and gave it a reassuring squeeze. "Then he and I will finish what we started this afternoon."

"And if he has a weapon with him this time?" Valerie asked. "You said his gun misfired the first time he broke in. Don't you think after two failed attempts to harm you, he's going to be more certain of his means next time?"

"Assuming there's a next time." Nash wiped his mouth on his napkin and dropped it on his plate. "I'll be fine."

"But if you stayed he—" Valerie began, when the jangle of Nash's cell interrupted.

He glanced at the screen and recognized the number as the main switchboard at the police department. Had he really talked to cops that many times in the last few weeks? Sheesh.

"Sorry, I should take this," he said, pushing his chair back from the table. Valerie followed him into the next room.

When Nash answered the call, a male voice said, "Mr. Colton, this is Officer Hagan. I have an update on your B-and-E case."

Nash's gaze shot to Valerie, and he quickly switched to speakerphone so she could listen. "I'm all ears. Did you catch the guy?"

"We did. He was picked up a few blocks from your house by a patrol officer just after I sent out the BOLO. His name is Mickey Gorman. That name mean anything to you?"

"No."

Valerie shook her head, her expression void of recognition.

"Why?" Nash asked. "Should it? He saying he knows me?"

"Nah. He's not saying much of anything. He punched

the arresting officer, so we've got enough to keep him until his arraignment. Maybe a night behind bars will loosen his tongue. Just thought you might know something that would help us fill in some blanks."

"Sorry. Never heard of him. That's all you know about him? His name?"

"Well, no. He was in the system. He's got a rap sheet for some petty theft, public intoxication and drug possession from places as far away as Florida and Georgia and as close as Ohio. Current address listed as Toledo."

Valerie's breath caught, her eyes widening.

Nash's pulse kicked. *Toledo.*

He held her stare as Hagan continued, "Anyway, we've been in touch with his parole officer, but thought you might have something that might shed some light on why he was in Chicago. And why did he target you, your house?"

Valerie's eyes were bright as she shook her head again, and Nash's grip tightened on the phone. "Nothing now, but I have your card. If I think of anything, I'll let you know."

"You do that," Hagan said.

Nash thanked the man for calling and disconnected, his eyes still locked on Valerie.

"Toledo," he said simply.

She shook her head once again, more firmly. "No. I know what you're thinking but... I can't—" Val raked her fingers through her hair and got up to pace across the room. When she spun back to face him, her mouth was firm, her jaw set. "My mother is a lot of things, Nash, but she wouldn't—" He saw the doubt that flickered across her face. "It's just a horrible coincidence."

He pocketed his phone and strolled toward her. "Are you trying to convince me of that...or yourself?"

When she didn't reply, he pulled her into his arms and kissed her forehead. Her body was shaking, and he wished he could do something to ease her mind, take away the hurt and confusion she had to be feeling. Even if her mother was completely innocent of any involvement in the recent attacks, the simple fact that Val could even suspect her mother had to be tearing her up inside. She was conflicted enough because of her relationship with him and her torn loyalties.

She tipped up her face, and Nash's heart broke when he saw the tears in her eyes. Finally she whispered, "Give me twenty-four hours. Let me make a couple calls, check some things before you say anything to Hagan. Please?"

He gave her a soft kiss. "Okay."

"I'm coming with you," Valerie said later that night as Nash was leaving. Snagging her coat from the front closet, she called over her shoulder to Vita, "We're gone. Good night!"

"Hold up." Nash sidestepped to block her path out of the Yateses' front door. "As much as I'd love your company, I think I'd feel better knowing you're safe here."

"Uh, Nash? Didn't you just spend the last five minutes convincing Vita your house was safe?"

He tugged her into his arms. "I'm willing to take any risk to show the person behind this I won't be cowed. But placing you in harm's way is a whole different story."

She tipped her head to the side as she gazed up at him. "What if I'm willing to assume the risk in order to be with you tonight?"

"Val…"

"Earlier today at the park, you said you'd be there for me. I believe you. I know you'll protect me, if needed." She kissed him gently, then added, "And I can help protect

you. Be a second set of eyes and ears keeping guard…"
She pressed her body fully against his and leaned in to
whisper in his ear. "Besides, I've been waiting all day,
weeks really, to get you alone and naked again."

He inhaled deeply as if preparing to offer another argument. She nipped his earlobe, and he half sighed, half
groaned. Taking the sound as assent, she scooted around
him and headed out to her car.

Back at Nash's bungalow, they checked the premises
together for signs of intrusion, ventilation success and
other mayhem before determining the house was clear,
if chilly from having the windows open all day.

Nash pulled an extra blanket from the linen closet and
wrapped it around Valerie's shoulders. "How's that?"

Looping her arms around his waist, she edged closer
to him. "Good. But you know what's better? Body heat.
Physical activity…"

"You don't need to ask me twice," he said with a low
growl in his throat as he swooped in for a kiss.

Valerie stood on her toes, stretching to reach his lips
and angling her head to allow him access to her throat.
He trailed his kisses from her jaw to her neck. "You're
beautiful, Val. You're all I've ever wanted."

The whispered words washed through her, a balm to
her frayed nerves. Today had been upsetting and tiring in
so many ways, but being here with Nash made it all seem
worthwhile. She could block out the smell of the natural
gas that lingered in her mind, push aside the concern of
whether her mother was staying on track and mentally
sound, and quell the fear of losing the man she'd come to
realize she didn't want to live without. Nash truly made
her feel safe. Anchored. Loved.

In a move that caught her daydreaming, he bent to
catch her behind her legs and scooped her into his arms.

He carried her across the bedroom and deposited her on the bed. He hesitated only long enough to kick off his shoes and shuck his blue jeans before following her down on the made bed.

"Come here, you," she said, folding the blanket he'd given her around them both as she hooked her legs around his. She met his kiss with equal passion and fervor. After their unexpected lovemaking weeks ago, the night of their overdue reckoning, she'd thought about being with Nash in so many stolen moments. While working with Sara. While driving. While showering...

An image, a scent, a word could carry her mind off to intimate moments she'd shared with Nash. As a teenager. On their recent night of passion. In her fantasies.

In truth, Nash hadn't been far from her mind in twelve years. And now he was in her arms. At last.

As he rolled with her, pulling her on top of him, she dragged the comforter with her, creating a warm cocoon around them. A dark nest that shut out the world. A snug cave where the woodsy scent of his body wash and the mint-toothpaste flavor of his kiss mingled and enticed her better than any aphrodisiac.

He helped her wiggle out of her slacks and pressed a line of toe-tingling kisses, nibbles and licks on her belly as he unbuttoned her blouse. Revealed her skin. One. Button. At. A. Time.

Slowly. Seductively. Maddeningly...

Her body was on fire by the time he inched the blouse off her shoulders and reached for her bra hooks. She writhed with pleasure as he freed her breasts from the satin bra and took her nipples in his mouth. She arched her back, wanting more, needing him...

"So sweet. Val, I—" He seized her mouth in another

deep kiss, and she welcomed him with a lusty sigh, a plundering tongue and an open heart.

When he fought to get her arms free of the bra and blouse, she rolled with him, pedaled her legs to kick free the blanket…and found herself more tangled than before. A laugh escaped, and he raised his head to shoot her a quizzical look. "What's so funny?"

"Us. We're hopelessly tangled in covers and clothes and limbs. I think we need a reset."

He touched his forehead to hers, chuckling, then kissed her once more before fighting off the blanket and comforter that had become more mummy than cocoon.

Giggling like naughty children, they finished stripping, straightened the bedcovers and climbed between the cool sheets.

"Brr. Bring that hot bod back here, mister." She tugged his arm as he moved closer to her. "I miss your heat already."

"Likewise, love." He covered her, and with their bodies aligned, flesh to flesh, woman to man, teasing was set aside for hunger, for intimacy. For love.

She may not have spoken the words, but she told Nash with every touch and caress how much she cared for him, needed him, wanted him.

As he joined their bodies, whispering her name, she knew a soul-deep peace. The journey had taken years, carried her through deep valleys of sorrow and nearly broken her spirit, but with Nash, she'd finally found her way home.

Chapter 17

Valerie waited until Nash went into work the next morning before making her inquiries concerning Mickey Gorman. She may have denied to him that her mother could have any involvement, but deep down, a terrible uncertainty nagged her. She sat on the bed where she and Nash had just made love, reconnecting, rebuilding the love and intimacy her mother had shattered years ago, and she steeled herself. With her back propped against the headboard and her knees drawn up to her chest, Val prepared herself.

The same red flags that had glared at her when Officer Hagan had called now replayed in her brain. Mickey Gorman. Toledo. Public intoxication. Drug use. Parole officer.

Could Mickey Gorman be a part of her mother's AA group as part of his parole requirement?

The one thing she knew for sure was she wouldn't get the answers she needed by stalling.

Taking a fortifying breath, she started with a call to Nancy, wanting to check on her mother's general condition before broaching a potentially dicey subject with her mother.

"She was actually much more upbeat the last time I spoke with her," Nancy said. "Seemed to feel more in control, less harried. She went to AA with me a few nights ago and was much more relaxed after the meeting. I think your visit helped. She makes no secret that she's looking forward to you getting back home."

Valerie's chest constricted. *If she went back home.* How did she break the news to her mother if she did decide to stay in Chicago with Nash? She shoved aside that problem to focus on what Nancy was saying.

"—planning to call her or stop by tonight."

"Oh, good. Thank you." Taking a deep breath, Val asked, "Nancy, has my mother ever mentioned knowing someone named Mickey Gorman?"

Nancy took a beat longer than normal to respond. "Val, you know that the content of my conversations and counsel with your mother are confidential. I can't divulge anything your mother tells me and vice versa. Privacy is a cornerstone of the AA program. Without it, our members wouldn't feel the freedom to truly be open about their addiction and recovery struggles."

Val's shoulders drooped. "Yeah, I know. I just thought...well, never mind. Thanks for keeping an eye on her. You take care, too."

After disconnecting the call, Val slumped down on the bed. While it was encouraging to get a good report on her mother, Nancy's non-answer due to privacy concerns wasn't the decisive *no* that would have put her mind at ease.

She mulled how to approach her questions for her mother. Dread ticked in her gut like the timer on a bomb. She didn't want to set her mother off. According to Nancy, she was on a more stable track at the moment. Neither did she want to learn truths that could blow her world apart. But ignorance, or ignoring a potentially devastating truth, wouldn't resolve anything, didn't protect Nash from a threat that was within her power to stop.

Finally, she lifted her phone again and tapped the screen icons to call her mother. After basic salutations and inquiries of general well-being both ways, Val got to the heart of the issue at hand. "Mother, do you know a man by the name of Mickey Gorman?"

As Nancy had, her mother took a beat before responding. "Why? Where is this coming from?"

"Just…answer my question. Do you know Mickey Gorman?"

"It sounds to me like you're accusing me of something." Her mother's timbre began to tighten and rise in pitch. Caution lights flashed in Val's mind.

"No accusations. I just need to know if—"

"If you *are* accusing me of something, just say it!"

That her mother would jump to such a conclusion was common for her paranoia, but Valerie was uncomfortable with the bridge between the mention of the suspect's name and her mother's defensiveness.

"Why do you assume I'm making an accusation? Have you done something to be accused of?"

Her mother grunted loudly. "*He* put you up to this, didn't he?"

"If you mean Nash, then no. But when I learned that the man who broke into Nash's home and tried to create an explosion that could have killed both Nash and me is from Toledo, it just rang all sorts of warning bells."

"Nash and *you*?" Horror filled her mother's voice. "You're *still* hanging around with him? After everything I've told you? Valerie! I warned you to *stay away* from him!"

A prickle bit Valerie's nape. "Why should I stay away, Mother? What danger am I in if I'm with Nash? Something you set up?"

Carol's huff was loud and long. "He's turning you against me! He's lying to you and stealing you from me! He's no good, Val. All of those Coltons are cut from the same cloth and will hurt you, hurt *us*. You have to listen to me!" Panic was rising in her mother's tone.

"Mother, take a breath. I'm all right. Nothing is going to happen to either of us."

"You don't know that. You don't—"

Valerie bunched the bedspread in her hand, swallowing hard to fight the nausea that roiled in her gut. Pitching her own tone low and slow, she repeated, "Do you know Mickey Gorman?"

Silence answered her, and the anxiety and suspicion knotting her gut grew.

"Mother, did you hire Mickey Gorman to hurt Nash?"

"For God's sake, Valerie! I don't have to listen to this. If this is the only reason you called, then I'm hanging up."

"Mother, it's a simple enough question. If you didn't—"

"Goodbye." The line went silent.

"Mother?" But, as expected, no one was there.

A heaviness sat on Val's lungs, its crushing weight rooted in one awful truth. Despite her exclamations of dismay and indignation, her mother hadn't denied a relationship with, or her hiring of, the man suspected of trying to harm Nash.

Valerie's suspicions brewed inside her over the next couple of hours, making her ill with worry. Her position, torn between her duty to her mother and her love for Nash, was difficult enough without adding the question of whether her mother was behind the attacks on Nash.

She and Nash had been ripped apart years ago by innuendo, supposition and assumptions, and she wasn't about to leave their attempt at reconciliation to the mercy of doubts and impressions. As much as learning the truth terrified her, Valerie decided the best way to put the issue to rest was to go to the source.

After a distracted morning of trying—and failing—to work on the final art for the Yates' Yards winter advertising campaign, Valerie headed down to the police station where Officer Hagan worked. She had the front desk call him to the lobby, and she was told he was out on patrol.

Her shoulders drooped, and disappointment, all the more potent given the courage she'd had to muster to come down to the station, lanced her spirits.

She was turning to leave the station when another familiar face entered the lobby. She straightened and hurried to catch up with the man's long-legged strides. "Detective Cartwright?"

Cartwright glanced at her, then, clearly recognizing her, brightened with a polite smile. "Hi, uh, Ms. Yates, right?"

She nodded. "I need to talk to you, or…someone."

His expression modulated. One eyebrow lifted, an indication she had his full attention. "About?"

"Well, Officer Hagan has been working with Nash Colton concerning the break-ins and sabotage intended to cause a gas explosion at his house. I understand the chief suspect has been arrested and is being held here until his arraignment."

Cartwright squared his feet and folded his arms over his chest. "He was. But Mr. Gorman has been transferred to the county jail now. He just had his arraignment. In fact, that's where I just was. Considering it seems the repeated attacks on Mr. Colton were attempts on his life, I've been given the case."

"Oh. Um… I see. And what happened at the arraignment?"

"He pled not guilty. Of course. But considering he broke his parole in numerous ways, he'll likely be sent back to Ohio later this week. We're still working out those details."

Valerie wiped her sweaty hands on the legs of her gabardine pants. "Can I see him?"

Cartwright tipped his head. "Pardon?"

"I'd like to talk to him. Ask him a couple questions."

The detective's spine straightened. "Do you have information about the case, Ms. Yates?"

"Not exactly. Just questions. Something I really need answered."

The detective's incisive gaze bore into her, and she shivered. "What questions?"

She glanced around the lobby, her anxiety climbing. "It's probably nothing. I mean I can't imagine—"

He hitched his head toward a door that led deeper into the building. "Let's go to my office and talk."

Valerie's pulse scampered. She couldn't tell the detective anything that would implicate her mother. That would be a complete betrayal.

And yet…if her mother was complicit, how could she *not* tell the detective what she knew. She had to think about Nash, his safety. And what was morally right. She wasn't responsible for her mother's bad choices. If she had done the unthinkable, hired a man to hurt Nash, she had to be stopped.

Her feet felt leaden as she followed Cartwright to his desk and perched on the edge of the chair opposite him.

"So…what is weighing on you in the case against Mr. Gorman?"

Even as he asked the question, Valerie sensed that the detective already knew what she suspected. The man was no dummy. If he'd done his research on the case, if he remembered anything she'd told him when she'd been interviewed after Axel's death, he'd put two and two together the same as she had. The keen look in his eyes told her he was two steps ahead of her.

Perspiration popped out on her lip, and she knew a moment of regret, of guilt. Swallowing hard, she said, "I understand Mickey Gorman is from Toledo."

Cartwright nodded. "Yes. That's his current home address."

She twisted her fingers in the strap of her purse. "I think… I mean there's a chance…"

The detective said nothing, waiting patiently, his gray-green gaze fixed on her.

"My mother lives in Toledo. She doesn't like Nash." Valerie had to pause and take a calming breath to keep her gorge from rising. Blood rushed past her ears in a whoosh that drowned out all the other noises from the police station. "In fact, she hates him. And all of the Coltons. She's under a doctor's care for mental illness, but recently, she hasn't been taking her medicines properly. So I'm concerned that, in a moment of irrationality…" Her throat clogged. She couldn't say the words. It was too awful. Tears stung her eyes.

Cartwright's expression shifted. The same compassion he'd displayed when Sara had fainted filled his face as he leaned forward and reached to cover her hand. "Take all the time you need. But I need to hear you say the words. Officially."

When she sniffed and wiped her cheek with her sleeve, he handed her a facial tissue from a box on the corner of his desk.

After she blew her nose and gulped oxygen, she blurted, "I think my mother, Carol Yates, hired Mickey Gorman to come after Nash."

Cartwright sat back in his chair, his expression calm and sympathetic. "Why do you think so?"

With nausea roiling in her gut, Valerie outlined her mother's history with the Coltons, her mental illness, her continued insistence that Nash would hurt her. "I know it's largely speculation and circumstantial, but when I heard Gorman was from Toledo, and was previously arrested for drug- and alcohol-related charges, and knowing my mother attends AA meetings and…"

Valerie paused, exhaled, squeezed the chair's armrests until her fingers blanched.

Cartwright lifted the receiver of his desk phone and pressed an extension. "Yeah, hi, Sally. Cartwright in Homicide. Can you bring Mickey Gorman up to an interrogation room for me, please. Yeah. I know. Yes, now. Thanks." When he hung up, he twisted his mouth and regarded Valerie with an intense scrutiny.

Valerie rubbed a hand on her chest where she thought her heart might crash through her ribs. Part of her wished she could take back her words, rewind and erase her traitorous suggestion to the detective.

"I can't imagine how hard it must have been to come in today, Ms. Yates." He pushed to his feet, signaling an end to the conversation. "But you did the right thing."

Valerie stood, too, although her legs were weak and her knees buckled. She squared her shoulders with more bravado than she felt. "I still don't have the answers I need."

Cartwright sighed. "Ms. Yates—"

"Detective," she interrupted, her stomach swooping. "I want to come with you. Be in the room when you question him. I want to hear what Mickey Gorman has to say."

Cartwright shook his head. "That's not—"

"Please. I won't say anything or interfere in any way."

Hands on his hips, his mouth pressed in a grim line, Cartwright stared at her silently for a moment. Finally, his eyes narrowing, he said, "If I let you watch from an observation room, you have to understand that if you divulge anything we learn, to anyone, including Nash Colton, I can have you arrested for impeding an investigation. If Gorman gives up your mother and you tip her off, I'll charge you with aiding and abetting. Your complete silence and discretion is imperative. Understood?"

Including Nash Colton. Valerie's lungs struggled for air. If she agreed, if she got the answers she needed, she was promising to keep secrets from Nash again, just when they had reached a turning point in their relationship.

"I—"

"I mean it, Ms. Yates. Letting you observe is outside normal procedure. I can sell it as you being an informant, already being privy to the information gathered, but I need your sworn word it goes no further."

Her insides were being ripped in a hundred directions,

her loyalties torn, and guilt chewed her soul. But she'd come too far to turn back. She'd set a boulder in motion that couldn't be stopped. Releasing a shuddering sigh, she gave Cartwright a nod. "I promise."

Chapter 18

"Hey, where are you?" Nash asked, when he finally reached Valerie on her phone that afternoon. "I left work, thinking we'd steal away for a long lunch, and when I went by the house to get you, the only one I found home was that dang calico. Why haven't you been answering your phone?"

"I, um, had it turned off." She laughed stiffly. "I didn't realize it until a little while ago. Duh!"

"Okay, well, I'm back at work now and already ate without you when I couldn't find you, so... I guess I'll just see you back at the house later?"

"Well, maybe. I... I'm not sure what—" Valerie stopped abruptly, and in the background, Nash heard a male voice that said, "We're ready."

"Who was that? What's ready?"

"Sorry, Nash. I have to go."

"Val, what's going on?" Silence answered him. She was already gone.

Nash hung up his office phone and leaned back in his desk chair, puzzling over her abrupt departure, her unwillingness to answer his simplest questions. Old familiar doubt demons nipped at him, and he shook his head, wanting with all his heart to confidently dismiss the nagging suspicions. But Hagan's call wouldn't leave him alone. The fear in Valerie's eyes, even as he'd promised to give her twenty-four hours to answer her own questions, haunted him. Now she was shutting him out again. Like before, when they'd been teens.

He wanted to quash the niggling suspicions, but his gut told him plainly that something was up and Valerie was keeping it from him. After promising to be open with him. Candid and faithful.

Already she'd broken her promise.

But he'd given her twenty-four hours to learn the whole truth and bring it to him. He needed to wait. To trust.

His chest squeezed, and he began the painful, tedious wait. He didn't care what the truth she'd discovered was. No matter how bleak the news might be, his first and only concern was that she keep faith with him. They could face any challenge together. But if Valerie chose deception, distance and doubt again, how could he believe they had a future?

He refused to go down that dark path again.

Valerie followed the uniformed officer who'd been assigned to sit with her in the observation booth next to the interrogation room while Cartwright questioned Gorman. They'd had to wait for the public defender assigned to Gorman's case to be called and arrive at the station. The PD, a woman named Jill Russell, had been at court, delaying matters. Valerie had spent the time pacing, second-guessing her choice and avoiding calls from Nash. Her white lie about having her phone off was only partly false. She had turned off her phone when he continued calling.

She'd only turned the phone on five minutes before getting his most recent call, because she'd wanted to listen to her voicemail. His increasingly concerned messages broke her heart, especially knowing she couldn't tell him the whole truth about what she'd been doing, what she'd learned. She prayed that Nash had enough faith in her to let a generic answer stand. Enough trust to let "I can't say more" stand.

The uniformed officer motioned to a chair from which Val could watch the interview. She shook her head, too hyped on adrenaline and nervous energy to sit still. When the lanky, wiry-haired man was ushered into the small, drab interview room, Valerie's stomach lurched. Regardless of whether her mother was behind the attacks, this man was undoubtedly the face she and Nash had watched on surveillance footage breaking into Nash's home. This man had tried to kill, or at a minimum, maim Nash with a gas explosion. Acid crept up her throat, and she thought she might throw up.

"Mr. Gorman," Detective Cartwright began, his deep voice resonating through the speakers in the observation booth. "We've received new information regarding your case and have—"

Gorman leaned toward Cartwright with a snarl. "I told you before, I don't got nothing to say."

"Do you know a woman in Toledo by the name of Carol Yates?"

Gorman's flinch was tiny, almost imperceptible, but

Valerie caught it. And she was certain Cartwright had, as well, because now he leaned forward, almost touching noses with Gorman, and said in a low, stern tone, "Don't take the fall for her. If Carol Yates put you up to this, paid you, blackmailed you, whatever, now is your chance to come clean."

Valerie held her breath. *Please deny it. Please...*

She held her breath. But any hope Valerie had that she'd misinterpreted Gorman's twitch as guilt or surprise evaporated when, after a few tense beats, the wiry-haired man sat back, his pale skin reddening. Gorman's mouth tightened, then he leaned toward Jill Russell, and whispered to his lawyer. Russell conferred with him, too quietly for Valerie to hear anything. But she didn't have to hear to know what they had to be discussing.

When both Gorman and Russell straightened in their chairs, the public defender faced Cartwright, placing her hands, fingers laced, on the table. "We'd like to discuss a plea. Mr. Gorman will answer all of your questions, in full, for immunity."

Valerie's knees gave out. Staggering backward, she slumped into the chair she'd refused earlier.

"Immunity?" Cartwright scoffed. "No way that flies with the DA. But we can see about a reduced sentence. We'll work with Mr. Gorman's parole officer and the courts in Ohio to get leniency."

As the negotiations in the interrogation room continued, Valerie's head swam, and a loud buzzing filled her ears. Gorman may not have said the words yet, but his turnabout, when faced with the truth, spoke for him.

Her breathing sawed from her in quick, shallow pants. Lifting a trembling hand, she covered her mouth, thinking she might be sick.

The uniformed officer squatted beside her. "Are you all right, ma'am?"

She lifted a blurred gaze to the policeman and shook her head. "No."

She'd defended her mother to Nash. Given her mother chance after chance. But her loyalty to her mother had been ill-placed.

Her mother was behind the attacks on Nash. Valerie didn't think she'd ever be all right again.

Vita answered the door when Nash arrived at the Yateses' early that evening. He'd worried about Valerie and her lack of communication throughout the afternoon, and, having not found her at his house when he left work and unable to reach her on her phone, he'd driven straight to the Yateses'.

"Oh, Nash, I'm so glad to see you." Vita ushered him inside, wiping her hands on her skirt. "Val's been upstairs in her room for the last two hours. She's clearly upset over something, but she wouldn't talk to us about it. Maybe she'll tell you what's wrong."

"Thanks." He took the steps two at a time and hurried to the closed guest room door. After knocking lightly, he called, "Val, can I come in? It's Nash."

He heard footsteps, then the door flew open, and she launched herself into his arms.

"Hey, hey," he crooned softly, rubbing her back as he held her. "It's okay. What's going on?"

Though she clutched him, her body shuddering as she nestled against him, she said nothing. He allowed her a few minutes to simply hug him and gather herself. When the trembling of her limbs calmed, he eased her back and guided her to the bed. She sank on the edge of the mattress, and he joined her. Angling his body to face her, he lifted her chin, trying to bring her eyes to his. "Tell me. What's going on? What happened today?"

She met his gaze only briefly before jerking her chin away and shaking her head. "I can't."

His stomach lurched. Were they over before they'd really started? He swallowed hard, working to rein in his gut reaction. "Can't what? What are you saying?"

She scooted closer, reaching for him. "Can you just… hold me?"

The fear that had gripped him eased. He wrapped her in his embrace again and leaned back against the stacked pillows, cradling her close. "Val, please talk to me. I hate seeing you like this." When she remained silent, he asked, "Did you talk to your mother?"

He felt her stiffen. Of course, her mood was about her mother. Val's mission this morning had been to find out if her mother was connected to the Gorman guy the police had in custody. She was always agitated after talking to her mother, so that explained a lot. But not all. Not the extent of her current distress. A different sort of tension curled in a hard ball inside him.

"What did your mom say when you talked to her? When you asked her about Mickey Gorman?"

Valerie buried her face deeper into the crook of his neck. Sighed brokenly. "She…never gave me a straight answer. She got hostile and defensive when she realized I suspected her of wrongdoing."

"Huh." He understood the subtle difference that Val had to be debating. "Do you think she was being deliberately evasive, as in she didn't want to admit the truth? Or was she so hurt by your assumption that she didn't want to dignify the question with a response?"

"I—" Her fingers curled into his shirt. "I also called her sponsor, Nancy. I asked her about Gorman, too. If my mother knew him, had mentioned him."

Nash noticed Valerie hadn't answered his question, but let it slide for the moment. "What did Nancy tell you?"

"Not much. She reminded me that privacy and discretion are cornerstones of the AA program."

"So if she knew something she was honor-bound to keep your mother's confidence?"

"Yeah."

Nash meditated on that briefly, then asked, "Even if she had knowledge of a crime?"

Val hesitated, then said, "Nancy did say that the last time she talked to my mother, she seemed in a calmer frame of mind. But otherwise, I—I really didn't learn anything else…from her."

Every time Valerie paused, as if carefully choosing her words, every time she avoided his questions, Nash grew more edgy. Coupled with her obvious distress over… *something*, he concluded she was withholding critical information.

"What aren't you telling me?" he asked, testing his theory.

Valerie was still, silent. Wouldn't look at him.

"You know you can trust me, don't you? If something has happened, if you learned something important—"

"Nash," she began, and he waited for her to continue. And waited.

"Valerie?"

"Just…stay with me tonight. Here. Hold me and… trust me. Please?"

He knew it was a leap of faith, but he nodded, pulled her close, kissed her head. "All right."

* * *

Valerie slept little that night. Her conscience plagued her for having kept Nash in the dark about her mother's involvement in the attacks. Guilt chewed her gut for having directed the police to her mother, and questions racked her about what was happening with the case. She'd wanted to go to Ohio, be with her mother when the police came for her, but Cartwright warned her not to. He wanted nothing to tip Carol off. Besides, Cartwright had contacted the police in Ohio about an arrest warrant for Carol, and Val couldn't have gotten to Toledo before it was executed. He had advised her simply to go to Rick's and wait.

But waiting was torture. Had her mother been taken into custody? Had she resisted arrest? Valerie had told Cartwright about her mother's mental illness, but too many things could have gone wrong.

And Nash. Dancing around his questions last night had torn her up. When Nash learned the truth, understood how much she'd kept from him, would it change his feelings toward her? At first light, afraid her tossing and turning would wake Nash, she finally tucked her cell phone in her pocket, slipped from the bed and went downstairs.

Vita was already awake and had coffee brewing.

"Good morning, dear," Vita chirped brightly. "You're up early. I hope that means you're feeling better."

Valerie didn't want to worry her aunt, so she forced the brightest smile she could manage. "Some better. Thanks. Have I had any calls?" she asked, knowing it was a long shot.

"At this hour?" Vita handed Val a mug of steaming coffee. "No. Are you expecting a call on the house phone?"

"I guess not." If there was news, both Cartwright and her mother had her cell number, and her phone hadn't been out of her sight since she left the police station yesterday. Just in case, she checked the home screen again for any indication she'd somehow missed a text or had a message.

Nothing. She wilted in one of the chairs at the kitchen table and raised her mug for a sip of fortification.

She heard the soft padding of feet behind her and turned, expecting to find Rick. Instead, Nash stood there, barefoot, hair rumpled and his clothes from yesterday wrinkled from being slept in. To Valerie, he looked sexier than any movie star or cologne model. Her heart swelled, and a bittersweet pang filled her chest. She wanted to wake up to groggy, rumpled Nash every morning for the rest of her life. But had her mother made that impossible?

He yawned widely and scratched his chin. "Does this house always get up so early?"

Vita filled another coffee cup and handed it to Nash. "Not always. Can I get you two breakfast?"

Even though she hadn't eaten dinner the night before, Valerie's stomach churned at the thought of food. "No, thank you."

Clearly her answer nettled Vita's maternal instincts, because she sent her a dubious look and sighed.

"Just coffee for me. I'll get a bite at home before I go into the office. I have to shower and change clothes—"

Valerie's phone jangled, sounding especially loud and harsh considering the early hour. Adrenaline charged through her and left her trembling, with dread close on its heels.

"Oh," Vita said, setting down her mug. "Maybe that's the call you were waiting for."

Nash frowned. "What call?"

Her caller ID read, *Chicago Police Department.*

Her mouth dried, but mustering her courage, Valerie rose from the table on wobbly legs and hurried out of the room to answer the call. It took two tries to scrape out a response. "Hello?"

"Ms. Yates? Detective Cartwright."

Her breath left her in a quavering exhale. "Yes?" she rasped.

"Have you been in touch with your mother since we spoke yesterday?"

Valerie hadn't a destination in mind when she'd left the kitchen to take the call in private, but she found herself on the back screened porch, the icy wind cutting through her thin sleep shirt. "I— No. You told me not to."

Cartwright grunted.

"Why?" She could barely hear herself over the thumping of her pulse in her ears. "What's happened?"

"Nothing. That's the problem. Officers in Ohio went to your mother's home, but she wasn't there. They waited all night for her to return, but she didn't."

A fresh kind of panic swept through her. Had her mother harmed herself? Had she overdosed on booze and pills? Given in to paranoia and despair? "Did—did they go inside? Are you sure she wasn't there?"

"They checked the premises. The house was empty. I just thought maybe she'd contacted you, given you some indication where she was?"

"M-maybe at her friend's house? Nancy, her sponsor?" Valerie forced her thoughts to settle enough to conjure Nancy's address from memory.

"Okay. We'll check it out. It should go without saying—if you hear from her, call me. Immediately."

"Right. Yes." She stood staring out at Rick and Vita's frozen backyard, shivering from the cold and her concern.

The early morning sun glinted off the frost like shards of broken glass. The metallic scent of snow hung in the air. In the icy breeze, a random flake or two wandered down from the pale sky, swirling haphazardly like Valerie's thoughts. Untethered. Spinning recklessly. Leaving her cold.

Her mother was missing. Wanted for hiring an assassin. Determined to destroy the one relationship where Valerie had found deep abiding love and joy. Set on tearing her from the family where she'd felt happy and supported.

With a keening moan, she bent at the waist, lashed by pain and wrenched internally. Because she still felt a duty to her mother because of Carol's illness. She wanted so desperately to break free of the millstone of chaos and hatred that was her mother's hold on her.

"Val, my God!"

She gasped her surprise, not having heard Nash's approach until he spoke. He placed something around her shoulders. Her coat, she realized as she straightened and caught the edges of it to pull around her.

"Love, it's freezing out here. Why don't you come in?"

She nodded but couldn't speak. Didn't move. Soon his arms were around her along with the coat.

"I wish you'd tell me what's going on. It's obviously tearing you up." He smoothed a hand along her cold cheek. "How can I help you, if you won't talk to me?"

"Just...stay here. Be with me." She reflected on all that would likely come down in the following days, hours, and added, "And give me grace."

"Grace?" Nash frowned, the dark tug of his mouth reflecting confusion over her odd word choice. And suspicion. He had to understand that something bad was coming. She saw the hurt in his eyes when she dodged answering his questions and put emotional distance between them with her lack of candor.

But grace was what she'd need most when the police found her mother, when Nash learned the whole truth about what she was keeping from him, when her reckoning came and she had to choose a way forward, inevitably betraying someone she loved…

She couldn't live like this, with divided loyalties. It was too much…

Eventually, if she didn't make a choice, it would break her.

Even if Nash hadn't been aware of how restless Valerie had been through the night, watching her across Vita's breakfast table left little doubt. She looked miserable. At the start of their reconciliation, her misery was not reassuring.

When he'd heard her plaintive wail, chills had sketched down his spine. Seeing her doubled over, crumpled with whatever pain tormented her, a rock had lodged in his chest. Not just because he hurt for her, but because she wouldn't share the source of her pain with him. Because she seemed to be moving away from him instead of closer. He was losing her, and he didn't know why. Or how to reverse course.

He could guess *who* easily enough, but her mother was a volatile subject. The big red danger button of their relationship.

He'd guided her back inside to Vita's breakfast table, but Valerie was clearly somewhere else. Though she held a mug between her hands, she stared silently into space. Nash studied the dark circles under Val's eyes, the worry lines etched between her brows, her faraway expression.

He was due at work in an hour, but every minute that

passed made it more obvious he should take another personal day to stay with Val. If he still had a job with Reed and Burdett Architecture when all the Colton family drama was resolved, he'd owe it all to his understanding boss, and the fact that he'd accumulated six weeks of sick leave and vacation days since starting at the firm.

He battled down the frustration of not knowing how to help her and said quietly, "Val, if you don't want to talk to me...fine. But I think you should talk to someone. Vita or Nicole? Rick? Maybe Faith?"

She blinked slowly and finally met his gaze. "No. I...can't."

"Well, I'm not leaving you like this, so... I'll call my office and tell them I'll be out today—"

She roused a bit then. He mug thunked to the table. "No. That's not... I don't..."

Gathering her hand in his, he kissed her knuckles. "We'll go somewhere together. Leave town. Maybe a change of scenery to distract us is what we both need."

She shook her head. "Not today. I need to be—"

Drawing a slow breath, his heart in his throat, he ventured, "What about Ohio? Do you want me to take you to Toledo?"

Her chin jerked up, her gaze bright with alarm.

Cautiously, he continued, "I'll go with you, if you feel you're needed there."

Tears bloomed in her eyes, and her hand squeezed his. "Thank you...for offering. But...no. That's not..." Putting an arm on the table, she buried her face in the crook of her elbow and groaned. "I hate this, Nash. I hate it!"

He clenched his back teeth and struggled to calm his internal battle between frustration and concern for her. Finally, he shoved back his chair and pushed to his feet.

"Come on. We're at least going for a walk. Get your coat—"

Now it was Nash's phone that rang. As odd as it was to get a call at this early hour, the panic that filled Valerie's face set Nash's pulse on edge, even before he pulled the cell from his jeans pocket. The name on the caller ID was his second shock.

He scowled, hesitated.

"What is it?" Val asked.

"Not what. Who. It's my dad. He never calls me."

When he continued to stare at the phone, Valerie took his hand. He could feel her trembling, heard the note of dread when she asked, "Are you going to answer it?"

He didn't want to. Something in his bones told him not to, warned him it would be bad.

"It could be an emergency," she said, rising from her own chair to move closer to him, her face pale.

He arched one light brown eyebrow and grumbled, "That's no selling point." But he stabbed the screen before the call could go to voicemail. With a deep breath, he said, "Hi, Dad. What's up?"

He heard his father clear his throat, then in a tight voice, Erik said, "Nash, we have a…situation."

Of course they did. Because the Coltons couldn't catch a break this year.

Nash gripped the phone tighter, his gut tight with dread. "What kind of situation?"

"Do you remember a girl named Valerie Yates? Used to visit Rick and Vita years ago as a kid? In the summers, I think." Nash's heart seemed to still as he shot a worried look to Val. He put the call on speaker.

"Of course, I know her. Dad, she was at Axel's funeral with me. Are you so self-absorbed that you don't even remember that? In fact, I'm dating her."

"You're what?" Through the phone connection, he heard a groan, some shuffling, a muffled second voice.

"She was my girlfriend years ago, too. You might have known that if you'd paid attention to anyone but yourself." But when had his father ever cared about his sons or anything that mattered to them?

Erik's voice remained strangely flat, yet with a thread of strain. "You may remember I had my hands full with your grandmother and the media at my brother's funeral."

"Yeah. Whatever. Your point?"

"My point is…right now, I'm with her mother," his father said slowly. The tension in his voice was more obvious now.

Valerie slapped a hand over her mouth, muffling a gasp, but her eyes were wide with confusion and alarm.

"You're…what?"

Erik sighed, his voice dipping lower. "You heard me. And she has a gun…pointed at my head."

Chapter 19

A shudder rolled through Valerie as Nash's face paled, and he muttered, "What the hell?"

"She is requesting your presence…here at my house," Erik continued. "Or she will— Ow, easy there, woman! I'm cooperating! No need to be—"

They heard a quiet *oof*, then Erik said, "She wants us both here. She says she'll kill me if you don't come. Right now."

Nash met Valerie's eyes with a pained expression. No words needed to be spoken to realize the danger of the situation, the reason behind her mother's drastic actions, or the consequences of handling the situation the wrong way. Valerie held out a trembling hand for the phone. She knew, perhaps better than anyone, how explosive the situation could become. Or maybe it was already teetering near DEFCON 1.

She wiggled her fingers, asking for the phone. "Let

me talk to her. Maybe I can get her to stand down. Use my phone to call the police."

"Dad…" Nash held up a finger, silently saying hang on.

"Who was that?" Erik sounded more panicked now. "I— Tell her no cops! Carol is adamant."

Valerie's hand shook as she brought up the number pad on her cell. Cartwright's number should be in her recent calls…

Muffled voices could be heard, then Erik came back on the line. "She says…if the cops show up, she swears she'll kill us both, no questions asked." His father growled under his breath, then whispered, "Nash, she's not right in the head. She— Ow!"

Valerie waved her hand again, silently begging for him to turn over the phone.

"Dad, put Carol on the phone. Valerie is here. Maybe she can clear this up."

"I— Okay. But you're coming? Right? She's serious, Nash. She wants you here. With me. She says it's the only way—"

Nash pressed the phone to his chest to cover their whispers. "We need to go. No matter how this plays out, we gotta at least try to—"

Val snatched the phone from him and said, "Mr. Colton, tell my mother to talk to me. Please!" But she nodded to Nash and picked up her purse as they headed out the door. She was still in her nightshirt, but they had no time for her to change. Vita's garden shoes by the door would have to do for her feet.

She followed Nash down the porch steps, tossing him the keys to her car as she waited for her mother to come on the line. She knew she needed to let Cartwright know where her mother was, what was happening. But she also knew what Cartwright would say about Val and Nash hurrying over to the scene, trying to handle the standoff between Erik and her mother themselves. But without help from the detective or some law enforcement, how—?

"Val'rie? S'that you?"

Valerie's pulse spiked as she climbed in the passenger seat. Her mother's voice sounded strangely high-pitched, slightly slurred. "Yes. Mother, please, you can't—"

"Are you with that Colton boy again after ev'rything I've said?"

Valerie closed her eyes. Took a beat to breathe in. Released it. Her mother had been drinking. She knew it in her bones, even without hearing her slurred speech—which made the situation all the more difficult to manage. Alcohol skewed everything. Despair stabbed her. She could imagine the familiar smell of alcohol fumes wafting off her mother. As with so many times as a little girl and a teenager, Valerie felt the roil of bile and acid in her stomach and climbing her throat. Fear, loathing and fury stirred in her core like a lethal cocktail.

Lethal. Poor choice of words. Or perhaps exactly right. Erik was convinced her mother intended to kill him. "Mother, you can't hurt Erik Colton. You need to walk away. Everything will be fine, but you have to put the gun down and—"

"No. No, no, no-o-o! I can't do that, Val'rie. It's all 'is fault. Ev'rythin'…started with him. He has to pay for what he did to us."

Valerie wanted to scream her frustration. The last few years of psychiatric counseling, drug therapy and rehab went out the window in an instant when her mother drank. She reverted to old thought patterns, paranoia and obsessions.

Nash cut a dark look toward her that showed his deep

concern. He took Valerie's phone from her other hand, and when they stopped at the first red traffic light, he thumbed in a number. Indicating his phone in her hand, he mouthed, "Mute. I don't want her to hear me."

"Mother, I'm on my way. We'll figure this out together. Like always. Just…don't do anything rash. Take a breath. You're all right. Hang on." After that last encouragement, she tapped the screen to mute her end of the connection. "Nash, wait! She doesn't want police. They'll set her off, Nash. You can't—"

The call Nash had made on her cell phone connected, and she heard a chipper male voice that said, "Hi, Valerie! What can I do for you, gorgeous?"

With the phone on speaker in Nash's lap, he continued pushing the speed limit and weaving through traffic. "It's Nash. I need your help, bro. Get over to Dad's ASAP."

"Why?" Damon asked. "What's wrong?"

Nash gave his brother a bullet-point explanation, while Valerie could hear her mother and Erik over the line from the phone she held.

"You lied to me! Cheated on me. You used me and threw me away like trash!" her mother ranted.

"I don't know what you're talking about! I never met you before—"

Val cringed, knowing how Erik's denial, his memory lapse, would go over with her mother. In a word, disaster.

"What!" Carol shrieked.

"Look, I'm at least thirty minutes out. You gotta call the police, a negotiator or someone in," Damon said. "This could turn ugly quick."

"Uglier, you mean." Nash sighed heavily and pounded his fist on the steering wheel when they got trapped behind traffic at a stop light.

"I'll handle the law enforcement, get us some backup,"

Damon said. "You need to stay away, Nash. We need Val's mom to calm down. Stand down. Your presence isn't likely to do that."

Nash nodded as if his brother could see the response. "Maybe. But Val's with me, and she might be able to help de-escalate things."

"Maybe. But it's still risky. Don't do anything rash, bro. I'm on my way."

Once Damon disconnected, Valerie took her phone back from Nash and unmuted her mother. Taking a fortifying breath, she said, "I'm still here, Mother. Talk to me."

"The bastard says he doesn't even know me! Thirty years ago he had his hand up my dress, and now he doesn't know me!"

Normally, when her mother had a high-emotion episode, Valerie had been counseled to firmly and calmly disengage. For both her mother's sake and her own, she'd been advised to take herself out of her mother's emotional spiral, not to feed into a cycle of delusion and uncontrolled emotion. But how did she do that when her mother had a gun to Erik's head?

"I've had my hand up a lot of dresses, lady," Erik said in the background.

Valerie gritted her teeth. *Oh, geez! Not helpful, Erik!*

"Mother, let me talk to Erik. Hand him back the phone, okay?"

"Why? Are you plotting with him against me? Don't you understand how—?" More muffled noises interrupted her mother, then the line went quiet.

"Mother? Mother?" When she got no reply, Valerie sent a terrified look to Nash. "She hung up."

He angled a sharp glance toward her and the silent

phone. "We'll be there in two minutes. Get them back on the line if you can."

Valerie nodded, but instead of calling Erik's phone, she switched to her own phone and called the last number she'd entered in her speed dial. She cut a glance to Nash, who was fully occupied negotiating traffic. Still, when Cartwright came on the line, she kept her voice low. "It's Valerie. She's at Erik Colton's house. Please hurry! She's holding him hostage."

Chapter 20

Nash wheeled into the driveway of his father's home moments later. A gray sedan with bumper stickers and a license plate identifying it as an Ohio rental had been left on the grass near the front door, not even in the driveway.

Val climbed out of the passenger side with her heart in her throat, studying the haphazard parking of the rental vehicle on the lawn. Of course, her mother had driven here. Drunk. And highly upset, which was bad enough. Her heart thrashed in her chest, and she fought to rein in the adrenaline coursing through her. She needed to think clearly and focus if she had any chance of righting this crisis.

She circled the front fender of the car and reached for Nash's hand, stopping him as he charged toward the front door. "Promise me you'll let me handle my mother my way."

He scowled as he laced his fingers with hers. "I'm

having a hard enough time not telling you to wait outside. I don't like the idea of you being around an unstable woman who's waving a gun around."

"I don't like it for you, either. But she's my mother. I know her best and how to handle her moods." They stopped at the bottom step to the stoop, and she tugged his arm to make him face her. The burn of acid in her throat made it difficult to speak, but she whispered, "She's more likely to listen to me than anyone else. Especially anyone with the last name Colton. Please, Nash."

A muscle in his cheek jumped as he considered her point. "Maybe we could stall until Damon comes? He has training with hostage—"

But before he finished his sentence, the front door flew open.

Erik Colton stood at the threshold with Carol inches behind him. Erik's stiff expression and the irritation bright in his green eyes told Valerie her mother still had her weapon trained on him, even though it wasn't visible.

After flicking her eyes over Nash with clear disdain, Carol's gaze went to Valerie. "Valerie, you need to leave. This is between me and the Coltons. This is their own fault."

Valerie raised both hands and took a cautious step toward the door. "Let's not talk about blame. Before we go any further, you need to put away the gun."

"No blame? Valerie, you know what they did to me! He has to pay!"

Beside her, Nash stiffened, and she squeezed his wrist, silently telling him to stay calm.

"Please, Mother. Put your weapon on the ground, and let us talk this through. Erik will apologize, and we'll—"

"Apologize?" Erik scoffed, and despite her dismay at

the man's lack of cooperation, Valerie maintained eye contact with her mother.

"Dad," Nash said in a warning tone. "We all want to settle this without bloodshed or scandal. Right?"

Valerie took another slow step toward the door, with Nash on her heels. Could she use distraction to buy them time until Cartwright or Damon arrived? She was afraid of what might happen if she didn't defuse things before Cartwright arrived. "Mother, please. Talk to me. Let's resolve this peacefully."

Carol shook her head. "No. Th's is long overdue. I won' have peace 'til he pays for e'rything, he—"

Knocking Val aside, Nash lunged toward the door.

Carol startled, stumbled. The gun fired.

Nash landed on his hands and knees on the stoop, and Carol jerked Erik back by his shirt collar as she tried to slam the door.

"No!" Valerie threw herself against the closing door and wedged her shoulder inside. "Mother, don't! Let me in…" She heard scuffling and a crash inside.

Twisting, she glanced down at Nash. "Are you all—?"

He waved one hand at her as he got to his feet. "I'm fine. Go."

She shoved hard on the door, and it swung open. The foyer was littered with coats and umbrellas from the fallen coatrack. She prayed that was the crash she'd heard and stepped over the debris as she hurried deeper in the house. "Mother!"

She found Carol and Erik standing in the center of the living room. She still had his collar fisted in her hand, the gun at his temple. Erik's cheek was now bleeding from a short gash.

"Damn it, Mother!" Valerie growled. "This is not the

answer to anything! You'll only make things worse for yourself if you hurt anyone."

Carol blinked, frowned. "Why d' you call me 'Mother?' You used to call me 'Mommy.' Are you trying to wound me, being so formal, so distant?"

Her response caught Valerie completely off guard. "I—I don't know. It's not—" Maybe it was a subconscious way of distancing herself. She hadn't felt warm fuzzies toward her mother in a long time, and the more formal moniker just…fit. Valerie waved a hand, as if batting away the distracting comment. "Mother, focus. Put the gun down, and then we can talk about anything you want."

Carol grimaced and shook her head slowly, wearily. "I'm tired of talking. That's all I've done for the last few years. It doesn't help. It doesn't change things."

Val's heart twisted. She knew the fatigue, the relentless ache her mother meant. "Mother, you've been doing better. Things were going okay. You can do it again."

"So tired of it—"

Deep down, Val knew it would always be this way. Her mother would never be "cured." Carol would be fighting this battle against her mental illness for the rest of her life. Every day would be the same battle to retrain her thinking, fight the temptation of alcohol and fight the negative thoughts that taunted her. "I'm going to help you. You're not alone."

"Liar! You left me! You're on their side!" Carol swung the gun toward Valerie. "This is your fault!"

"No!" Nash shouted.

A strong, hard body tackled her from behind. Another ear-shattering blast echoed through the house.

The seconds that followed stretched like minutes.

Erik grappled loose from her mother's grip.

Nash shifted his body in front of Val's.

Carol panicked and sent another wild shot over their heads.

"Mother, stop!" Valerie shouted, her own panic rising. *No. Not good.* She quickly put a lid on her emotions. The key to getting through this was keeping everyone, her mother especially, from giving in to extreme emotion.

"We have to get that gun away from her," Nash mumbled under his breath.

"I know. I'm trying," Valerie whispered back.

"Well, your way is not working," Nash said tightly, "and I'm not going to sit back and let her kill—"

They heard a scuffling, a grunt, and Valerie whipped her head around to find Erik fighting Carol for the gun. The weapon discharged again, and Nash shoved from the floor and charged toward Erik. "Dad!"

A cry of frustration ripped from Val's throat. This was exactly the kind of chaos that would feed her mother's paranoia and spiraling anxiety. "Please, stop!"

Somehow, Carol managed to wrest control of the gun again, just as Nash inserted himself between the pistol and his father.

Erik swiped sweat from his face, aiming a finger at Carol, and yelled, "You are batshit crazy, lady!"

"Dad, can it!" Nash growled.

Seeing the ire rise in her mother's eyes, Valerie staggered to her feet and rushed forward, hands raised. She had to do something that would make a difference. Fast. "Mother, stop this now, and I'll come home with you!"

"What?" Nash barked. The hurt and shock in his voice reverberated to her marrow, but she had to focus on her mother. On saving them all from potential disaster.

"What do you say, Mother? You and I walk out of here now. Everyone safe?"

"It's too late," Carol whined, the gun still waving precariously in her hands. "It won't end until *he's* gone." She aimed the weapon at Erik, then moved it to Nash. "And him. You went back to him. Just like I knew you would."

"Mother…" She took a breath, searching for that something to make a connection. "*Mommy*, I need you to stop. Please."

"I h've to." Carol's face crumpled with anger and grief. "If that idiot Mickey hadn't botched things up…"

She sensed more than saw Nash tense. Her gut pitched, but Valerie kept her gaze locked on her mother. "No one needs to get hurt, Mommy."

"I hav'ta set things right, Val. They stole you fr'm me."

"You hired Mickey Gorman to kill me, didn't you?" Nash asked, his voice hard.

Val shot him a quelling look.

"You sh' be dead. But Mickey screwed e'ry thing up."

"Mother, we can work this out. Just—"

"And you knew, didn't you?" Nash asked, the disappointment heavy in his tone.

Valerie faced Nash, her heart sinking. She knew her guilt was written on her face, but she didn't have the strength to hide it.

"What the hell's going on?" Erik demanded. "Are you saying that she hired a killer? Did she murder Axel?"

"I wish I had." Carol scoffed. "One less Colton t' plague th' world."

"That's what had you so upset last night and this morning, isn't it?" Nash asked.

"I—" Val's voice stuck in her throat.

"Why didn't you tell me?" The question carried a world of pain, accusation and frustration.

"I'm sorry, Nash. I couldn't…"

"Couldn't or wouldn't?" he snapped. "My God, Val! I thought we were past all the hiding and secrets."

"Hello? Could you two have your lovers' quarrel later? There's still a crazy woman with a gun pointed at us!" Erik growled.

His father's chastening seemed to snap Nash back to the danger her mother posed, but Valerie knew the matter was far from settled.

"No." Carol swayed, and the gun drooped. "Let them argue. Let her see how treacherous and unfaithful her Colton is!"

Nash's green gaze darkened to deep jade as he narrowed his eyes on Carol. His body tensed, and Valerie read his intent in his expression the instant before he lunged.

"Nash, no!"

He seized her mother's wrist, shoving the hand that held the gun into the air. Shots fired and plaster rained down from the ceiling. Fear stole Valerie's breath. Then a sense of urgency, a need to protect, compelled her forward. She darted to the grappling pair and tried to insert herself between them. Reached for her mother's shoulder, trying to tear her attention away from Nash. "Mother! Mommy, don't! I'll come with you! Let's leave now!"

"Dad!" Nash shouted, "Get. Val. Out of here! Both of you go!"

Hands grabbed her around the waist, dragged her back, even as she fought and called to Carol. "Mother! Mother, please don't!"

As Erik bodily lifted her and carried her outside, Valerie's energy left in a wave. Defeat and despair drained her, and she went limp as a sense of failure crashed down on her. She was numb as Erik led her into the icy morning, past the parked cars and toward the street.

But the crunch of tires in dead leaves on the street roused her. Detective Cartwright emerged from his vehicle, a squad car pulling in behind him.

A bittersweet bubble of hope swelled. Cartwright's arrival was both a godsend and the beginning of the end. She struggled free of Erik's grip and staggered to the detective. "They're in the living room. Please hurry! She's trying to kill Nash!"

Chapter 21

Nash kept a firm grip on Carol's wrist, holding her arm up and keeping the gun pointed at the ceiling. Now that his father and Valerie were out of harm's way, he looked for an opportunity to overpower her. It wouldn't be difficult. He could already feel Val's mother weakening. The trick would be in not hurting Carol in the process.

He hooked a leg around Carol's, hoping he could trip her, knock her off balance and then take her to the ground with a wrestler's move. But just as he made his move, Val's mother smacked her forehead into his face. Pain exploded behind his nose, and the warm leak of blood dripped onto his upper lip.

On some level he heard the new voices approaching, but his focus was on maintaining the upper hand with Carol. Disarming her…

"Police! Drop your weapon and get down on the ground. Hands behind your head!"

Relief flowed through Nash, an odd counterpoint to the adrenaline and anger that had fueled his struggle with Carol. On the heels of the relief came surprise. The man charging into the room, leading with his own weapon, was not Damon.

"Drop the gun and get down!" Harry Cartwright repeated, his tone commanding.

Carol turned a startled look toward the detective as if she'd only just noticed him, and Nash used that instant of Carol's distraction to wrestle her to the floor.

But she clung tenaciously to the pistol. Even as Cartwright continued barking orders, Carol struggled.

"Colton, damn it, move away from her and get on the ground!"

Raising a silent prayer, Nash released Carol's wrist, then eased to the floor and rolled behind the couch. He heard a wail, and as he righted himself and turned to watch, Carol lifted the gun to her own temple.

"Get away from me! I'll do it! Don't touch me!"

Heart thundering, Nash held his breath.

"I don't want to hurt you, Carol," Cartwright said. "Everything will be fine. I just need you to place the gun on the floor and lie on your stomach."

A movement at the other side of the living room caught his attention. A uniformed policeman moved into the room silently, weapon drawn.

Carol wept, her hand trembling, the gun shaking. "No... No, no, no...get away from me!"

Nash held perfectly still, not wanting to do anything to unbalance the precarious situation.

Cartwright stayed put, as well, speaking in a low soothing tone, clearly trying to keep Carol's attention on him as the uniformed officer inched forward behind her.

And then in a matter of seconds, a swift move that disarmed Carol and another that wrestled her to the floor, it was over. She continued to sob and snarl invectives about the Coltons, but Valerie's mother was in custody.

Cartwright stepped over to check Nash for weapons before he allowed him to stand, then started firing questions at him. On the other side of the adrenaline rush, Nash shuddered.

"You're bleeding. What happened?" Cartwright said.

"She headbutted me. Don't think it's broken." When Nash raised a hand to his nose, it was his torso that protested with a sharp, stinging pain. He grunted and looked down to find a red stain around a tear in his shirt. "I'll be damned. She winged me. I didn't even realize."

"That happens sometimes, in the heat of the moment." Cartwright angled his head, appraising the wound, when Nash raised his shirt to examine it himself. "You need an ambulance?"

Nash pressed his hand to the bleeding gash, hissed at the pain the pressure caused. "Nah. I'll get my dad or Val to drive me."

"I have to get statements from both of them. You, too. But yours will wait until you've seen a doctor."

Across the room, the uniformed officer had Carol on her feet, her hands zip-tied behind her. With a firm hand on her arm, he led her from the room.

"What will happen to Valerie's mother?" he asked, knowing how this turn of events would devastate Val. He had only to think of her brokenness last night and this morning for confirmation of that, and he ached for her.

But remembering Val's mood also reminded him how she'd hidden the truth from him, how she'd promised her mother to leave the scene with her, how she'd had the opportunity to choose him and had sided with her mother.

Again. Her mother, who'd hired a killer to murder him. Who'd taken his father hostage and held a gun to them all.

Bitterness and disappointment swirled in his gut. Even after everything they'd shared and discussed, Valerie continued to deceived and forsake him. To shut him out.

"Nash!" Damon entered the room, his DEA shield out identifying him as law enforcement. He flashed the badge toward Cartwright, who must have remembered him, since he barely glanced at the ID. "Are you all right? Val said shots were fired!"

Nash lifted his hand from his side and Damon's face paled. "My God!"

"Flesh wound... I think." Nash raised a querying glance to the detective. "Permission for my brother to take me to the ER?"

Cartwright nodded. "Go on. I'll catch up with you later."

Holding his side, which had begun to throb, Nash walked outside with Damon, scanning the lawn for Valerie. His father was leaning against a squad car on the street, talking to another uniformed officer. Erik lifted his head as Nash came out and gave him an up-and-down look, and when his gaze went to the bloody stain on Nash's shirt, he frowned. He excused himself from the officer he was speaking to and started toward his sons.

Nash continued toward Damon's car, still looking for Valerie. He needed to know she was safe, that—

The screech of a female voice drew his attention to the police cruiser, where the policeman who'd taken Carol into custody was trying to put her in the back of his squad car. Valerie stood near her mother, watching as the officer tried to get cooperation from Carol.

Seeing Valerie across the yard, her attention focused on Carol rather than on him, spiked the churn of harsh emotions that gnawed his gut. Even when her mother had so clearly betrayed Valerie, she still gave her mother preference over him. He gritted his teeth, trying to quell the petty jealousy and irritation. But deep down, Val's choice spoke to a deeper uneasiness and uncertainty within him, a years-old sense of being discarded and devalued.

Clearly upset herself, Valerie said something to Carol that Nash couldn't hear. Val turned to the officer, motioning, and got a short answer from the uniformed man. With a nod, she closed the distance between herself and her mother, touched Carol's face tenderly, then gave her a hug. In response, Valerie's mother snarled something and jerked away.

"She's a piece of work, that one, huh?" Erik said as he approached.

"She's mentally ill, Dad. A little sensitivity, please?" Nash turned to his father and sized him up. "You're all right? You're gonna get that looked at?" He nodded his head toward the cut on Erik's cheek.

His dad waved him off. "I'm fine. How bad is that?" Erik pointed to Nash's wound.

"Headed to the ER now," Damon said, sidestepping toward his car in a not-too-subtle hurry-it-up gesture. "We'll let you know."

"Yeah. You do that." Erik's gaze stayed on Nash. He seemed...worried?

Nash hesitated, sensing Erik was about to say more. Erik pursed his mouth, making the frown lines etched in his face deeper. His complexion looked sallow. His hair grayer. His face thinner. The recent events in the family, losing his brother and Father Time had aged Erik.

"You comin', Nash?" Damon called.

As Nash turned to leave, he cut one last glance to Valerie. Her focus remained on Carol, who was finally being put in the police car. With a sigh, he fell in step with Damon. "Yeah, let's go."

"Nash."

He turned back to his father when he called to him.

Erik pulled back his stooped shoulders. "Thanks. For coming when I called. I—"

His dad didn't finish the sentence, but the stiff words of gratitude were more than Nash had expected. "Of course. That's what family does."

Valerie stood shivering in the cold Chicago morning, watching with a shattered heart as the police car with her mother inside drove away. Her efforts to defuse the situation hadn't been enough. Her years of trying to protect and defend her mother hadn't been enough. Nothing she'd sacrificed or offered her mother had been enough to prevent this tragedy. After all these years of trying, hoping and doing her best for her mother, Carol Yates still resented her, blamed her, didn't care enough to consider how her actions affected her daughter.

Valerie squeezed her eyes shout and inhaled the icy air deeply. *Stop.* That's ten-year-old Valerie thinking. Eighteen-year-old Valerie. Pre-counseling, pre-educating-herself-on-the-realities-of-borderline-personality-disorder-and-alcoholism thinking. She worked to push aside the raw hurt and conjure her counselor's voice, oft-repeated refrains, advice for coping.

Not your fault. Not your responsibility. Her choices. Tough love.

She heard footsteps crunching in the frosty grass and blinked away the moisture in her eyes.

"You okay?" Detective Cartwright asked as he stopped beside her.

Not Nash, as she'd expected. She twisted, glancing to

the curb where she'd seen Nash talking to Erik earlier. He wasn't there. Disappointment plucked at her as she exhaled a cleansing breath that clouded in the November chill. Cartwright was waiting for an answer. "Um, yes and no."

"If it helps," he said, angling his body to face her, "you did the right thing."

Valerie hesitated, trying to believe him. "Did I?"

He nodded. "Look, I know it's hard now. I'm guessing you're feeling kinda guilty about turning her in. But she was a threat to herself and others. You know that, right?"

Valerie let her shoulders droop. Nodded.

"If it helps you deal with things, you can blame me for giving you no choice."

She sighed. "Shifting blame is just another way we lie to ourselves, Detective. My counselor tells me facing hard truths head-on is the only way to affect real change and healing."

"You have a counselor. Good. I was going to recommend that."

Valerie twisted her mouth in a thoughtful moue. "I haven't talked to her in a while, but…it looks like I will be again. Soon."

"You should. This is—" he waved a hand down the road in the direction the squad car had left "—a lot to process."

His expression reflected more than just concern for Val's well-being. It seemed to her he was processing his own dark pain, but she didn't feel she had the right to ask him about it. So she simply nodded and muttered, "Yeah."

"And…it's Harry."

She sent the detective a puzzled look.

"I will follow her case, advocate for her, make sure that her mental illness is accounted for throughout her time in custody, the legal process and any detention. She'll be given a psych eval, of course. But rest assured, I'll see that she's cared for properly."

She tried to form the words of appreciation that knotted in her throat, but was distracted when a warm coat, redolent with an expensive-smelling cologne, was draped around her shoulders.

She cut a startled glance to Erik, who flicked a dismissive hand and said only, "I figured you were cold. I could see you shaking from across the lawn."

The gesture, so reminiscent of Nash's earlier that morning, resonated in her core with a bittersweet pang. "Where's Nash?"

"Left."

"He left?" Confusion and sharp disappointment sliced through her. She'd expected Nash to be upset with her, expected she'd have to explain her actions to him, but she'd never imagined he'd leave her. He had to know she was struggling with the issues of her mother's actions. He'd promised to be there for her but had fled the scene at the first sign of disagreement. "But... I don't understand..."

Erik shoved his hands deep in the pockets of the bathrobe he wore. "Damon took him to the ER a couple of minutes ago."

Valerie stiffened with alarm, and she took an involuntary step closer to Erik, grasped his arm. "The ER? He was injured? How badly? Which hospital?"

Erik shrugged. "Didn't ask which one. But don't panic. It wasn't life-threatening. The bullet really only grazed him."

Erik's cavalier disregard for his son's injury stunned Valerie. But it shouldn't have. Nash had told her for years how disengaged and disinterested his father had been throughout his life. They made quite the pair, she and

Nash, each with their own distant and dysfunctional parents. But at least they had each other. Or did they?

A fresh wave of pain blindsided her. She had to find Nash and explain her recent actions.

As she turned to get clearance from Cartwright to leave the scene, she tuned in to what he and Erik were discussing…and was hit with another shock.

"She left no question she hated me and my son. All Coltons, she said. Why couldn't she be the one who killed Axel?"

A ripple of anxiety swept through Valerie. Was it possible?

Cartwright made a noncommittal motion with his hands. "We'll look into it, of course, but we're currently following other leads that seem more promising."

"Such as?" Erik asked.

Was it her imagination or did Erik seem jittery? He *had* just been held at gunpoint, but still…

Cartwright schooled his face and gave his head a small shake. "Not at liberty to divulge specifics in an active investigation, Mr. Colton." The detective shifted his gaze to Valerie. "I think I'm about done here. Can I do anything for you before I go?"

She pulled Erik's coat around her shoulders tighter, gripping the edges closed with one hand. "No. Thanks. Just…look out for my mother?"

He gave her a grim nod before returning to his car and driving away.

"I'm going to the emergency room to find Nash." She glanced at Erik, pausing, hoping he'd redeem himself by expressing a desire to accompany her to check on his son. When he didn't, she squelched a spark of irritation and added, "May I keep this coat for a little while? I'll return it later today."

Erik flicked a hand. "Sure. Now if you'll excuse me, I have calls to make. Lawyer, insurance, builder. Thanks to your...*mother*—" He paused, his grimace telling her he'd debated what derogatory adjective to use and finally curbed the notion. But his tone said what his words didn't. "I have bullet holes to repair in my home."

By the time Valerie got to the urgent care clinic where Damon had taken Nash, he had been treated for the bullet wound, given an antibiotic to prevent infection and released. She met them in the parking lot as they were leaving the clinic, which Damon had opted for instead of the ER since Nash's injuries weren't life-threatening. When she saw the bruise already darkening Nash's face where her mother had head-butted him, she winced. He didn't have a broken nose, thankfully, but he was clearly in pain and moving slowly, carefully. But more frightening to her was the cool look in his eyes when he spotted her. He was angry. Hurt. Understandably so. She had work to do to salvage the mess she'd made.

"I'll take him home," Val offered, trying to ease under Nash's arm to help him to her car.

He waved her off. "I got it. And Damon's already said he'd take me." When she opened her mouth to protest, he nodded at her dishabille. "Besides, don't you want to go home and dress?"

She glanced down at herself. She was still in her sleep shirt, Vita's garden shoes and Erik's coat. Hair uncombed. No makeup. She must look a mess. But none of that had mattered when she thought Nash was injured. It still didn't, compared with her need to heal the damage she had done to their relationship.

"It's not a problem for me. And we need to talk..."

He stiffened and avoided eye contact. "Yeah, we do."

The hard edge in his tone cut Valerie to the quick.

Damon sent her a sympathetic look and shrugged as Nash hobbled past her and out the door. "I'll get him settled at his house and have him call you." He took a step, then gave Val a feeble smile. "He cares about you, but he's stubborn. You may have to fight to get past his walls, but don't give up on him. You were meant to be together. Even I can see that."

Damon's reassurances buoyed her, but after twenty-four hours of calling and having him ignore her calls, she decided she had to employ the move she'd used three weeks earlier. She'd arrive at his house unannounced and confront him.

Chapter 22

Nash wasn't surprised to find Valerie on his front porch late the next afternoon, but he was surprised how relieved he was to see her. Even so, his teeth still clenched, his chest still hurt and his thoughts still spun when he thought about what appeared to be another betrayal, another secret between them. Despite all that, knowing she hadn't ducked and run back to Ohio without hashing things out with him was encouraging.

He yanked open his door, wincing when the motion pulled the muscles in his side that had been damaged when he was shot. Grazed, really, but he still felt quite sore. And the stitches were beginning to itch.

"Hi," she said and exhaled heavily as if she'd been holding her breath. As if she'd been unsure whether he'd answer the door or not for her.

"Hi, yourself." He glanced past her when a movement caught his eye. The calico emerged from his bushes and meowed as if complaining about the cold. Returning his attention to Val, he appraised her mood—brow puckered, eyes wary, smile tremulous.

"Can I come in?"

He'd been staring. Nash blinked hard, cleared his throat and stepped back to let her in. He stuck his foot out to stop the cat when he tried to follow Valerie inside. "Go home, goofball. You don't live here."

"I tried calling," she said. "Several times."

"Right. I saw. I should have at least texted back. But I…" He scratched his cheek.

"Why didn't you?" she asked when he faltered.

"Well, when I got home from the urgent care clinic, I took one of the pain pills they gave me. It made me real sleepy, and I ended up napping the rest of the day. Turned my phone off. I've kinda had night and day backward since then and…"

And he hadn't had time between calls from all of his family checking on him to think, to process what he was feeling, what he wanted to say to Val.

"How are you feeling?" Valerie asked as she shucked her gloves and shoved them in her pockets. She turned, looking for an empty peg where she could hang her coat.

"Is this the small talk portion of your visit or are you diving right to the part where we talk about how you wounded me with your broken promise?"

She cut a guilty look over her shoulder, coat still in her hands. "I…meant your injuries. Your bullet wound. But…" Val finished hanging up her coat and turned back to him, her countenance reminding him of a scolded puppy. "If you'd rather cut to the chase…" She waved a hand, inviting him to elaborate on whatever he chose.

Nash closed his eyes. Sighed. "Sorry. That was… harsh."

After rubbing his gritty eyes, he forced aside his gruffness. He hadn't slept well and hadn't taken a pain pill recently, but he shouldn't let fatigue and discomfort color this discussion. He had a gut feeling his future happiness hung in the balance, and he needed to play fair or live with regrets the rest of his life.

"Yeah. It was." Valerie squared her shoulders. "For the record, I didn't set out to deceive you or break any promises. I was…cornered by circumstances. Caught in the middle."

Cornered by circumstances? Irritation niggled at the possibility she was trying to dismiss her actions with lame excuses. Swallowing the questions that stirred in him, he hitched his head to the living room. "You wanna sit?"

Valerie followed him to the couch and sat on the edge, leaning toward him as her fingers fidgeted. He took the opposite end of the couch, and, moving a pillow in deference to his injured side, he angled his body to face her. "You knew your mother had hired Gorman to come after me before we got the call from my dad, didn't you?"

"Nash, I couldn't—"

"Yes or no?"

She pressed her mouth in a taut line. Her eyes reflected pain as she lifted her chin. "Yes."

"So even though you promised, just a few days ago, to be forthcoming and honest and not to keep secrets from me, you did just that about something as important as an assassin hired to kill me. Is that about right?"

"It's not that simple. You make it sound like I wanted to hurt you. I hated keeping the truth from you!"

"But you did."

"I couldn't tell you! You haven't given me a chance to explain what happened!"

"Explain what? The bottom line is, when push came to shove, you picked your mother over me. You chose secrecy and undeserved loyalty to her over our relationship and the promises you made me!"

Val shook her head, her eyes bright with conviction. "That's not how it happened. I wanted to tell you, but Cartwright told me I *couldn't* say anything to anyone about what we'd found out. Including you."

Nash gritted his back teeth as he mulled that information. "Detective Cartwright?"

She nodded. "After I talked to my mother and Nancy by phone, asking them about Gorman, I was left with very uneasy feelings. I had to know the truth. The limbo was agony. And I wanted to *protect you*!" Her voice broke.

The half sob that snagged her words caused his own throat to tighten. A sharp ache crept through his chest like a growing fissure in a rock.

"Nash, I couldn't ignore the real possibility that my mother was trying to hurt you. I had to know, so I could stop her." She paused for a breath, wet her lips. "I went to the police and told Cartwright everything. He questioned Gorman, and Gorman gave my mother up in exchange for a plea deal."

"You should have told me all this that night when I asked you. You remember, I specifically asked you what you'd learned about Gorman!"

"Yes, I remember! But Detective Cartwright could have charged me with all kinds of things about messing up his investigation or aiding and abetting my mother or—" Clearly flustered and exasperated, she waved a dismissive hand. "Whatever it's called. But he told me, in no uncertain terms, that I couldn't say anything to anyone while he followed up with locating my mother. Including you."

"Not even when my dad called, and we rushed out to handle that whole disaster? You don't think a little heads-up about what you knew would have been helpful? Even then you were trying to hide the truth about your mother! Protecting her. Putting her first."

Valerie's mouth opened, and she goggled at him. "I chose you over her when I called Detective Cartwright, giving up her location, on the way to your father's house!"

"Wait… You called Cartwright?" He frowned, shook his head. "No. We called *Damon*. And you had my dad and your mother on the other line."

"But after she hung up and I couldn't reach them again, I called Cartwright. I gave him your dad's address. Don't you remember? You were there, driving the car! You had to have heard me."

A vague memory of Val making a brief cryptic call flashed in his memory. "That was Cartwright you called?"

"Who did you think it was?"

"I don't… I was focused on getting through the traffic and worried about my dad. I guess I didn't…" He expelled a breath in a loud gush and raked fingers through his hair as he considered what she'd told him, let it mesh with blurry memories of the frantic moments.

"When I left the police station the day before, Cartwright told me to let him know if I heard from Mother. If I learned anything."

She wrapped her hand around his, refocusing his attention on what she was saying. When he met her eyes, his heart jumped.

Val held his gaze with a teary, but determined, stare. Her expression radiated intent, gravitas and pleading. "I could have disobeyed Cartwright's order. I could have tried to protect Mother or helped her escape justice, but *you* meant more to me than making more excuses for my mother. She made her choice when she came after you, after your dad. And I made mine. I turned her in because I choose you, Nash. I want you in my life, now and always."

I choose you. He'd spent most of his life waiting to hear those words, waiting to feel that he'd been wanted. Not discarded or ignored. Not taken in out of pity. Not ghosted or avoided.

Wanted.

He took a moment, flopping back against the cushion while the notion digested. Settled and filled him with a warmth and love.

"What about you?" she asked, jostling him from his inner thoughts.

Nash frowned. "What about me?"

"You promised to trust me. You said you'd give me twenty-four hours to work things out. To find answers and deal with my mother."

He sat taller, a wariness prickling him. "And I did. All you told me the night before your mom showed up in town was that she hadn't denied anything, had avoided your question with redirection and taking offense."

She turned up a palm. "But trust shouldn't have a time limit, Nash. Either you trust me, trust that I have your best interest at heart, or you don't."

Nash stilled. She had a point. One he needed to address. "I do! I—"

Realizing he'd answered reflexively, defensively, and that his answer was as key, as fundamental to their future happiness as anything she could promise, he paused. Nash swiped a hand down his face as he took a mental step back and thought, really thought, about his feelings for Val, their past, his reasons for doubting her in days gone by.

"If you don't trust me, then what are we doing?" she asked, heartache weighting her voice. "That day in the park, we said we wanted to build a future. We said we could let bygones be bygones, make a fresh start."

He shoved off the couch, and his rib muscles throbbed a protest. Nash ignored the pain as he paced toward his back window. He stared out at the yard Vita and Nicole had helped him plan and plant. Nicole, who'd become like a second mother to him over the years. He hadn't warmed to her immediately. Even that relationship, which was so much a part of his current sense of love and a familial foundation, had been built slowly. One day, one loving gesture, one forgiving mercy at a time. Nicole had stepped in where his father had failed and showed him what real family, faith and grace meant. It all started with a rooted love. And if the past weeks with Valerie had shown him anything, it was that he'd never stopped loving her. His love had changed, matured. And in the past days had grown with respect and admiration and understanding. And passion, born of more than teenage hormones.

Nash exhaled a breath that seemed to free him of demons that had chased him for years. His old feelings of rejection by his father didn't have to shape his days. He had more powerful, more permanent and stable relationships to sustain him. His brother. Nicole.

Valerie.

"Nash?"

When he faced her again, he saw more than just the beautiful face and frightened eyes that waited for his response. He saw a woman who'd shown immense strength, caring for a mentally ill mother. Determination, as she educated herself and pursued her love of art and graphic design. And courage, having been the one to take the first step to end the painful abyss and misunderstanding that had separated them for years. And today. Valerie had risked rejection coming here today to fight for the love they were building together.

A knot formed in his throat and choked the words he knew he needed to say. The anxiety and doubts filling Val's face spoke for the hurt she had to be suffering as she waited for his reply.

His first job was to ease her mind, calm her fears. He strode quickly back to the couch and pulled her into his arms. As he cradled her head against his chest and pressed kisses to the top of her head, he rasped, "I trust you. I do. I'm sorry. I let this business with your mom mess with my head and…"

She squirmed free of his embrace in order to look him in the eye. "My mother will not come between us again," she said with the firmness and solemnity of a person taking a vow.

He nodded. "I talked to Detective Cartwright earlier. He said she'd be charged with attempted murder and a variety of other felonies, but that based on her psych evaluation, pending a judge's ruling, she'd likely be going to one of the secure state mental health facilities."

She nodded. "That's right. But that's not what I mean." Her grip tightened on his arms. "I will not let my allegiances to her override my allegiances to you ever again. For years, I met weekly with a counselor in Toledo who helped me sort out all the confusion and guilt I had surrounding my mother's drinking and mental health. I'd let that slide lately, but not again. The number one takeaway my counselor gave me, which I'd let myself forget in recent weeks, was that my own mental health has to be my first priority. So I'm going to find a therapist here in Chicago."

"Here?" he asked, hope swelling in his chest.

She smiled. "That's where I plan to be living." She sobered a bit, then added, "To be clear... I'm not cutting ties with my mother. I'll visit her wherever she's sent, keep tabs on her treatment, talk with her doctors. But my priority will be my life, finding my own happiness."

A smile spread across his face as he studied Val's countenance. "You are incredible, you know that?" He pressed a hand to his chest. "I really admire you. Your strength and wisdom."

Tears bloomed in her eyes. "Thanks. They're hard-earned." Dabbing the moisture clinging to her lashes, she whispered, "In case you were still wondering, you are what makes me happy. You are why I'm moving to Chicago, and you are the home I want to build for the future."

He cut his gaze to the wall where the drawing of a bungalow that they'd made together all those years ago hung. Her gaze followed.

Framing his face with her hands, she pressed a soft kiss to his lips. "Sorry, Mr. Architect. A house is just a building. Four walls with flowers out front. It's the people and love inside that make a home."

He hummed his agreement as he kissed her again, then something in her statement plucked his heart and caused a strange buzzing to fill his core. "You love me?"

Valerie's brow dipped as if she hadn't heard him correctly. "You don't know that?"

Her answer wasn't a straight *yes*, but her astonishment said what she didn't. He was searching for his voice when she plowed her fingers into his hair and let her tears flow. "Yes, I love you, Nash Colton. I have since I was a teenager, and I always will. Don't you ever doubt or forget that."

He cleared the constriction from his throat and cradled the back of her head with one hand while drying her tears with his other. "And I love you, Valerie Yates. Deeply and forever. I don't ever want to spend another day without you. Promise me you'll grow old with me? Do life with me?"

She canted back slightly and arched a delicate eyebrow in query.

He laughed. "Yes, I'm asking you to marry me."

"In that case, I promise. I'm yours, Nash. For life."

Epilogue

Four months later

Three minutes. Just three minutes.

Good God, who knew three minutes could last so long?

Valerie tried to clear her mind, shift her focus, but waiting was still not her strong suit.

She bent over the paper in front of her and resumed sketching. Since moving to Chicago, she'd shifted her talents toward freelance work and was already building an impressive client list thanks to her many connections through the Colton family. She'd done graphic-design work for True, Colton Connections, a local bakery, a temp agency and the Peoria Parks and Recreation department. She'd even had a call from a distant Colton cousin in Whisperwood, Texas, who wanted a new logo for his wife's expanding private detective agency.

As a face began to take shape on her sketch pad, she had a flash of the last time she'd waited for a test result. She'd used drawing to distract herself then, too. She smiled as she filled in the squarish oval she'd started. Eyes, nose, lips…

Soft, demanding lips. Skilled lips that still *made her breath catch and her toes curl.*

She glanced across the room to the man pacing the bedroom floor.

"How long has it been?" Nash asked.

Valerie checked the timer on her phone screen. "Minute and fifteen seconds."

Nash stopped and scowled at her. "That's all? You're sure?"

She showed him the screen, where the numbers glowed on her cell.

"I'm going to look. I can't take this…" He started for the bathroom and she rushed over to intercept him, laughing.

"Patience, my dear. We swore we'd wait it out together." She rose on her toes to press a kiss to his tense mouth. By the second kiss, his lips relaxed and he pulled her closer, hugging her tightly.

When he raised his head, he whispered, "Have I told you today how much I love you?"

"Three times, not counting the sweet nothings during our lovemaking this morning." Her grin reflected all the joy that had filled her heart the last four months.

Although seeing her mother committed to the mental health correctional facility had been painful, she also knew a sense of relief. Her mother would get the medical treatment and counseling she needed. Valerie could rest easy knowing her mother was safe. And because of that, Nash was safe. And with Nash, her future was safe...and certain.

"Good. I don't ever want you to doubt how I feel about you again." He kissed her and angled his head to glance at her phone. "Geez! Still forty seconds."

"What if it says I'm not pregnant?" she asked.

"Then we have the pleasure of trying again until you are." He tapped a finger on her nose. "And then doing it all again. I'm thinking three kids is a good number."

She gave a quiet sigh, but kept smiling.

As usual, he read her mood despite her pretense. Lifting a dark blond eyebrow, he frowned. "Wait. Where is this coming from? Don't you want to start a family?"

"I do. But...because of the complications I had last time, when I miscarried at seventeen, my doctor warned me I could have trouble conceiving again. Scar tissue and—"

"We'll cross that bridge when—"

The soft jingle of her phone timer stopped Nash, mid-sentence. His eyes widened. He swallowed hard. His fingers gripped her arms a little firmer. "Oh, boy. This is it."

She laced her fingers in his and led him into the bathroom. When they were both standing at the sink, she gripped the edge of the facial tissue she'd placed over the test stick and counted, "One, two, three!"

She whipped the tissue away, and they bumped heads as they leaned over to read the indicator.

"Well..." she said.

"So..." he said.

She pivoted on her heel to face him. "Congratulations, Daddy."

He looked stunned. Then a wide grin split his face. "I'm going to be a father!"

She laughed and nodded.

Nash whooped and lifted her from her feet as he hugged her. "Have I told you today that I love you, Val?"

She nodded, happy tears blooming in her eyes. "Yes. And I love you, too."

* * * * *

Don't miss the exciting conclusion of the Colton 911: Chicago series:

Colton 911: Under Suspicion *by Bonnie Vanak*

After a long beat of silence, Amina sighed dramatically and leaned back to look up at him. A slow smile tugged the corners of her lips. "Well, when you put it that way, I guess I should pick a restaurant, huh?"

He grinned and handed her the menus. "Yes, and I'll take the bags upstairs, then change clothes. When I come back down, we can order." He stood and headed for the stairs again but stopped when she called him. "Yeah?"

"Thanks for coming to the house. It meant a lot to have you there with me even though I know it was the last place you wanted to be."

He studied her for a moment. "That might've been the case at first, but I want to be wherever you are, Amina. And I'll always be here, there or wherever for you. Remember that."

Don't miss
His to Defend *by Sharon C. Cooper,*
available January 2022 wherever
Harlequin Romantic Suspense
books and ebooks are sold.

Harlequin.com